Hannah Ives Mysteries
from Marcia Talley

IN DEATH'S SHADOW
OCCASION OF REVENGE
UNBREATHED MEMORIES
SING IT TO HER BONES

MARCIA TALLEY

A HANNAH IVES MYSTERY

In Death's Shadow

AVON BOOKS
An Imprint of HarperCollinsPublishers

AVON BOOKS
An Imprint of HarperCollins*Publishers*
10 East 53rd Street
New York, New York 10022-5299

Copyright © 2004 by Marcia Talley
ISBN: 0-06-058738-5
www.avonmystery.com

First Avon Books paperback printing: September 2004

Avon Trademark Reg. U.S. Pat. Off. and in Other Countries, Marca Registrada, Hecho en U.S.A.
HarperCollins® is a registered trademark of HarperCollins Publishers Inc.

Printed in the U.S.A.

10 9 8 7 6 5 4 3 2 1

"Even the death of Friends will inspire us as much as their lives. They will leave consolation to the mourners . . . and their memories will be incrusted over with sublime and pleasing thoughts, as monuments of other men are overgrown with moss; for our Friends have no place in the graveyard."

Henry David Thoreau, *A Week on the Concord and Merrimack Rivers: Wednesday* (1849)

"Come like an evening shadow, Death!
So stealthily, so silently!
And shut mine eyes, and steal my breath."

CAROLINE SOUTHEY (1787–1854), *To Death*

ACKNOWLEDGMENTS

A million thanks:

To my husband, Barry, who supports me every day in every way.

To my writers groups—Sujata Massey, John Mann, Janice McLane, and Karen Diegmueller in Baltimore, and Janet Benrey, Trish Marshall, Mary Ellen Hughes, Ray Flynt, Sherriel Mattingly, Bert Brun, and Janet Martin in Annapolis—for tough love.

To my editor, Sarah Durand, who rescued Hannah when she was "between publishers" and loves her as much as I do.

To my agent, Jimmy Vines, who never gave up on Hannah, either.

To Joe Jacobs, who has been an insurance professional for more than two decades, working as an independent broker for many fine companies. If I got it wrong, it's my fault, not Joe's.

To my friends, Bob and Pat McNitt, who lent Mrs. Bromley their apartment, and to my many other friends at Ginger Cove who bear absolutely no resemblance to any of the characters in this book.

x • ACKNOWLEDGMENTS

To April Henry. There isn't anything she doesn't know about vanity plates, and she writes darn good mysteries, too.

To Barbara Parker, lunch buddy and web maven extraordinaire. (http://www.marciatalley.com)

And to Kate Charles and Deborah Crombie, dearest of friends, confidantes, and advisors, who read every word, sometimes more than once.

In Death's Shadow

CHAPTER 1

Chemo brain.

That black hole in my cerebellum that's sucked up my PIN number, my password on Yahoo.com, the location of my car keys and the answer to questions like why am I standing in front of the refrigerator holding the door open? How else to explain why I didn't recognize the woman when she bopped up to me in Dr. Wilkins's waiting room with a cheerful, "Well, Hannah Ives! How wonderful to see you!"

I looked up from my magazine—*Family Circle* was advising me to rub cornstarch on salad dressing stains—into a pair of designer sunglasses that reflected my own startled eyes back at me and the most gorgeous mop of apricot curls I think I've ever seen.

And drew a complete blank.

"Oh, hi!" I enthused, matching her delight for delight. "How *are* you?"

"Just great," she said, plopping herself down in the empty chair to my right. "And you?"

"Terrific," I said, stalling for time. She'd come from the direction of the staff lounge. *A nurse?* I nodded toward the lab where one of the hematology technicians had just separated me from several ounces of my blood. "Especially now that Vampira is finished with me."

Frowning, she drew shiny pink lips into an O and

peeked under the Band-Aid on her own, gloriously sun-tanned arm. "Tell me about it."

Not a nurse then. A patient. But where had I seen her before? While she pressed the Band-Aid back into place, I looked her up and down, desperate for clues.

Everything about the woman screamed *Sex and the City,* like she had a key to Carrie Bradshaw's closet. Late twenty-something, she wore a light blue, distressed denim jacket over a white cotton tank top, the hem of which hovered a good three inches above the waistband of a pair of olive-colored Sharagano low-rise flares with floral patches. Perfectly manicured toes were cradled in a pair of Kors sandals. I checked out her hands. Yup, fingernails to match, and . . .

. . . a wedding ring!

"So," I ventured, praying she wasn't recently widowed. "How's married life?"

She hugged her handbag, a kidney-shaped leather pouch, to her chest. An envelope from Farmers Bank of Maryland peeked from an outside pocket, and I found myself praying for a diversion—a fire alarm, an earthquake, a total eclipse of the sun—anything that would distract her long enough for me to slide the envelope out and read the name and address, but no such luck.

"Brian has just been incredible," she gushed. "You won't believe what he did!"

Brian. Was she a faculty wife, then? I raised my eyebrows to encourage her to go on with whatever unbelievable thing it was that Brian had done while I skimmed through a mental Rolodex of my husband's colleagues at the Naval Academy. Paul was a math professor. Did he work with anyone named Brian? I remembered a Bruce and a Bob, but no Brian.

"Well, Hannah," she drawled, turning sideways in her chair to face me. She grinned, relocated her sunglasses from the bridge of her nose to the top of her head and threw me an exaggerated wink. In a flash, I recognized her. Valerie Stone. Ovarian cancer. Stage IV. Advanced. The last time I'd seen her, she'd been thirty pounds thinner and completely bald. We'd bonded over a toilet bowl at Anne Arundel Medical Center.

"Valerie! You look absolutely wonderful! I almost didn't recognize you, with . . . with . . ." I was tap dancing as fast as I could.

"With hair?"

I laughed. "Yeah. The last time I saw you . . ." I paused again, searching for the right word.

"The last time you saw me, I looked like an extra for *Night of the Living Dead*."

"Not exactly." I smiled. "But close."

"The doctors were telling Brian I should get my affairs in order. I took it as a challenge. You know me!"

There was a time when Valerie and I knew each other very well indeed. We'd shared a hospital room during chemotherapy, but after she checked out, she moved back to her parents' home in New Jersey and we'd lost touch. I remembered Brian now, a gangly, fair-haired type. If Sweden had cowboys, they'd look like Brian. The couple had a daughter, too, but we'd never met. The little girl had been shipped off to Grandma's house and hadn't been allowed to visit her mother in the hospital.

"I did it for Miranda," Valerie said, as if reading my mind. "I heard about this clinical trial at NIH, so I applied . . . and now, praise God, it's a miracle. My cancer's in remission." She giggled. "Heaven will just have to wait!"

"I'm *so* glad," I said, leaning back in my chair and setting the magazine aside. "My breast cancer's in remission, too. Or so they tell me!"

"Have you gone back to work yet?"

I shook my head. "I got riffed. At first I was in shock. Then I got angry. I was all set to organize the breast cancer lobby and sue Whitworth and Sullivan up one side and down the other. Make 'em pay for laying me off." I sighed and leaned back in my chair. "Now I think losing my job's the best thing that ever happened to me. Life's too short to spend it commuting from Annapolis, Maryland, to Washington, D.C., just so some idiot office manager can dump all over you." I laid a hand on my chest. "I hyperventilate just thinking about it. Now I do volunteer work. Pick up a temp assignment now and then. How 'bout you?"

"I'm staying home with Miranda."

"How old is she now?"

"Four. And I'm going to see that little gal walk down the aisle if it's the last thing I do!"

I have a daughter, too, but Emily is twenty-four. The closest I'd come to seeing her walk down the aisle was a digital picture—sent via e-mail attachment—of Emily and Dante smooching in front of a wedding chapel in Las Vegas. At least there had been no Elvis impersonators mugging in the background. That would be a moment to cherish: "The Hawaiian Wedding Song" performed by a live professional singer from the Las Vegas Strip.

"Miranda's wedding will come sooner than you think," I reassured her. "Kids. One minute you're handing them a pacifier, the next minute it's the car keys." I chuckled. "But you were going to tell me something about Brian."

"Wait till you hear this, Hannah!" Valerie bounced in her chair like an excited child. "Brian took me on a cruise. Around. The. World!" She tapped my hand. "What do you think about *that*?"

I thought it was absolutely marvelous and told her so.

"On the QE2," she continued. "One hundred and twenty glorious days! And every minute of every day I was pinching myself. I just couldn't *believe* it."

While she raved on about the Caribbean, the Panama Canal, Hawaii, Pago Pago, and Fiji, I multiplied a couple of hundred bucks a day, times two, times 120, and couldn't believe it, either. Who could afford such a trip? "Pago Pago?" I asked. "There really is a place called Pago Pago?"

She nodded, her bright curls bouncing. "In Samoa. It was *dee*-vine."

"I've dreamed of visiting the South Pacific," I said. "But a four month cruise? I'd have to talk my husband out of a sabbatical."

"You could always play the cancer card," she suggested.

"Cancer card?"

"You know." She put a hand to her forehead and fluttered her eyelashes. "Oh dah'ling, ah'll jes' be miserable if ah can't see the Great Barrier Reef before ah die!"

I laughed out loud. "You didn't!"

"Oh, but I *did*," she said, "And it worked just as well for my new car." Her eyes ping-ponged about the waiting room as if checking for eavesdroppers before she leaned toward me and confided, "A Mercedes SLK320. Convertible."

"Hannah? Hannah Ives?" A nurse had wandered into the waiting room, brandishing my pink sheet.

"Oops, gotta go." I hooked a thumb in the direction of the examination rooms. "The Inquisition awaits within."

"Wait a minute." Valerie scrabbled around in her bag, retrieving a hairbrush, a lipstick, and a Palm Pilot before producing what looked like a business card. She pressed it into my hand. "Here's our phone number. Please stay in touch, Hannah."

I studied the card: BRIAN STONE, it read, FREELANCE WRITER. Brian's logo was a cartoon elephant seated at a typewriter, its trunk rolled up in the platen. Cute. I waved the card and tucked it with elaborate care into my purse. "I'll call you next week," I promised. "We'll do lunch."

Valerie smiled. "I'd like that. Very much."

Freelance writer, I thought, as I followed the nurse toward the examination room. I kicked off my shoes and stood obediently on the scales while she slid weights back and forth along the bar. *I wonder what he writes?*

"One twenty-five!"

"Huh?"

"One hundred twenty-five pounds." She consulted my

chart before making a notation. "You're almost up to your prechemo weight."

"Hallelujah," I said, stepping backward off the scale onto the cool linoleum.

"Open up," she said, and poked a thermometer into my mouth. I held it under my tongue, still thinking about Brian and Valerie Stone. That cruise must have cost a small fortune. How did they do it? *Maybe he's writing travel articles for* Condé Nast Traveler. The thermometer beeped. Next came the blood-pressure cuff.

Maybe he's got a trust fund, I thought as the cuff grew plump around my arm. Or a rich relative who obligingly croaked.

By the time I'd shucked my clothes, draped myself in a hospital gown—"ties up the back, please"—and settled myself uncomfortably on an ergonomically hostile examination table, I'd decided that unless Brian was ghostwriting thrillers for Tom Clancy, there was no way on earth he could have paid for that trip.

Not that it was any of my damn business.

CHAPTER 2

When I got home, I made a beeline for the com-puter and Googled "QE2" on the Internet: £16,999 per person. $25,500 U.S., plus change. And that was for an *inside* cabin. A Room with No View.

That night, over a second helping of his favorite lasagna—my late mother's special recipe—I asked Paul what he thought about circumnavigating the globe on a luxury liner. "In your dreams," he mumbled, eyes closed, clearly savoring his last meatball.

"Spoken by a man who has no *prayer* of getting dessert," I commented, rising from my chair to collect his empty plate. I slid the dirty dishes into the sink, then crossed the kitchen to the blackboard that Emily had decorated with sunflowers as an art project in third grade. Paul, supervised by Emily, had installed it to the left of the back door, where it had hung ever since. *Milk*, I wrote in bright pink chalk, *½ n ½*. At the bottom I scrawled: *lottery ticket*. One never knows.

Paul was using an iced tea spoon to mine the bottom of a freezer-worn, nearly empty carton of vanilla ice cream, and I was finishing up the dishes, when the telephone rang. Paul tipped the carton to his mouth, tapped the bottom and ignored the ringing. I kissed his cheek as I went by. "You are pitiful," I teased.

The caller was Janey Madigan, begging out of Saturday's Race for the Cure in Washington, D.C. Over the past several months, I'd put together a Go Navy/Beat Cancer team that would participate in the annual race to raise money for breast cancer research. Not only had I counted on Janey, I'd counted on her van. But, unfortunately, her mother had just broken a hip and Janey and Kip were heading off to her place in Maine. Janey was absurdly confident I'd find somebody to run in her place.

Ha. Ha. Ha. I'd already strong-armed Paul, his sister Connie, and her husband, Chesapeake County police lieutenant Dennis Rutherford, into joining the team. Not to mention my daughter Emily, with my grandchildren in tow. The rest of my family had bailed out.

Dad was on an Elderhostel, exploring Anasazi archaeological ruins at Mesa Verde National Park when he wasn't filling our mailbox with tacky postcards featuring wigwam-style motels with marquees promising !!A TELEPHONE IN EVERY ROOM!!

My sister, Ruth, claimed to be tied up doing inventory at Mother Earth, the New Age shop she owns in downtown Annapolis. A lame excuse, I thought, but even so, I never considered Ruth seriously. The closest Ruth ever comes to exercise is this Indonesian thing she's into—Pancha Tanmantra—picked up from a Buddhist monk on her last trip to Bali.

And, poor Georgina! My younger sister was pregnant. Again. As if she didn't have enough to do what with six-year-old Julie, and Sean and Dylan, the hyperactive twins, who had just turned eight. Somebody ought to wrestle Georgina's husband, Scott, to the ground and tie *his* tubes!

"Damn." I poured myself a second glass of merlot and carried it into the living room where Paul had settled down in front of the television with the newspaper and a cup of decaf. I sprawled on the sofa, resting the stem of the wineglass on my chest. "Damn," I said again, hoping he'd notice this time.

Paul peered at me over the top of the paper. "Who was it?"

"Janey and Kip have to go to Maine," I complained. "Who do we know with a van?"

"Just about everybody has an SUV," Paul muttered into the Business section of *The Capital*. "Nobody drives a regular car these days."

"I don't mean an SUV, Paul. I mean a van van, like one of those Ford Econolines."

"Whatever for?"

"Getting everybody to the race on Saturday."

Paul shrugged. "Use cars."

I shook my head. "Parking will be impossible in the District." I sipped my wine and thought for a moment. "Maybe I'll ask everyone to meet at New Carrollton and we'll ride the Metro in."

Paul nodded. "Suits me."

I relaxed into the cushions. "Well, that solves one problem, but who do I get to run in Janey's place?"

"How about that new friend of yours? The one you ran into at Dr. W's?"

"Valerie?" I hadn't considered Valerie. I didn't know what shape she was in after her cancer treatments, for one thing, although she certainly *looked* healthy. Then again, what did I have to lose? If Valerie didn't want to run the race, I thought, maybe she could join in the Fun Walk with Paul and the grandkids.

I got up to find the business card Valerie had given me.

Purses should come with locator devices, like cordless phones. Mine had eluded me again. I spent several frustrating minutes searching for it in all the usual places—the kitchen, our entrance hall, the powder room tucked into the triangle under the front stairs—before finding it where I'd dumped it, next to the sofa I had just been sitting on. Chemobrain had struck again.

My purse has more pockets than a pool hall, and I spent

some time rummaging through them. I was about to give up and call directory assistance when the card finally surfaced, sandwiched neatly between my Giant Shoppers card and a similar one from Sam's Club.

I took it to the phone, then paused, my finger hovering over the 4 button. Was I being presumptuous in assuming that Valerie might be well enough to join us? I remembered days following my reconstructive surgery when I could barely climb the stairs to my bedroom. Even weeks later, walking all the way around the block had been a triumph. I didn't want to put Valerie on the spot. But she'd driven herself to the doctor's office, I reasoned, and she seemed enthusiastic about meeting me for lunch. And I *had* promised to call. Besides, I was fresh out of friends whose arms hadn't been twisted practically out of their sockets.

I dialed her number.

After six rings I was expecting the answering machine to kick in, when a child I took to be Miranda picked up the phone. "Hello?" she whispered.

"Miranda?"

"Yeth?"

"Is your mommy there?"

"Yeth."

"Can I speak to her?"

"Yeth."

I listened to Miranda's gentle breathing on the other end of the line, and after a long minute, when there seemed to be no indication that the little girl was going to summon her mother to the telephone I said, "Miranda?"

"Yeth?"

"Will you go get your mommy, please?"

"Okay."

The phone thumped against a wall; as I waited, a clock chimed seven and I could hear a television playing the *Law and Order* theme song. Clearly, Miranda was going to keep me on hold for eternity. To pass the time I reread

Brian's business card and considered sending Valerie an e-mail.

A door slammed. There were footsteps, raising my hopes, followed by the distinctive sound of a coffee grinder, water running, the squeak of a tap being twisted. Eventually the room grew quiet.

"Hello?" I shouted, hoping to penetrate the silence on the other end of the line. "Hello? Hello? Hello?"

A muffled, "What the . . ." and hurried footsteps.

I had attracted someone's attention at last.

"Who's there?" From the soft drawl and the way "there" became a two syllable word, there was no doubt the speaker was Valerie.

"It's me, Valerie. Hannah Ives."

"Hannah, I'm *so* sorry! Have you been waiting long?"

"Couple of hours."

"You're . . ." She paused, then giggled. "You're kidding, right?"

"Right."

"I'm *so* glad you called! Usually when somebody says 'Let's do lunch,' it never happens."

"It's not lunch that I'm calling about, exactly. I was wondering if you'd ever heard of the Komen Race for the Cure?"

"Of course I've heard of it! Brian and me, we're from Dallas. There isn't anybody in Dallas who hasn't heard of the Susan G. Komen Breast Cancer Foundation. My mother participated in the very first run, in fact. Golly, that must have been twenty years ago, long before they moved to New Jersey!"

I told Valerie about my Go Navy/Beat Cancer team and invited her to participate in the race. To my surprise, not only did she agree, but she volunteered Brian to fill in for the absent Kip. "I *think* he'll still be in town," she added. "He's driving to West Virginia to interview someone for a story, but I'm pretty sure that's not until Monday.

"What do we do about getting T-shirts and bib numbers?" she asked, suddenly shifting gears.

I lifted my eyes heavenward and mouthed a grateful *Thank you.* "You must have run marathons before!"

"Oh, yes. I was training for the Marine Corps Marathon before . . . before I got sick," Valerie told me. "I hope to qualify for the Boston one day, God willing. It's slow, but I'm gradually coming back. This race will be good for me," she added. "Is it 5K?"

"Approximately. They modified the route because of beefed-up security around the White House, so it's about eight hundred feet shorter, but it still counts as a 5K race."

"It'll be fun," Valerie enthused. "It depends on whether I can get a babysitter for Miranda, of course."

Of course.

The dreaded B-word.

Reliable babysitters were harder than ever to find these days, and of the reliable few, how many would agree to show up at Valerie's house at the crack of dawn? Before allowing my newly snagged volunteers to slip away, I improvised. "Paul is doing the walk with our grandchildren. I'm sure they wouldn't mind including Miranda." As I said this I glanced at Paul, who waggled his fingers and grinned toothily. "Paul says sure. We'll pick you up," I added, "but it will have to be early. I'm participating in the Parade of Pink, which starts at seven-fifteen, so we'll need to get to the Metro by the time it opens. I hate to tell you this, but that means we'll be knocking on your door at five-thirty A.M."

Valerie chuckled. "Not a problem. We're up before then anyway. Brian's muse is pretty demanding. She rousts him out of bed around four every morning."

"How lucky for you."

"It is, really," she replied with a laugh. "I just love sitting on the porch with my coffee and the newspaper, watching the sun come up."

The last time I'd watched the sun rise was . . . frankly, I couldn't remember. Since abandoning my grueling commute, rising early had not been high on my agenda. I assured Valerie that I'd bring the bibs and the T-shirts, and then, because Brian's card had listed only a post office box number, I asked where they lived.

"We're in Hillsmere," she said, and gave me directions.

I knew Hillsmere Shores, a well-established, middle-class neighborhood on the Annapolis Neck peninsula, adjoining Quiet Waters Park. The park had a café, art gallery, playgrounds, a skating rink, and a paved bike/jogging trail, five miles long if you took all the loops.

"I feel bad about asking you to drive all the way out here," Valerie added.

"Don't be silly," I said. "There won't be any traffic at that time of morning."

"True . . ." Valerie let her voice trail off, as if she weren't really convinced. "Hannah?"

"Yes?"

"Thanks. Thanks for thinking of me."

I had to pause and clear my throat to let my next words out. "I should have stayed in touch."

"We both had a lot on our minds," she said simply.

That was an understatement. Immediately following my chemotherapy, I'd gone to stay with my husband's sister, Connie, on the family farm to wait for my hair to grow out. Instead of the rest and relaxation I was looking for, I found a body in a well. Things got a bit crazy after that.

When I had time to think about Valerie again, months had gone by. Her prognosis had been so poor that I was afraid she'd already died. And if I didn't bother to track her down, nobody could give me the bad news.

"Hannah? You still there?"

"Sorry. I thought I heard someone at the door," I lied.

"We'll do better this time around, won't we?"

"You can count on it," I promised.

CHAPTER 3

At 4:00 A.M., Saturday morning, the alarm clock practically self-destructed, but I refused to budge until the smell of coffee drifted upstairs from the high-tech coffee maker Connie had given me the previous Christmas. Consisting of one glass globe perched atop another, it operated on the vacuum principle—quietly hissing and gurgling, then erupting like Mount St. Helens—turning coffee-making into a spectator sport. Usually I was downstairs to enjoy the show, but I opened my eyes only long enough to see that it was still dark outside, turned over in bed, and drew a corner of the quilt over my head.

When I opened my eyes again, Paul was already awake, sitting up in bed with his pillow folded double behind him, watching the Weather Channel with the sound turned off. "Bad news, Hannah. It's supposed to rain all day."

I wriggled across the sheet until I was nestled next to him, propped my chin on his chest and stared at the screen. An amorphous green blob hovered over a satellite map of the greater Baltimore/Washington area. "Rats!" I muttered. I waited for the image to refresh itself, praying for a change, but the blob just sat there, if anything, denser and greener. "I can't watch. It's too horrible."

Paul grunted.

"Want coffee?" I asked.

"Yup." Paul tapped a button on the remote and switched to CNN. "You sure the race is still on?"

"They said 'rain or shine,' " I grumbled as I slid out of bed and reached for my robe.

"Okay by me, but I'm not so sure I want to take the kids out in this weather."

By "kids" Paul meant our granddaughter, Chloe, age three, and her little brother, Jake, who was ten months old. And Miranda, of course. "I'm sure Emily will bring rain hats and slickers," I called out over my shoulder, "but if the weather gets too bad, you can always hang out in the Old Post Office Building, terrorizing tourists in the food court."

I had fetched the coffee and climbed back into bed when the first phone call came. Paul's friend from the history department bugging out. "Another one bites the dust," I grumped. "What's the matter? Afraid he'll get his beard wet?"

"Well, at least he'd already paid," Paul said.

"There's that," I agreed, sipping my coffee. "Paul?"

"Hmmm?"

"How do you suppose Valerie and Brian managed that cruise?"

"Cut it out, Hannah. You're obsessed with this woman's bank account."

"Not obsessed," I protested. "Just curious. Two years ago Valerie drove a ten-year-old Honda. Now it's designer clothes, a Mercedes-Benz, and trips around the world. Like they said in that movie, I want what she's having."

"Why don't you ask her?"

"Ask her what?"

"How she did it."

"I wouldn't have the nerve."

Paul snorted. "You? Don't make me laugh, Hannah. You have more nerve than a snake charmer."

I set my cup on the bedside table and rolled over until

my cheek rested against Paul's shoulder. I flung my arm loosely across his chest. "Sometimes I worry that . . ."

Paul's lips moved against the top of my head. "What is there to worry about?"

With my finger, I traced little circles in his slightly graying chest hair. "Maybe you're too polite to say it, but I worry that you're upset with me for not going back to work full-time."

He turned on his side to smile at me. "What's the matter, Hannah? Tired of being a kept woman?"

"No. I just need to be sure you're comfortable with my hanging around the house, working temp jobs for peanuts."

"What's not to like?" he said, gently caressing my cheek with his thumb. He tipped up my chin until I was staring straight into his bottomless cup of coffee eyes. "Back in the Bad Old Days you would already be on the road, halfway to D.C. by now." His lips brushed my mouth.

"Mmmm. This *is* better," I said, melting into him.

Needless to say, we got a late start.

While I showered and threw on my running clothes, Paul dressed, grabbed two apples out of the fridge, and filled a thermos with hot coffee. By the time I flew out the front door, wasting a few precious seconds to turn around and lock it, Paul had already fetched the Volvo from where he had parked it—directly across from the William Paca House, halfway down Prince George Street—and was waiting for me with the engine running.

Dawn had turned the morning pale gray, just light enough to distinguish malevolent thunderclouds piling up darkly on the horizon. Paul turned right on Maryland Avenue, squinting through the condensation on the inside of the windshield. I turned the defroster up a notch.

He circled Market Space at a crawl, pulling cautiously

through intersections where traffic lights that would normally hold us up for five minutes at a time were solemnly blinking amber. By the time we crossed the Spa Creek bridge into Eastport, the rain was sluicing sideways against the windshield, and Paul had to switch the wipers from fast to frantic.

Outside, the pavement glistened like wet coal, curving gently as it wound through Hillsmere's alley of tall cedars, mature trees that had once marked the approach to the old Smith estate. Now the drive was lined on both sides by single-family homes on well-maintained, heavily wooded lots. Just past the Key School, Hillsmere Drive ended in a T at the river. On an ordinary day we would have had a panoramic view of the South River all the way across to Turkey Point. That day, though, the rain came down so hard it flattened the whitecaps and frightened away the usual sails that dotted the bay. As the wiper swept across my window, I was just able to distinguish the orange hulk of a container ship making its slow way up the bay to Baltimore harbor.

I consulted the directions Valerie had given me over the phone and instructed Paul to turn east on Bay View. On both sides of the street, modest, ranch-style homes hunkered down, dead center on quarter-acre lots. I wiped the inside of the windshield with my hand, squinting through the monsoon, trying to make out the numbers on the mailboxes. "They'll be on the right," I said, "just past the marina." As I spoke, the road curved gently to the left and I spotted a short gravel road with a cluster of masts at the end of it. "Gotta be around here somewhere," I muttered as we drew even with a dark green mailbox partially hidden by a plush boxwood hedge. "Wait! Turn here!"

Paul wheeled past the mailbox and into the driveway, tires spinning dangerously on the wet gravel. Before I could catch my breath, he slammed his foot on the brake, hard, jerking the vehicle to a halt just inches from the door of a massive three-car garage. If I hadn't been held so tightly against the seat by my seat belt, I'd have slid into a heap on the floor mat.

"Golly," I said when I pulled myself together, looked up and saw Valerie's house.

In the footprint of what had probably been a modest, sixties-style vacation home, Valerie and Brian had built a brand-new, Mediterranean-style, white stucco McMansion. Palladian windows flanked a central three-story atrium, a two-story wing meandered off into the left distance, balancing the hulk of the garage on the right, and the whole, huge wedding cake was topped by a roof of terra-cotta tile that would have looked more at home in Sardinia than on the shores of the Chesapeake Bay.

A house on steroids, I thought. It stretched nearly to the property line, towering over the water and its neighbors. The place next door looked like their toolshed.

"Golly, indeed," Paul agreed. "Now that's making a statement."

"What statement?" I asked, unfastening my seat belt.

Paul tugged on the zipper of his windbreaker, zipping it all the way up to his chin. "Nah, nah, nah-nah-nah," he singsonged. "I've got more money than you do!"

I had to laugh. "I don't think I'd want that monster garage defining the front of *my* dream house."

"Me, either," Paul agreed. "Unless you're sending the message that your cars are more important than your home itself."

"Probably needed to save room out back for the patio," I mused, growing ever more envious of Valerie's good fortune. "And the swimming pool."

On the way over we had agreed that Paul would brave the elements and make a dash to the door and ring the bell, but after seeing the exterior of the Stone estate, there was no way I was going to miss sneaking a peek inside. "Wait for me!" I called. Pulling my raincoat over my head, I dashed after him up the flagstone path that snaked through Valerie's impeccably landscaped lot.

Before Paul's finger could find the doorbell, Brian swung the door wide. Damn. I had just bet Paul that it would play Tchaikovsky's 1812 Overture, complete with cannon.

"Hi, Hannah," Brian said. "Come in, come in." He extended his hand. "You must be Paul."

While Paul shook Brian's hand I stepped over the threshold, dripping rainwater all over Valerie's spotless marble foyer. At first I thought that Brian had cut his hair short, but when he turned his head, I noticed he'd pulled it back into a neat ponytail at the nape of his neck. He'd grown a mustache, too. He looked like a spokesmodel for IKEA.

"Valerie will be down in a second," Brian told us. "Miranda was a little late getting out of bed this morning."

My eyes followed the gentle curve of the staircase as it wound its way up to a balcony-style landing. Over my head an ornate chandelier, dripping prisms, blazed in the early morning light. Why on earth did Valerie need to get a babysitter? I wondered. I could only assume that the Stones were between nannies.

"Gorgeous house, Brian," I commented dryly. "How long have you lived here?"

"Just moved in," he said, pointing to the living room where several packing boxes sat open on the parquet near a casual grouping of overstuffed white leather furniture. The north wall was dominated by a floor-to-ceiling fieldstone fireplace, and on the opposite side of the room, a picture window overlooked the bay. Even in the wretched weather, the view was spectacular. I could see now why Valerie liked to drink her coffee on the patio.

"Big," said Paul.

Brian laughed. "Yeah. Why just the other day I went looking for my glasses and discovered a bedroom I didn't even know we had!"

"Oh, Bry, you are *impossible*!" Valerie called down

from the landing. "Don't you believe a word of what he says! It's only thirty-five hundred square feet, and Brian designed every square inch of it."

"Impressive," I said. I wasn't particularly good at math, but counting the atrium, and with twelve foot ceilings everywhere else, I figured the *cubic* footage of Brian's humble abode probably approached that of Buckingham Palace.

With a hint of a smile on his lips, Brian turned to watch his wife and daughter skip down the stairs. Miranda's white-blond hair was bound with fat, pink rubber bands into two ponytails that coiled like springs on either side of her head. She hopscotched across the tiles, then stood, feet primly together, on the plush Bokhara carpet.

Behind her, Valerie looked fresh-scrubbed and radiant in a hot pink Spandex jogging bra and matching shorts, an outfit that rendered my husband temporarily speechless. I jabbed him in the ribs with my elbow. "Paul, this is my friend Valerie."

Valerie bent at the waist to whisper in Miranda's ear. "Say hello to Mr. and Mrs. Ives, Miranda."

Miranda looked up at me sideways through a fringe of colorless lashes. "Hello." She stuck out a foot. "I have new shoes."

"Indeed you do," I said. "What a pretty pink."

Miranda tapped her foot on the carpet, and the heel of her tennis shoe lit up like an emergency vehicle. "They flash."

Brian laid a broad hand on the top of his daughter's head. " 'All the better to see you with, my dear,' " he quoted.

Valerie produced a Little Red Riding Hood slicker from the hall closet and helped Miranda into it. All the child needed was a basket of goodies and she'd be ready to set off through the woods to grandmother's house.

Valerie slung a duffel bag over her shoulder. "Ready or not, here we come!"

"Prepare yourself," I said.

Laughing, Brian scooped Miranda up in his arms and we followed him out, into the fury of the storm.

CHAPTER 4

It could have been wetter, I suppose, like at the bottom of the Chesapeake Bay.

Our team, whittled down to a dozen waterlogged, but spirited individuals—I shared DNA with half of them—rendezvoused at the Washington Monument, where we slogged around in puddles up to our ankles and fortified ourselves with the water du jour—Dasani—and containers of Yoplait served up with plastic spoons by volunteers in official yellow Race for the Cure T-shirts.

Somewhere down on Constitution near the Ellipse, we'd left the children, damp but happy, in the capable hands of Emily and her father, but we'd long ago lost track of Brian and Dennis, who had gone off in search of a battery for Brian's digital camera. One of those underwater models would have been far more practical.

The rest of my team was packed—elbow-to-elbow, along with 55,000 of our closest friends—into two blocks of Constitution Avenue that normally accommodated eight lanes of rush hour traffic. I sipped my water, intrigued, as the crowd began to sort itself into distinct clusters around me.

Behind Connie, a man and a woman waited with their arms wrapped protectively around their daughter, not yet thirty, but, sadly, already wearing the pink T-shirt that identified her as a breast cancer survivor.

Next to them, a husband snapped photograph after photograph of his wife as she mugged for the camera, switching the bill of her pink ball cap forward, backward, and sideways, laughing merrily into the lens.

A Neanderthal in short-shorts barged past to join a pack of eight or nine individuals, all running—their bibs proclaimed—in honor of Marjorie. As I watched, a woman who had been bent over retying a shoelace stood, and I could read the writing on her shirt: I'M MARJORIE.

I was thinking, *Way to go, Marjorie!* when Connie nudged my arm with the hand she was using to hold her water bottle. "Look behind you," she whispered. "That just breaks my heart."

I turned slowly, casually, to see what Connie was talking about.

A thirtyish guy with a profile right off a Roman coin knelt on the wet pavement, helping his daughter, around four, adjust her rain cape. Through the plastic, the little girl's bib read: IN MEMORY OF MOMMY.

I swallowed hard, thinking how close Emily might have come to running this race in memory of me. My throat tightened as I recalled that awful day when, still groggy from the anesthesia, I'd awakened in the hospital to hear Emily sobbing in the hallway just outside my room.

I stole a glance at Valerie and knew, instantly, even before she spoke, that she was thinking the same thing. "That little girl's mother must have fought very, very hard," Valerie whispered.

I found Valerie's hand and squeezed it, too choked up to speak. I stared into the distance instead, toward the huge balloon archway that marked the starting line, then back into the mob of runners—north, south, east—in any direction other than that of the sad-eyed little girl and her handsome father.

My eyes skimmed the crowd. On the fringes, near the curb, stood a woman, her pink shirt showing through a clear plastic raincoat. Even from ten feet away I could tell her eyes were rimmed with red.

I nudged Valerie. "Look. See that woman over there? Is she all by herself?"

"Don't think so. See those two guys? Just behind her?"

But as Valerie spoke, the men moved away, confirming my suspicion that the woman was alone. She hugged herself, arms laced tightly across her chest as if trying to contain some private grief.

"Here, hold my water for a minute, will you?"

I elbowed my way through the mob until I was even with the woman. "You okay?" I asked, stepping up on the curb.

Even the rain couldn't hide the tears that coursed down her cheeks. "My sister was supposed to run with me today." She drew a ragged breath, gulping air. "But she . . . she died last week."

It was probably my imagination, but the rain seemed to fall harder then, drumming a dull *rat-a-tat-tat* on the bill of my cap. I slipped my arm around the woman's shoulders. "It's been four years for me. How about you?"

"Six years in September."

"You *are* a survivor," I said. We stood in companionable silence for a few minutes as packs of runners ebbed and flowed around us. Water that had collected on the twisted hem of her slicker poured onto her jogging shoes, but she didn't seem to notice.

"Your sister would have wanted you to run today, you know."

"I know. It's just so hard to . . . to . . . go on."

"But that's what it's all about, isn't it? Just going on."

She turned to face me then, swiping at her cheeks with the back of her hand. "You're right," she said. "You're absolutely right."

"Come run with us." I waved to my team, huddled in a pathetic blue and gold clump about ten yards away.

"Thanks. I'm okay. Really."

The woman squeezed my arm gently then turned and, before I could stop her, was swallowed up by the crowd.

I stood there for a moment, staring after her, praying she'd live to run the race again next year, when I noticed Connie trying to attract my attention by making exaggerated gestures, pointing to the starting line and to her watch.

Way up front, in the sea of runners, heads began to bobble. "They're off!" Connie called. But the crowd was so dense that, just like traffic jammed up on the beltway, I knew it would be five minutes, or even more, before we'd move even an inch in the direction of the starting line.

As I rejoined my group, the rain began to descend in torrents. Connie shrieked, then began laughing. "I'm soaked clear down to my underwear!" Someone began to cheer, and before long everyone around us, drenched and dripping, was laughing and cheering, too.

I nudged my way forward and stood next to Valerie, who had added a digital MP3 player to her running ensemble. I tapped her on the shoulder. "What are you listening to?" I asked.

Valerie smiled, removed one of her ear buds and handed it to me. "Listen."

I held the ear bud to my ear and concentrated, trying to identify the music over the deafening roar of the crowd. It wasn't hard. Lindsey Buckingham's gorgeously twangy guitar was slipping and sliding all around the lyrics of "I'm So Afraid," one of the tracks on Valerie's favorite Fleetwood Mac album, *The Dance*. " 'Days when the rain and the sun are gone,' " I sang out loud, tearing up again as bittersweet memories washed over me. Valerie had a boom box in the hospital room we shared. We must have played *The Dance* CD a thousand times, singing along, each confined to our separate beds, until we knew the lyrics to every song by heart.

Who could have predicted that, years later, Valerie and

I would be bonding again on a street in Washington, D.C. Like twins, each connected by our own umbilical cord to Valerie's MP3 player, our heads bobbing together in perfect rhythm as we sang: " 'So afraid/Slip and I fall and I die.' "

The song ended. Almost reluctantly, I handed the ear bud back to Valerie. Instead of screwing it back into her ear, though, she let it dangle and reached out to wrap me in a bear hug. We might have stood there forever, oblivious to the crowd, the noise, and even the pounding rain, if Connie hadn't whomped me on the back.

The runners in front of us had begun jogging in place.

I picked up my feet. "Valerie, can I ask you a rude question?"

"Sure," said Valerie, jogging in place beside me.

"When we first met, you were worried about how to pay your medical bills, so when I heard about the cruise and saw your house . . ." My voice trailed off. "You win the lottery or something?"

Valerie took off her cap and shook the water out of her hair. "Ha ha, I wish." She grinned broadly. "We had kind of a windfall."

"Yeah?"

"An insurance settlement."

"You won a lawsuit?"

"No, not a lawsuit." As space opened up, we began to jog forward. "Look, it's complicated. I'll explain later." Valerie adjusted her cap, screwed in her ear bud, and with a friendly wave jogged away.

"What was that all about?" asked Connie, running up to take Valerie's place beside me.

"It's complicated," I said. "I'll explain later."

Side by side Connie and I jogged south on 17th Street and west on Independence Avenue. *An insurance settlement*, I mused. *Very in-ter-rest-ting*. I barely noticed the water rushing along the roadway as I ran, until the stream became a torrent, carrying with it raw sewage from a storm drain that had overflowed. With Connie trailing close behind, I eased through the foul-smelling bottleneck, trying not to breathe. I'll never wear these shoes again, I thought, plodding on and on toward the Lincoln Memorial.

An insurance settlement. Chug-chug-chug. *Malpractice, maybe.* Chug-chug. *With an out of court settlement.*

Pulling slightly away from the pod of runners behind us, Connie and I looped west toward the Tidal Basin. As I dashed over Kutz Bridge, with my socks squish squish squishing, I found myself hoping Valerie would spill all, nondisclosure agreement, if any, be damned. I glanced right and couldn't resist waving to Thomas Jefferson, standing in the shelter of his memorial. Old T.J.'s Nikes, at least, were dry.

We zipped past the Holocaust Memorial, picking up speed near the Freer Gallery, so much so that the netting set up by Park Police to keep back the spectators became a blue peripheral blur. At the Hirschorn Museum, I slowed to concentrate on massaging a painful stitch out of my side, but Connie, recklessly throwing away any chance she might have had of setting a land speed record—as if—declined to run ahead, staying with me as we turned north on 7th Street. Runners streaked by, cutting and weaving, as we passed the Sculpture Garden and rounded the corner onto Pennsylvania Avenue. Just ahead, like a carrot on a stick, was Freedom Plaza and the black banner and digital time clocks that marked the finish line. Endorphins kicked in, and I sprinted the last hundred yards.

A few seconds later a loudspeaker blared, "Hannah Ives has crossed the finish line. She's a breast cancer survivor," and I thought my lungs would burst, whether with pride or from exhaustion, it would be difficult to say.

Valerie was waiting, as promised, on the steps of the Old Post Office Building. We gave each other a high five, then I collapsed onto the wet marble.

"Seventy-six minutes, more or less," I wheezed. "Gawd, I'm exhausted!"

Connie bent over, her hands resting on her knees. "How'd you do, Val?" she said, addressing her shoes.

Valerie beamed. "Twenty-seven."

Connie straightened. "Twenty-seven minutes? My God, girl. You on drugs?"

Valerie smiled. "I've been working out."

Breathe, Hannah! In through the nose. Out through the mouth. In through the nose. Out through the mouth. "I am so out of shape," I panted. I stood up, stretched and windmilled my arms. "I thought once around the Naval Academy seawall three times a week would prepare me for this. . . ."

"Do you have a running partner?" Valerie asked.

"No," I admitted. "I suppose it would be easier if I went running with someone."

Connie raised both hands, palms out. "Don't look at *me*, sweetheart! I've got a business to run."

That was certainly true. An article in the Sunday Arts & Leisure section about Connie's folk art dolls, made entirely out of gourds she grew herself on the Ives family farm, had brought in a flood of orders, so many that Connie had hired a part-time assistant.

"You got Thursdays free?" Valerie asked, ignoring my sister-in-law.

I nodded.

"I'll run with you," she volunteered. "Meet me at Quiet Waters Park around ten."

"Thanks," I said, enormously grateful. "I'd like that."

Connie had been drinking from her water bottle when she stopped in mid-swig and looked around as if she'd lost something. She had. Her husband.

"Where are the guys, Val? Surely they've crossed the finish line before now."

Valerie hooked a thumb toward the arched doorways that led into the building. "Brian and Dennis have gone to find Paul and the kids. I suggested we meet at the Hotel Washington on 15th Street. We can catch a cab to the restaurant more easily from there. Don't know about you, girls, but I'm ready for some *serious* carbohydrates."

A vision of the Thai Room's delectable Bean Thread Jelly Mushroom shimmered large before me, like an oasis in the desert, especially after my skimpy breakfast.

"C'mon," I called, my stomach rumbling. "Last one to the hotel is a rotten egg roll!"

CHAPTER 5

The doorman at the Hotel Washington gamely
held a black umbrella more or less uselessly over Paul's
head as he leaned his elbows against the passenger side
window and bargained with the cabby. Dressed in an in-
ternational yellow foul-weather suit he normally reserved
for sailing, Paul looked like the Gloucester Fisherman, but
whatever this fisherman was selling, the cabby, it was
clear, wasn't buying. I could tell from the expression on
the driver's face that he wasn't keen about taking a group
of shipwreck survivors on board. His eyes darted from
one of us to the other, clearly weighing the advantages of
a three zone fare, plus a dollar fifty for each additional
passenger, against how wet his seat covers were going to
be by the time he got us to the intersection of Connecticut
and Nebraska and paid him off, plus tip.

At the restaurant, two cabs later, we peeled off our sod-
den rain gear and left it to drip dry in the glass-enclosed
vestibule. The hostess led us past the booth seating to a
long rectangular table covered with thick, white table-
cloths where the rest of our party were already pulling out
chairs and getting settled.

Miranda didn't care for the booster seat the waitress
had brought her. She tucked her chin to her chest and
whined, "I'm a *big* girl, Daddy." Brian smiled apologeti-
cally and waved the waitress away, watching with a pater-

nal grin as Miranda hauled herself up onto the chair. Brian pushed her in, but her dimpled chin barely cleared the edge of the table. Her lower lip quivered. "I can't *see!*"

Connie shot Dennis a look that said, plain as day, *Thank heaven she isn't* our *kid,* and I caught Dennis winking back.

Valerie leaned toward her daughter. "Would you like to sit on a phone book, sweetheart?"

Miranda nodded, and in a few minutes was elevated to eye level with the rest of us, perched on a copy of the Metropolitan Washington yellow pages, seriously studying her menu. It was upside down.

Paul ordered wine, then surveyed the group over the top of his reading glasses. "Everybody like spicy?"

"I do," said Valerie, "the spicier the better. But not for Miranda. Do they have something milder, like Pad Thai?"

"Is the Dalai Lhama Buddhist?" Dennis quipped.

Connie cocked her arm and aimed a playful jab at her husband's rib cage. "He's been working too hard," she said. "Poor boy needs a vacation."

Dennis had, in fact, been working hard. A series of robberies, the last resulting in a triple homicide, had every convenience store clerk from Glen Burnie to St. Mary's City clamoring for bulletproof vests.

Dennis poured his wife a half glass of pinot grigio, then turned to Valerie. "We haven't been away, really away, since our honeymoon." He filled Valerie's glass, then passed the bottle to Paul.

I dipped the corner of my napkin in my water glass and used it to wipe liquefied Goldfish crackers off Jake's chin. "Brian and Valerie just got back from a fabulous trip," I said.

Emily smiled across the table at Valerie. "I was wondering where you got the terrific tan!" She folded a large cloth napkin into a triangle and tied it loosely around Chloe's neck. "Where'd you go? The Caribbean?"

Valerie laid her menu on the table. "We went on a cruise."

Before she could continue, the waitress appeared to take our order.

Brian looked up from the menu he'd been sharing with Miranda and said, "What do you recommend, Paul?"

"Everything's good," Paul replied.

"Why don't you order for us," Dennis suggested. "Community table, right?"

Nods all around. Soon Paul was locked in a serious discussion with the waitress, who, scribbling furiously, took down every word he said in Thai script.

"Dennis and I honeymooned in the Caribbean," Connie commented after the waitress had disappeared into the kitchen with our order. "What islands did you like best?"

"Actually," said Valerie, "we never stopped in the Caribbean. We went straight from Lauderdale to Cartagena in three days! Can you believe it?"

"Where's Cartagena?" Emily asked.

I stared at my daughter in mock horror. "Where's Cartagena? After four years at Bryn Mawr you have to ask? *That* was money well spent!"

Emily stuck out her tongue.

"It's in Colombia," Brian told her, laughing. The wine had reached our end of the table and he paused to pour me a glass. "On the Atlantic side of the canal."

By "canal," I presumed Brian meant the Panama Canal. No geography whiz myself, I was confused. I'd seen *Romancing the Stone* three times. I thought Cartagena was in Chile. Maybe there were two of them.

While Valerie and Brian described highlights of their cruise, interrupting each other excitedly from time to time, I nibbled on my Thai Room Special Chicken—a crab-stuffed drumstick, deep fried to a golden brown—and wondered about Valerie's insurance settlement.

During the Stone travelogue, platter after platter was

brought to our table. In addition to Pad Thai and the delectable bean threads I'd been lusting after, there was Lemon Grass Soup, Larb, Satay, Beef with Ginger Root, Chicken with Hot Chili and Garlic, Pork with Spicy String Beans, the sort of rough-hewn, lip-blistering fare one might encounter at the home table of an expatriate Thai cook. As each new dish arrived, we'd ooh and ahh and somehow rearrange the table to accommodate it, before falling upon it with dueling chopsticks like ravenous villagers. I thought I'd died and gone to heaven.

Meanwhile, I tried to figure out a tactful way to bring up the question of Valerie's good fortune. *Say, Valerie, speaking of the Shrimp in Red Curry Sauce, weren't you going to tell us about your recent windfall?*

Instead I ate silently and studied portraits of the Thai royal family that hung on the wall behind the well-stocked bar, while Valerie went on and on about the beauties of New Zealand, the mysteries of the Orient, the oppressive heat of India and Africa, and how disappointed she was that they got to spend one day—only one day!—in England, and in Southampton, at that. What was there to see in Southampton, for pity's sake?

"Wow!" said Emily simply after Valerie had talked the QE2 from Southampton back to New York Harbor. I jabbed my chopsticks into a spicy squid salad that was delicious but so spicy that it made my eyes water.

"Wow, indeed," said Paul.

"And you . . ." I pointed my chopsticks in Paul's direction. "You never take *me* anywhere!"

Paul held up a hand. "Not true! Remember the BVI?"

I settled back into my chair and chewed thoughtfully on a carrot curl before replying. "Yes. Well, there was that."

Several years before, Paul had been accused of sexual harassment by one of his students, an allegation both the Academy—and I—had taken very seriously. After putting everyone through months of hell, she'd withdrawn the charges. Exhausted by the ordeal, we'd chartered a sailboat in the British Virgin Islands, where, floating silently over the crystal blue, impossibly clear water of Manchineel Bay, the rifts in our troubled marriage had finally begun to heal. I smiled, remembering Paul's daily ritual: standing on the bow in his bathing trunks, gazing down the Sir Francis Drake Channel as the sun rose over the hills of Cooper Island behind him. How he'd turn to me with a goofy grin and sing like Jimmy Buffett, "Ah! Just another shitty day in Paradise."

According to Valerie, they'd had 120 days—none of them the least bit shitty—in Paradise.

Connie and Dennis were gazing meaningfully at one another. Based on our recommendation, they had honeymooned in the BVI. From the signals that were passing, like electricity, between them, I was betting their memories were X-rated.

I blushed and turned away, noticing that Chloe was using her fingers to arrange individual grains of rice into a design on her plate, making sure the noodles didn't touch the rice.

"Damn!" Dennis patted his waistband, pulled out his beeper and checked the screen. "Sorry, all. Gotta make a call."

Connie pouted. "Perfect timing, as usual."

Dennis kissed the top of his wife's head as he eased between her chair and the wall. "Don't worry, sweetheart. I'll be back before dessert."

I spooned rice into Jake's mouth while he reached for the dish holding the spicy squid. Jake would eat anything. Emily tried to persuade Chloe to try a shrimp, but my granddaughter was having none of it.

I turned to Brian. "Valerie tells me you've won some sort of lawsuit."

Brian glanced up from his noodles. "Not exactly." He gave Valerie a narrow-eyed look that would have turned Leona Helmsley to stone.

Valerie ignored him. "We cashed in my insurance."

"Your life insurance?"

Valerie nodded.

"I didn't know you could do that," I said.

Brian reached out and covered Valerie's hand, where it rested on the table, with his own. I knew the type. Now that she'd let the proverbial cat out of the bag, he would go all masculine and take charge on her. "It's a plan that became popular during the AIDS epidemic," he explained. "Here's a theoretical for you. Let's say I'm gay, terminally ill, with no dependents. And I've got this monster life insurance policy. Who's going to get it when I die?"

Connie balanced her chopsticks on the rim of her bowl. "Your family?" she suggested.

"That's one scenario," Brian continued. "But suppose your nearest and dearest believe that homosexuality is an abomination before the Lord? Suppose they've disowned you? What if you don't want them to get one red cent?"

"Change your beneficiary," Paul said.

Brian pointed a finger. "Exactly! That's exactly it! Change your beneficiary."

When we looked puzzled, Brian pushed his plate aside and leaned forward. "So let's say you're gay, you're terminally ill, your family's a bunch of homophobic shits, and your medical bills are sky high. You've also got a $500,000 life insurance policy. Why shouldn't you get to use that money now, when you need it most?"

"It's called a viatical," Valerie interrupted.

"Viati-what?" said Emily. She unwrapped a straw and plunked it into Chloe's milk.

"Viatical. It comes from 'viaticum.' That's Latin. It means preparations for a journey," Valerie said.

Brian nodded. "So this is how it works. You get a doctor to certify that you're going to die, you take that information to a financial services company that specializes in viatical settlements, and they buy your policy from you. Cash on the counter."

"I get it," said Paul. "You sign your policy over to them,

they pay you for it, and when you actually die, they get their money back."

"Right. And you get to spend the money any way you want," Brian added. "Medical bills. Clothes. Cars. Trips. Whatever."

"Wait a minute!" Paul held up a hand. "How does the company make any money on the deal?"

"Well, they don't pay you the full value of the policy, of course. It's on a sliding scale, based on their estimate of how long you have to live." He patted his wife's hand. "As you know, Valerie's prognosis was grim. The doctors gave her six months. A year, max. So the payout was about eighty percent."

Valerie shifted in her chair, as if uncomfortable with the turn the conversation had taken. "Yes," she chirped with artificial cheerfulness. "But I didn't die, did I, darling?" She smiled. "So we paid off my medical bills, and with the money we had left over . . ." She paused, glancing at Brian as if seeking his permission to go on.

"We bought the house and splurged on the trip," Brian finished for her.

"It's ironic, really," Valerie added, grinning broadly. " 'Viatical' means preparation for a trip. Well, it was for a trip." She giggled. "It's just that I didn't end up at the morgue."

CHAPTER 6

In the days immediately following my first marathon, I ran another marathon . . . of sorts. I vacuumed the house; paid the bills; tossed out my jogging shoes and bought a new pair, on-line, from LadyFootLocker.com; sanded and repainted the patio table in a color grandly named "manor green"; and helped Paul get ready for another famous race, this one from Annapolis, Maryland, to Newport, Rhode Island. On a sailboat. Following a gala reception on Friday evening, Paul would step aboard *Northern Lights* with the rest of her crew, making sure every sail, halyard, sheet, line, and cleat on the old Pearson 37 was shipshape and ready for a perfect getaway when the starter's pistol sounded in Annapolis Harbor on Saturday at noon.

Wednesday morning I was down in the basement, up to my eyebrows in laundry, doing my part, when Paul materialized behind me. "Do I have any clean underwear?"

I'd been rooting for a stray sock in the dryer and bumped my head on the way out. "Ouch!"

"Sorry, love."

I stood up, rubbing my head. "That's okay. I'll live."

"I'm packing and couldn't find any underwear."

"That's because it's all down here." I handed him a laundry basket. "Sort away."

Paul's idea of sorting was to paw through the basket

and select items he recognized, leaving the rest—my permanent press slacks and knit tops, for example—in a tangled heap. I watched him lay waste to three basketsful before asking, "Do you need a duffel bag?"

"No. Just a pillowcase."

I rummaged through a basket on the dryer and came up with three. "Which do you want? Laura Ashley, Ralph Lauren, or Bart Simpson?"

He added a neatly folded T-shirt to his pile, rested a paternal hand on top, looked down at me and smiled. "Ralph, I think."

"Ah-ha," I said, handing it to him. "Designer luggage."

I watched with amusement as Paul slid three neatly folded piles of clothing into the pillowcase, gathered up the open end and swung the pillowcase over his shoulder like a buccaneer, making off with his plunder. Sailor's luggage. A matter of pride with my husband. Anything that wouldn't fit into a pillowcase stayed home.

To tell the truth, I was missing him already. The house seemed so vast and empty when Paul was away, so I'd made plans to keep busy. There was my project at St. John's, of course. And shopping for drapery fabric with Emily. I might even take in a movie or three.

I'd gotten in touch with Valerie, too, confirming my promise to join her on Thursday for a run through the park, followed by lunch at Domino's. It'd be missionary work for Valerie, of course. She'd have to gear down, for one thing, running with me, like driving 40 in a 65 mph zone. As soon as they were posted, I'd checked the race results online. Valerie's time had been truly amazing: 212th in the twenty to twenty-nine age group. I was an embarrassing 1,394th in mine.

After Paul and his pillowcase set out for the Academy, I headed over to the St. John's College library, where I was wrapping up a long-term project organizing and cataloging the extensive collection of the famous mystery writer, L. K. Bromley. The author, a sprightly eighty-something whose real name was Nadine Smith Gray, had retired several years ago to Ginger Cove, an upscale retirement community just outside Annapolis. Since I began working on her collection, we'd become friends.

Presently I was tasked with tracking down Mrs. Bromley's short stories—most of which had appeared in *Collier's* and *The Saturday Evening Post* during the fifties and sixties—with the aim of reissuing them in a single volume. Working through Mrs. Bromley's literary agent, a taciturn New Yorker with a smoker's cough whose clients had mostly predeceased him, we'd identified several publishers, and he was now pressuring me for a proposal.

It had been slow going. We didn't have a title, for one thing. When I'd brought this up the last time we met for lunch, Mrs. Bromley had promised to think about it and get back to me. I was still waiting.

I grabbed a cup of coffee in the staff area of the library, then retreated to the quiet room at the southeast corner of the main floor that served as my office. Since she hadn't called me, I would call her.

"How about that title?" I asked the author after the usual pleasantries.

Mrs. Bromley moaned. "I'm simply *no* good with titles, Hannah. It's a sad, sad truth, but my publishers always picked them for me."

"There's a review here somewhere," I said. "It describes you as . . . just a minute." I scrabbled around in the folder marked *Reviews*. "Ah, here it is. 'She is the consummate wordsmith,' " I read, " 'whose writing style always has touches of poetry even when her subject is greed, power, murder, and retribution—and, as in *Death Be Not Proud*, the story of one woman's search for justice.' " I paused. "I am *so* disillusioned!"

Mrs. Bromley laughed. "How about 'The Collected Short Stories of L. K. Bromley,' then?"

"Borrrrrr-ing!" I paused for a moment. "You are a writer," I chided. "Words are your business."

"They've dried up, I'm afraid. When I traded in my pen for a paintbrush, Hannah, something happened. I'm having a hard time even remembering names."

"They say the proper nouns are the first to go," I chirped, regretting the words the instant they fell out of my mouth.

"That's supposed to be reassuring?" She chuckled, so I knew she hadn't taken it the wrong way. "So, Hannah, what do 'they' say about looking at your wristwatch and calling it a clock. I did that yesterday." She sighed. "Even the common nouns are deserting me. Discouraging."

"Noun deficiency anemia?" I quipped.

She laughed. "Yes, you might say that. Perhaps I should take up crossword puzzles. Use it or lose it, you know."

I doubted Mrs. Bromley had time for crossword puzzles. For the past year she'd been teaching art classes at Anne Arundel Community College three days a week. This semester, I knew, it was watercolors. Her students adored her.

"Okay, Mrs. B. Let's use it," I prodded. "First, I think we've got enough stories for two collections. Thirteen stories each."

"Really?" she said. "I'm amazed I wrote that many."

"More," I told her. "This is just the cream of the crop."

We batted titles around for a while, each more ridiculous than the last, before settling on "Maryland Is Murder" and "Chesapeake Crimes," the Collected Short Stories of L. K. Bromley, Volumes One and Two, respectively. We laughed, agreeing that the publisher would probably change the title anyway, to something more sexy, like "Bra Full of Bullets," and put a cartoon of a French maid blowing smoke off a revolver on the cover, but at least I'd checked one more thing off my To Do list.

Around four o'clock I took a break and brewed myself a cup of tea. Tina, the student aide, had just brought a copy of *The Capital* into the staff lounge. She checked the show times for movies at Annapolis Mall, then slid the newspaper toward me across the table.

Sipping my tea, I scanned the headlines. I don't know why I bothered. The SARS epidemic was still raging in the Far East. U.S. and British forces were still under fire in Iraq. Construction was still tying up traffic on the Chesapeake Bay Bridge. Depressing. With my cup to my lips, I turned the pages, checking the local news, gradually making my way back to the Letters to the Editor, which in our town were usually good for a laugh.

Since my recovery, I didn't normally read the obituaries. Too depressing, like Iraq. *Three years to live*, I'd think, if the deceased were older than me or, *Whoops, should have been dead five years ago*, if not. I hadn't any intention of reading the obituaries that day, either, but while skimming an article about a brave local dog that had lost his leg to cancer, a picture halfway down the right-hand side of the page caught my eye. A woman who looked a lot like Valerie Stone. Fuller face, though, and longer hair.

I stared at the picture, hard. I set my cup down unsteadily, sloshing hot tea all over the table. *It looks like Valerie Stone because it* is *Valerie Stone, you idiot!* I started to hyperventilate.

No, I told myself. It can't be Valerie. You just talked to her!

I folded the paper until I was staring at the headlines again. I counted slowly to ten, breathing deeply. Maybe I'd dreamed it.

But when I opened the paper to the obituaries again, there she was: Valerie Padgett Stone. On Monday, June 9, after a long battle with cancer. There was more, of course, about her father, the Honorable Fletcher J. Padgett of Saddle River, New Jersey. About the family receiving visitors on Friday at Kramer's Funeral Home. Something about in lieu of flowers that seemed to separate into individual letters that swam around the page, rearranging themselves like Scrabble tiles until they lost all meaning.

I blinked, eyes dry, too stunned, I think, to cry. *Valerie can't be dead! We're going running tomorrow!* I pictured Valerie as I'd seen her on Saturday, smiling at me and waving from the doorway of her beautiful new home, holding Miranda, who was sound asleep, in her arms.

Not Valerie, who could run a mile in six minutes flat. Not Valerie with her yoga-in-the-morning-Pilates-in-the-afternoon body. Not Valerie. No way. Valerie was in perfect health.

Still in denial, I scurried to my office and dug my cell phone out of my purse. I stared at the buttons for a while, then paged through my phone book until VAL-CELL appeared in the lighted window. I'll call her, I thought. She'll pick up.

But deep down I knew she wouldn't. I threw myself into my chair and dialed Paul at his office instead. It wasn't until I heard his cheerful voice saying "Ives" that I came completely unglued. "Valerie died!"

"What? Hannah, calm down! I can't understand a word you're saying."

"It's Valerie!" I sobbed. "Valerie Stone is dead."

CHAPTER 7

Paul didn't want me to go to the funeral home alone. Or so he said. Then he smiled with sad cocker spaniel eyes, like a boy whose trip to Disney World was about to be spoiled by an airline strike. No way *I* was going to ruin his precious sailboat race!

"Go! Shoo! Scat!" I said, flapping my hand at him for emphasis.

I wanted, no, *needed* Paul to be on his way. In the two days that had passed since we learned of Valerie's death, he'd been smothering me with attention. You'd think he'd been assigned to suicide watch.

"Valerie was my friend, not yours," I reminded him.

He opened his mouth to protest, but I closed it with a kiss. If he said one more comforting, oh-so-understanding thing to me about Valerie, I knew I'd break down and start bawling again.

"Besides," I added a moment later, reaching up to ruffle his hair, "it'd be embarrassing to have you moping about the funeral home with a bumper sticker pasted to your forehead that says, 'I'd Rather Be Sailing.'"

After Paul had set off for the Annapolis Yacht Club, I put away my cheerful smile and dragged myself up to the bedroom. I stared into my closet—could have been minutes, could have been hours—grieving over Valerie, worrying about Miranda, and wondering about Brian.

No one could make me believe that Valerie had died of natural causes. But if I followed that thought to its logical conclusion . . .

I shivered. The husband was *always* suspect. But what could Brian's motive have been? Valerie's insurance money was long gone: the house, cruise, and car were proof of that. Besides, Valerie had died on Monday. Didn't Valerie tell me Brian would be out of town that day?

I sat down, hard, on the edge of the bed. I frowned. That meant Miranda . . .

Please, God, don't tell me Miranda found her mother's body! My eyes filled with tears for the third time since morning, and I scurried into the bathroom to splash cold water on my face. In mid-splash I caught sight of myself in the bathroom mirror and wished I hadn't. Puffy eyelids, bloodshot eyes with purplish pouches underneath. If I knew a makeup artist, I'd be using the emergency entrance.

My hair wasn't too bad, though. The week before the race, I'd had it cut in a wash-and-wear bob and high-lighted, just for kicks. I fluffed it with my fingers. A wash and some mousse and I'd be ready to go.

If I ever figured out what I was going to wear.

Back at the closet, I pulled out a pants suit I hadn't worn since I quit the job in Washington, D.C. Charcoal gray. It matched my mood.

To keep my mind off the funeral home—*Please, God, don't let there be an open casket*—I rummaged through my jewelry drawer looking for something to brighten up my lapel. I have fifty boxes, I swear, marked AURORA GALLERY. I opened the one labeled CAT PIN and thought, not for the first time, that I should own stock in that store. If something happened to me, Aurora Gallery would have to declare Chapter 11.

I pinned on the cat and added a pink paisley scarf.

I plopped back down on the edge of the bed, checked my watch. Five o'clock. The family had been gathering at Kramer's for over an hour. Who would I know, besides

Brian? And Miranda, of course, if someone thought to bring her along. I suddenly wished I hadn't been so eager to send Paul on his merry way. With Paul along, at least I'd have someone to talk to.

I rummaged in the closet, found the Ferragamos I used to wear with the gray suit, and slipped them on. They pinched. I switched to a pair of Easy Spirit pumps. Wrong color. I retrieved my Clark T-straps from under the bed and eased my feet into them. Ah, much more like it.

I could have procrastinated away another ten minutes—a hat, perhaps? I had half a dozen hat boxes—proper round ones, too—stacked on the top shelf of the closet, but I chided myself for being so ridiculous.

It's just that I have a problem with funeral homes. Especially funeral services in funeral homes. Like sending a loved one off to heaven from the lobby of a hotel. Before my mother died, she'd insisted on cremation. There'd been a service at St. Anne's—Book of Common Prayer, Rite One—with Bach and Mozart on organ and flute. Two days later, at sunset, we'd taken Mother's ashes out on Connie's sailboat and sprinkled them over the Chesapeake Bay. If you have to go, it doesn't get much better than that.

I sighed, gathered up my courage and my handbag, double-locked the front door, and wandered up Prince George to the intersection with Maryland Avenue. I turned left, killing a few more minutes by browsing the shop windows, still trying to work out in my head what I would say to Brian. I wanted to know how Valerie had died, for one thing. It seemed tactless to come right out and ask, but then, my friends will say I've never let a little thing like tact stand in my way.

For more than a century Kramer's Funeral Home had been tucked away on Cornhill Street, one of half a dozen seventeenth century streets that radiate out from State Circle like spokes. Once a grand Georgian mansion owned by a wealthy colonial tea merchant, the house had been enlarged over the years to accommodate Robert Kramer's ever-expanding services to the dead, dying, and bereaved.

I entered the lobby and looked around. A rich, red oriental carpet. A mahogany highboy. A highly polished table, perfectly round, supporting a vase containing an elaborate flower arrangement the size of a Volkswagen Beetle. I touched a lily. It was cool, slightly damp, and very real.

To my right, an ornate, carpeted staircase led up to the second floor, but a red velvet rope prevented anyone from actually venturing upstairs. I circumnavigated the table, looking for someone who could point me in the right direction, and then I saw it. One of those signboards on a tripod, black, with white snap-in letters that usually spell out things like Soup du Jour: Cream of Broccoli.

Today's special was Valerie Padgett Stone. Blue Room. With an arrow pointing to the right.

It was so bald, so matter-of-fact, so . . . final. I gulped for air, glancing around the entrance hall, looking for a place to sit down, but apparently Mr. Kramer didn't want me to sit down in his lobby because he'd provided no chairs. I breathed in, and out, then followed the arrow to a room that was, as the sign said, blue. Relentlessly so. Blue carpet. Blue chairs. Blue draperies. Blue walls. Even the Kleenex boxes were blue.

And in spite of the fact that the newspaper had requested no flowers, baskets of delphiniums, as deeply blue as the South Pacific Ocean and just as beautiful, were arranged against the far wall.

Among the flowers, on a stand in front of a blue and gold brocade curtain, sat Valerie's casket, made of rosewood and so highly polished that I could see in it the reflection of the blades of a ceiling fan as it rotated slowly overhead. I took another deep, steadying breath. The lid was open.

I froze in the doorway, dreading the next half hour.

"Welcome." The voice belonged to a tall guy loitering in the foyer immediately to my right. Because of his blond hair, I figured he was related to Brian. He extended his hand and I took it, covering his hand with both of my own. "I'm so, so sorry," I said. I didn't find out till later he was the funeral director's son.

"Have you seen Brian?" I asked.

Kramer, Jr. pointed.

Brian, dressed in a dark navy suit with a red and white polka-dotted tie, chatted practically forehead-to-forehead with a grandmotherly type wearing a pink A-line skirt, a matching sweater set, and a short strand of fat, Barbara Bush pearls. Her fingers dug deeply into his sleeve. I knew the type: she would prattle on forever.

"You might sign the guest book," Junior suggested. "While you wait."

Using a silver pen actually attached to the book by a chain—can't be too careful, those Kramers—I scrawled my name, and Paul's, on the top line of a new page. At least thirty people had signed the book before me; not a single name I recognized. They were scattered throughout the room now, sitting pensively on chairs, staring at their hands or the walls. Some were standing, clustered in groups of three or four, making small talk.

When I looked his way again, Brian was holding court next to the casket, talking to a young woman wearing a sleeveless dress with poppies splashed all over it. If I wanted to speak with him now, I'd have to go up there. Next to the body.

I hesitated, my hand clutching the back of a chair, the metal cold beneath my fingers. Now that I'd signed the guest book, perhaps I could slip away before anyone noticed me? Then Brian caught my eye, and I was doomed.

I weaved through the crowd to join him. "I'm so, so sorry, Brian," I said after he released me from a hug.

Brian turned to his companion. "Corinne, this is Hannah Ives, one of Valerie's friends."

Corinne offered me a wan smile and a limp hand before flouncing off to join a group of other twenty-somethings huddled behind the lectern. They looked disgustingly fit, like the aerobics instructors they probably were.

Brian rested his hands on my shoulders and studied me with dry, bloodshot eyes. "Why did she have to go and die on me, Hannah?" His voice broke and he croaked, "What am I going to do?"

"I know how hard it is," I said. "I lost my mother a couple of years ago and a day doesn't go by that I don't think about her. Sometimes I hear a joke and I pick up the phone to tell her because I know she'd laugh her head off. . . ." My voice trailed off. "It gets easier to bear, over time, but the pain never goes away, Brian. I miss my mother terribly."

A huge tear rolled down Brian's cheek.

"Oh, damn! I didn't mean to upset you." I snatched three tissues out of a nearby box and handed them to Brian, who used all three to blow his nose.

"I wasn't there," he said, crumpling the tissues into a ball. He turned to his wife, lying motionless in her casket, and in a voice that was barely audible managed to choke out, "I wasn't there for you, darling. I wasn't there when you needed me."

Under the circumstances, there was no way I could avoid looking at Valerie, too.

Even in death Valerie was beautiful. She was dressed all in white: in satins, seed pearls, and lace. I cringed. It must have been her wedding gown. Her hands, as beautifully manicured as they had been in life, were folded at her waist, and between her fingers was twined a long golden chain with an engraved, heart-shaped locket on the end of it. I knew, without opening it, that the locket held pictures of Brian and Miranda, face-to-face, unaging, for all eternity.

I stared at Valerie's cheeks: plump, flushed, warm. Logically, I knew they weren't. Logically, I knew that if I worked up the nerve to touch her—as some of the other mourners had done—Valerie would feel cold as stone. Stone. I swallowed hard. This was hardly the time for puns.

Still, I couldn't persuade myself that Valerie was dead. She looked peacefully asleep, eyes closed, cheeks flushed, just as she had during our hospital stay.

Awake, Valerie had always been vibrant, bouncy . . . so, so . . . there was no other word for it, so *alive*. I found myself staring at Valerie's chest, willing it to rise and fall and feeling astonished when it didn't.

I was standing with Brian, praying silently, when I became aware of the music, wafting in from speakers carefully camouflaged within the decorative hexagonals of the wainscoting. Mozart, I thought, then a jarring segue into "You Light Up My Life." After a bit, electronic violins swooped and soared into "On Eagle's Wings." How Valerie and I would have laughed over that!

I reached out and took Brian's hand, squeezed it. "What killed her, Brian?"

"Her heart just stopped," he whispered.

"Her heart?" I couldn't believe it. "But Brian," I said, turning to look at him, "she trained. She could run a mile in nothing flat. How could a heart as healthy as that simply stop?"

"It was the chemo," he said, simply. "All those drugs, most of them experimental. They said it could weaken her heart. It was a known risk."

I remembered the consent form they made me sign before starting my own chemotherapy, the catalog of warnings about side effects that ranged from aggravated hangnails to death. I nodded. "Oh. Yes. I see."

But I didn't see. How many people did I know of who were actually killed by their chemotherapy? Not very many.

And if chemo didn't kill her, who did?

Not Brian, surely. He was no longer the beneficiary of

Valerie's life insurance policy, I reminded myself. Whoever bought it was.

Whoever bought it. A frisson spawned of pure, cold evil shuddered up my spine.

"Brian, can I ask you something?"

Next to me, I thought I felt Brian stiffen, but his answer was disarmingly casual. "Sure. Shoot."

"Losing Valerie so suddenly like that reminds me that time is precious. I want to make the most of every minute I've got." I paused, waiting for Brian to finish shaking hands with a tweedy couple in their mid-seventies. "I've been thinking," I said after the couple had moved on. "I've got a life insurance policy. Not as much as Valerie's, I suppose, but it's gotta be worth something. Maybe I should do what you and Valerie did? Cash it in? Take a cruise?"

"Yeah?"

"Yeah. With that . . . what did you call it, viatical thing?"

"Viatical. That's right."

"Who did you work with on that, Brian?"

Brian patted his breast pocket. "I've got his card . . . whoops, wrong suit." He flashed me a crooked grin. "The guy's Jablonsky. First name, Gilbert. Has an office up in Glen Burnie."

"Thanks," I said. "I'll look him up."

"You do that," said Brian. "The man's a prince."

I strongly doubted that any princes lived in Glen Burnie, Maryland, a five-mile-long corridor of chain stores, fast food restaurants, and car dealerships, punctuated by traffic lights at every single intersection.

"It was really worth it," Brian added thoughtfully.

"Cashing in her policy?"

"No, I mean the chemo. It was hard on Valerie, for sure, but it gave us another year together. Didn't it?"

"I'm sure Valerie never regretted it," I said, thinking of Miranda. I was one hundred percent sure about Miranda. Although the Stone marriage seemed strong, at least on the surface, Valerie had never discussed her relationship with Brian, so how she might have felt about her husband in the privacy of her own home was another thing altogether.

I squeezed his hand. "Where's Miranda now?"

"Kat is bringing her."

"Kat?"

"Katherine. Valerie's mom."

"From New Jersey? I read that in the paper."

Brian nodded. "Valerie's father is a judge up there." He dropped my hand and turned to face the others. "What am I going to say to all these people, Hannah? Tell me, what am I going to say?"

I touched his shoulder with the palm of my hand, letting it rest there for several seconds, feeling the soft, damp wool. "Let them do the talking. You just nod and say, 'Thank you.' Nobody expects any eloquent speeches from you, Brian."

Brian nodded. "Kat's been a godsend. She wants Miranda to stay with them for a few weeks. They've got ponies. . . ." Brian paused, looking puzzled, as if trying to remember who he was and what he was doing there.

"I think that's a fine idea," I said. I'd never met Valerie's parents, of course, but unless they had just been let out on parole or were dabbling in satanic cults, Miranda might feel more secure with them than batting around a big empty house with a father who was, to put it mildly, distracted.

"There they are now," Brian said.

Valerie's parents—a handsome couple of the "I'm running for political office and you're not" persuasion, swept into the room and were immediately surrounded by a gaggle of sympathizers. The Honorable Judge was a handshaker. Mrs. Padgett nodded and smiled, nodded and smiled, like a bobble-head doll. A professional multitasker, she somehow managed to control a purse strap that wanted to slip off her shoulder, a wayward strand of auburn hair that, in spite of all the hair spray, tumbled over an eyebrow, as well as a squirming Miranda, whose right hand she kept firmly clamped in her own.

"But I have to *go!*" Miranda wailed.

Valerie's mother bent down and without disturbing her permagrin, warned, in a hoarse whisper that somehow carried clear across the room, "Not *now,* Miranda."

Miranda's legs turned to cooked spaghetti. She hung, suspended, an uncooperative lump on the end of her grandmother's silk-clad arm.

I smiled, almost feeling sorry for the woman. "Looks like your mother-in-law has her hands full."

"Yeah," said Brian. "Guess I better go bail her out. Excuse me, will you?"

I laid a hand on his arm. "No. I'll go. You have other things to do."

Brian flashed a grateful smile and tipped an imaginary hat. "Thanks, Hannah. Later." He turned to trade a low-five with a middle-aged hunk who'd been hovering nervously at his elbow for a minute or two. The guy bulged uncomfortably in his churchgoing suit, as if he couldn't wait to get home and trade it in for jeans and a T-shirt. I left Brian and the bodybuilder to trade fitness tips, and went to introduce myself to Valerie's mother.

Physically, Katherine Padgett was a hard-edged, more shop-worn version of her daughter, but there the resemblance ended. Mrs. Padgett, as it turned out, was more than willing to allow me, a perfect stranger, to take Miranda off her hands. With a vague, distracted smile she probably reserved for loyal retainers, she passed the little girl over to me, then immediately resumed the conversation I'd so rudely interrupted. I'd never met Ellen Moyer, the mayor of Annapolis, but I recognized her from pictures in the paper.

So don't introduce me to the mayor, you insensitive clod! I'm just the nanny. I sent a half-hearted curse in Mrs. Padgett's direction—*May lipstick stains defile your teeth*—then turned my attention to her granddaughter, my knees popping audibly above the strains of "My Heart Will Go On" as I knelt on the carpet next to the child.

"Hi, Miss Miranda. Do you remember me?" I didn't want her to think I was some creepy stranger.

"Yeth. You're Mrs. Hannah."

"That's right. I came to your house one day and your mommy and your daddy and you and me all went running in the rain!"

Miranda nodded sagely.

"So, why don't I call you Miranda and you can call me Hannah, just like friends."

"Okay."

Switching into grandmother mode, I asked, "Do you need to go potty, Miranda?"

Miranda nodded, her ponytails bouncing like springs.

Kramer, Jr. pointed us in the direction of the ladies' room which, when we found it, was decorated in soft peach tones, a welcome relief from the relentless sea of blue. Miranda and I discovered that one of the two stalls was already occupied by a pair of slim ankles in bright red, high-heeled sandals.

I ushered Miranda into the other.

To my surprise, Miranda was wearing disposable pull-ups.

"Mommy's gonna buy me big girl panties," Miranda chirped as I boosted her up onto the commode.

"Wow," I said, trying to sound impressed. After two weeks of potty training, Chloe, at three, had already reached that milestone. I suspected she could have nailed it in two days flat, but Emily was bribing her with M&Ms, so the little scamp had drawn it out, milking it for all the M&Ms she could get.

Miranda sat primly on the toilet, producing nothing but the tap-tap-tap of her patent leather heels against the porcelain. "Don't watch me," she said.

"Okay." I pulled the stall door toward me and held it closed while Miranda tinkled, waiting for the telltale rumble of toilet paper spinning off the roll. From the stall next door came an unmistakable sound. The owner of the red shoes was quietly retching.

"You okay in there?" I asked.

"Fucking clams!"

"Is there anything I can do?"

The red shoes turned, heels facing out, and a bright floral hem floated down, gently covering them. I knew the next sound, too: the dry heaves.

When I'm sick to my stomach, nothing feels better than a cool washcloth across my forehead. I was heading for the paper towel dispenser when I noticed Miranda had hopped off the toilet seat and was crouching on all fours, peering under the partition into the adjoining cubicle. "That lady's throwing *up!*" Miranda crowed.

"Go away!" the lady whimpered.

I tried again. "Are you sure there's nothing I can do?"

"Just get that damn kid out of here and leave me the fuck alone!"

I grabbed Miranda's arm and eased her gently to her feet. "C'mon, Miranda. The lady wants some privacy."

With one chubby hand Miranda tugged at her pull-ups. "What does fuck mean, Mrs. Hannah?"

I bent to help Miranda with her panties. "It's a very, very bad word."

Miranda smiled up at me slyly. "My mommy says I should never say fuck. Only bad people say fuck."

"Your mommy is right, Miranda," I said, fighting the urge to giggle. Whatever explanation Valerie had given her daughter, the child was clearly seeking a second opinion.

"Is that lady bad?" Miranda asked, pointing toward the occupied stall.

"No, the lady's not bad. She's just not feeling very well."

"My mommy gives me ginger ale," Miranda offered helpfully.

"Maybe somebody will give the lady ginger ale, too, Miranda," I said. But, I thought, it sure as hell ain't gonna be me.

CHAPTER 8

In olden days, a woman waved her sailor off with a perfumed handkerchief and a kiss, then paced the widow's walk until his sails reappeared on the horizon.

Nowadays, we send them off with plastic bags full of Snickers bars and wait for a call on our cell phones.

But nothing has changed about the kiss. I planted a good one on Paul, then stood on the seawall and watched until *Northern Lights* was a tiny white triangle against the far, dark shore of Kent Island.

Then I went home to look for my life insurance policy.

I started with the Bombay chest in the living room where Paul keeps Important Papers—capital I, capital P. Frankly, I don't go there very often. It holds our old checkbooks, of course, so you'd think I'd open the drawer from time to time, but after I got cancer, I gave up balancing checkbooks. Numbers had never been my friends, and as it appeared that my days *themselves* could be numbered, I didn't want to spend a single one of them fooling around with numbers.

Besides, Paul can extract square roots in his head. He does our accounts on Quicken. And he *loves* his Turbo-Tax. "It's the most challenging computer game in the world," I've often heard him say. "If you play it right, you get money back. If you play it wrong, you go to jail."

H&R Block and I? We love that in a man.

I sat cross-legged on the rug, pulled open the drawer and began to paw through its contents. I found checkbooks going back to 1985, the deed to our house, titles to the cars; and in the back, held together by a green rubber band, were Emily's report cards from elementary school. In kindergarten, I noted, my daughter "played well with others." She still did, I mused. There was a lot to be said for that.

Why Paul would want to hold on to a deed to one square inch of land in Alaska from a 1950s Ralston cereal promotion was completely beyond me, but underneath our precious toehold in the Klondike, I found what I was looking for: a fat brown folder marked, in Paul's neat square capitals, INSURANCE.

Inside there were pockets for House, Car, and Life, and an empty, achingly optimistic pocket labeled "Boat." I pulled an accordionlike document with my name on it out of the "Life" pocket, unfolded and read it through, including the fine print.

If I died tomorrow, Paul would be a quarter of a million dollars richer. He could buy that boat, I thought, and a nice one, too, although I prayed he would wait a decent amount of time before allowing some *other* woman to lounge about the bow in her tankini like a hood ornament.

I tucked the insurance documents into my handbag, then wandered upstairs to put the rest of my outfit together.

What's appropriate when bartering with strangers for one's life? I decided on a lime green frock with splashes of white because it gave me a demure, slightly vapid look. I wiggled into some panty hose, then buckled on a pair of white-white sandals with two-inch heels and tottered over to the Imari dish on my dresser where I keep my hair ornaments. I selected a rhinestone-encrusted bobby pin and slid it into the cluster of curls over my right ear.

I was done.

No I wasn't. A vision of my life insurance policy poking out of that lumpy brown leather object presently masquerading as a handbag in my entrance hall sent me back to the closet for a small white clutch that had once belonged to my mother. I pulled out the spaghetti-thin strap that was tucked inside and suspended the bag from my shoulder. I minced over to the full-length mirror hanging on the back of our bathroom door to check the results. If my sister Ruth could see me now, she'd be laughing her caftan off: Mary Tyler Moore, circa 1965, on her way to make life miserable for Alan Brady.

I certainly hoped so.

I drive an old LeBaron, an orchid-colored convertible that I wouldn't trade for anything—unless a sweet deal on a vintage Mercedes 450SL happened to come along. Making the most of a beautiful day, I cranked down the top and let the wind run riot through my hair as I sped north on Ritchie Highway as fast as traffic would allow.

I had looked up Gilbert Jablonsky in the yellow pages and discovered he worked for an outfit called Mutually Beneficial Financial Services Group. MBFSG had offices in Bowie, Laurel, and Greenbelt, Maryland, but Jablonsky hung his hat in a building in Glen Burnie, not far from the Maryland Department of Motor Vehicles.

Jablonsky's building, when I found it, was newly constructed of pink polished stone, rising smugly above the squalor of the neighborhood. If Jablonsky and Co. hoped they were setting a good example to which their neighbors would rise, they must have been sadly disappointed. A bank kiosk, a gym, a pizza parlor, and a store called Party City occupied an adjoining strip mall that might have been state-of-the-art in the 1970s. On the opposite side, a brushless car wash and detailing center had spruced up a bit with colorful murals and tree-sized potted palms, but it would take more than a good example, I thought, to get Manny to remove that wrecked car from the roof of his auto body shop.

I parked in the shadow of Manny's, gathered up my

purse and cell phone, and, leaving the top down, went off to see whether the inside of Jablonsky's building would live up to the outside.

It did.

MBFSG had a suite of offices on the sixth floor, lushly decorated in peach, celadon, and cream. Framed prints from the National Gallery of Art decorated the walls, and, standing proud and tall in an oriental-style pot on the receptionist's desk, was a lipstick red amaryllis in full bloom.

"Is Mr. Jablonsky in?" I asked.

The receptionist considered me with cool, green eyes. "Do you have an appointment?"

"No," I admitted. "But I was in the neighborhood and was hoping I would catch him in."

"Who shall I say?" she asked, plucking a ballpoint pen from a MBFSG coffee mug—red with white letters—sitting next to her monitor.

I told her my name and she jotted it down on a yellow Post-it pad. "Have a seat," she said. "I'll see if he's available." She ripped the Post-it off the pad and wandered down a short hallway with the Post-it stuck to her thumb.

A few seconds later she was back, without the Post-it. "He'll see you now," she said, and ushered me into a small but attractively furnished office with a picture window overlooking the parking lot. If he leaned back in his chair, Gilbert Jablonsky could easily sail paper airplanes through the front door of Amore Pizza. Right now, though, he was on the telephone.

"I think we need to cut our losses on that one, Alex." Jablonsky stood and covered the mouthpiece with a beefy hand. "Sorry," he whispered. "I'll just be a moment." He nodded vigorously at something the person on the other end of the line was saying, but his eyes were all over me. "Please. Sit." He waved vaguely at a pair of upholstered chairs placed side by side, facing his desk.

I smiled.

I sat.

I arranged the skirt of my dress modestly over my knees, folded my hands on top of my handbag and gazed demurely at Jablonsky as he continued his conversation. His voice was deep and resonant, so resonant that I thought he could moonlight doing voice-overs. Darth Vader came to mind, or the voice of God in *The Ten Commandments*.

Gilbert Francis Jablonsky, Jr., CFO—or so it was engraved on the nameplate on his desk—was tall and tanned, with a generous shock of salt and pepper hair which he'd recently had trimmed, causing his ears to stand out like handles on a sugar bowl. He wore a blue and white striped long-sleeve shirt tucked into the waistband of slim, beltless navy blue trousers held up by a pair of pink paisley suspenders. He had neatly draped his jacket over a hook on a wooden coat tree near the door.

As Jablonsky talked—to someone in Florida about reverse mortgages—he paced. "Nuh-uh," he said evenly. "C.J.'s a big boy. Don't you think it's time he learned to pull his own chestnuts out of the fire?"

Apparently, Jablonsky didn't like what he heard, because he frowned. "Well, sir, just ask him to think it over and get back to me." And he hung up quietly without saying good-bye.

Jablonsky eased into his chair and leaned forward. "So," he said, turning his full attention to me at last. "What can I do for you, Ms., uh . . ." He glanced at the Post-it. ". . . Ms. Ives. May I call you Hannah?"

"Sure," I said.

"Gil."

"I beg your pardon?"

"Gil. Please call me Gil."

"Oh, sorry." So far I was coming off as something of a dingbat. *Begin as you mean to go on*, Mother always used to say. "Gil," I began, trying it out. "Well, *Gil*," I continued, easing into my role, "I was talking to this friend of mine? And she said . . ." I flapped a hand. ". . . well, never mind what she said, but she told me all about viaticals and, well, I've got this *life* insurance policy? So I—"

Jablonsky held up a hand. "Whoa! Back up a minute!" He smiled, revealing a row of straight, ultrawhite teeth. "Most people have never even heard the term 'viatical,'" he commented. "I'm impressed. So, how did you find out about me?"

"My friend, Valerie Stone?" I said, lacing my fingers together and twisting them nervously this-way-and-that. "Valerie and I talked about it a lot. Before she . . . before she died."

"Valerie Stone," he repeated thoughtfully. The crease between his brows deepened. "Ah, yes. I remember Valerie well. Young. Very young. Such a pity."

I nodded.

"She had a child, too, didn't she?"

I nodded again. "Yes. Miranda. She's four."

"That's the hardest part about this job, Hannah. Losing my clients."

"But Valerie was sick," I reminded him. "*Real* sick."

"Most of my clients are." Jablonsky's chair creaked, protesting, into an upright position. He rested his forearms on the leather blotter and flashed me a solicitous smile, as if it had just occurred to him that I might be one of those moribund customers, too. "But," he added quickly, "as Valerie's friend you probably know that her death, regrettable as it may have been, was, all too sadly, inevitable. With the money we were able to negotiate for her, though, she was able to live out her last days in comfortable fashion." He paused. "*Very* comfortable fashion."

I blinked rapidly, fighting back tears that were all too real. "That's what I'm here to talk to you about, Mr. Jablonsky."

"Gil," he reminded me.

"Gil." I studied my thumbnails. "I've got cancer, too, you see."

Jablonsky sucked in his lips, closed his eyes and shook his head slowly from side to side. "Damn," he said simply.

I fumbled for my purse, pulled out my policy and laid it on his desk, smoothing out the creases. "I saw what you did for Valerie and figured you might be able to do something for me, too."

With two fingers, Jablonsky slid my policy toward him across the desk. He folded his hands on top of it, making no move to read it. "Tell me about yourself, Hannah."

So I hit him with my whole medical history, skating just a bit over the question of my prognosis, which was probably much too excellent for his purposes, thank you very much.

Jablonsky made listening noises—*uh-huh, gee, um, oh-yes, I see*—at all the right places, and when I got to the part about how disfigured I felt after surgery, he closed his eyes, tapped his tented fingers against his lips and said, "That must have been rough."

I took a deep breath and let it out slowly. You had to hand it to the guy: *great* bedside manner. Next thing you know, he'd talk me into letting him remove my appendix with his letter opener.

He raised an encouraging eyebrow, so I rattled on and on. When I ran out of steam, Jablonsky thanked me, then skimmed over my policy, flipping through pages at a furious rate, explaining the fine points of viatical settlements to me as he went along. "I see your husband is beneficiary."

"That's right."

"Should we bring him on board?"

"Oh, Paul's away on business," I cooed, "but if he were in town, he'd be sitting right here next to me." I patted the seat of the empty chair to my right.

In point of fact, if Paul *had* been listening, he wouldn't

be sitting anywhere. He'd be flat out on the floor, having a coronary.

Jablonsky examined the last several pages. "Mostly boiler plate," he murmured, picking up a pencil, "but there are some goodies in here." He jotted something down on a pad of lined paper, then looked up at me with a sober smile. "We'll need a certificate from your doctor, of course."

"Of course." I nodded sagely.

"Then, depending on what he says about your prognosis, we should be able to do something very nice for you."

"Can't you tell me how much my policy's worth now?" I asked. "I'd like to surprise my husband when he gets back."

Jablonsky chuckled, as if I'd said something amusing. "I don't buy the policies myself, Hannah," he explained, "I'm just a broker. More like a matchmaker, really." He grinned. I swear to God, the guy practically *twinkled*! "What I do—with your permission, of course—is shop your policy around to the various viatical settlement firms I usually do business with. When we hear back from them, I'll call you in, we'll sit down at a table, look over the proposals and take the best offer."

"Can you give me a ballpark figure?" I pressed. "You know. For my husband?"

Jablonsky tapped the eraser end of his pencil on his notepad. Then the pointy end. Then the eraser. "Well, don't *hold* me to this, now, but considering your medical history, you might qualify for as much as sixty-five or seventy percent."

"And that's . . ." I squinted at the ceiling through half-closed eyes. "I'm not very good at percents, Gil," I said.

"One sixty-five, one seventy thou." He spread his fingers and rocked his hand back and forth. "More or less."

"My goodness!" I squeaked, all the while thinking that goodness had very little to do with it. If Mrs. Gilbert

Francis Jablonsky Senior's little boy was donating his services out of the pure goodness of his heart, then step aside Camilla Parker-Bowles because *I'm* going to be the next Queen of England.

"So," I inquired sweetly. "How much do you charge, Gil?"

Another thousand-watt smile. "Ten percent."

I paused, digesting this bit of information. "Well," I said, standing and gathering up my belongings. "It sounds like a win-win situation to me."

"You bet your life," he replied.

Jablonsky escorted me to the door. He laid a hand gently on my upper arm. "I'll be in touch," he promised.

Halfway down the hall, I turned. Jablonsky still stood in his office doorway, looking after me.

He tipped an imaginary hat.

I waggled my fingers.

You bet your life.

"That's exactly what I'm afraid of," I whispered to the amaryllis as I passed it by.

CHAPTER 9

No matter how many times I do it, there's some-thing magical about being able to sit in the comfort of my own backyard and surf the Internet.

The previous Christmas, Paul had bought a network card for my laptop computer and set about installing a wireless network in our basement office. I had to smile, remembering how he scuttled up and down the basement steps, fiddling with the antennae, testing the coverage by wandering all over the house with my laptop, looking for hot spots. He can't do on-line banking in the living room, as it turns out, or in the guest bedroom, but he can transfer funds to his heart's content from the upstairs bathroom.

Technology, ain't it grand?

The signal's hot, too, on the patio, so that's where I went on Sunday morning with my laptop and a glass of fresh brewed iced tea to see—in the good old American "if it sounds too good to be true it probably is" tradition— what I could find out about viaticals.

A half moon floated in the blue of the late morning sky as I powered up Google and typed in "viatical": 36,000 hits.

I sat back, stunned. Thirty-six thousand hits for a word I'd never even heard of until a week ago? Where had I been? Living under a rock?

I typed in "Tammy Faye Bakker." Only 8,660 hits, and *everybody*'s heard of Tammy Faye Bakker. I'd *definitely* been living under a rock. On the planet Pluto.

I clicked the back button, returning to "viatical."

Skimming through the first screen of entries more or less confirmed what Valerie had told me: viatical settlements had been introduced in the early years of the AIDS epidemic, largely for humanitarian reasons, to improve the final days of AIDS patients. If you have a *life* insurance policy, the reasoning went, why not use it for *living*?

What Jablonsky had neglected to mention was that with the advent of protease inhibitors and other powerful medications that help prolong the lives of AIDS patients, the pool of qualified applicants had begun to dry up. In response, viatical settlement firms cast their nets wider, targeting individuals with illnesses such as cancer, diabetes, or heart disease. Then the viatical market virtually exploded, spreading beyond the terminally ill to reach out to the elderly—the older and more affluent (and sicker!), the better. *Who could lose?* The seller gets a large sum of money immediately; the broker collects a commission for his efforts; the buyer snags a life insurance policy at a discounted rate and collects the face value of the policy upon the individual's death. And because death is inevitable, there can be no default on payment. Right?

I figured there had to be a catch.

I rose from my chair, picked up my glass of tea, and began a slow stroll around my garden, just to mull it all over. More or less absentmindedly, I deadheaded a rose, picked three leaves out of the birdbath, and was setting up the sprinkler to water a patch of droopy hollyhocks when I noticed the garbage bag that had flattened my primrose border.

I knew the culprit, Lillian Perry, a lovely but confused seventy-five-year-old suffering from mid-stage Alzheimer's disease. She shared the house next door with her attorney son, Bradford, who had moved to Annapolis several years ago. In her own mind, Lillian had never left her Tennessee farm, and she continued to dispose of her garbage in the approved Thomasboro, Tennessee, way— she chucked it over the barbed-wire fence and into a sinkhole.

As a way of getting acquainted with your neighbors, tossing garbage over the fence left a lot to be desired. But it launched—so to speak—our friendship with Brad, so until it got out of control, neither Paul nor I were inclined to complain.

I dragged the Perrys' garbage over to our can and stuffed it in.

When I returned to my computer for another go, a drop-down window was flashing like a billboard on Times Square in the upper right-hand corner of my screen. I clicked to get rid of it, but my aim was off, so I opened the window instead. Some Ph.D. with more abbreviations after his name than there were letters in the alphabet desperately wanted me to buy his book on viatical fraud.

Inspired by the good doctor, I clicked back to Google and typed in "Viatical fraud."

Seven thousand hits. Plus. Holy moley!

I picked an article at random. In it, a state regulator reported that a patient with a life expectancy of ten months was paid twenty percent of the death benefit of his policy, which, had he been less sick, desperate, and ill-informed, could have netted him eighty percent or more. In general, though, sellers had few complaints. It was the buyers further up the food chain who often got screwed.

In the mid-nineties, I learned, the word went out—in venerable publications such as the *New York Times*, *U.S. News & World Report* and the *Wall Street Journal*—that investing in viaticals was that rarest of animals—a no risk thing. The *New York Times* reported that with profits on investments averaging nearly twenty percent, it was a business that had become "too attractive to ignore."

Indeed.

And when celebrities like Phil Donahue and Morley Safer jumped on the bandwagon, the industry boomed like plywood sales during hurricane season. It was A Sure Thing! They said so on *60 Minutes*! Everyone wanted in. Investor demand rapidly outstripped the ability of brokers to supply viaticated policies for investors to buy.

Some out-and-out crooks were raking in investor money so fast they didn't even bother buying policies with it, spending the money instead on beachfront homes, cigarette boats, fast cars, and airplanes, or squirreling it away in the Cayman Islands. But everyone else was scrambling. Pretty soon, brokers began stooping to just about anything, and I mean *anything*, to get their hands on policies they could resell.

I sat back and sipped my tea, imagining the scenario.

A guy's got AIDS and no life insurance policy. No insurance company in its right mind is going to sell him one. But his friends are selling their policies right and left, so he goes to a broker like Hooke, Lyne & Sinker and complains that he wants a policy to cash in on, too.

"So apply," Hooke tells him. "Just don't tell them you have AIDS."

"But what if they require a physical exam?" the guy might ask.

"Easy," says Mr. H, smooth as silk and twice as slick. "We'll make the policy for $100,000, so you won't even need a physical."

"But I need more money than that," the guy complains. "I can't work, and I gotta pay for my meds."

"We have people who will take the physical for you."

"Whoa," our guy says, "ain't that dishonest?"

"Well, sure," Hooke says, "but who's it going to hurt? The insurance company's rolling in dough. They won't even miss it."

So, our guy gets the policy, waits a decent amount of time, and then—ohmahgawd, what a surprise!—is diagnosed with AIDS and viaticates it.

Clean-sheeting, they call it. Happens every day. Some AIDS-inflicted entrepreneurs had turned "wet ink" policies around so fast, they started calling them "jet" policies.

The insurance companies were not amused. Tens of thousands of investors lost everything when the insurance companies discovered the fraud and rescinded the policies.

On www.watchoutforthis.com there was a picture of Mrs. Mildred Page Belton, age seventy-five, dressed in her red vest, still greeting customers at a Wal-Mart outside of Sun City, Arizona. Mildred's life savings—her comfortable retirement—had vanished. I stared at her care-worn face and work-worn hands and swore that if some S.O.B. did that to *my* grandmother, I'd kill him. Something lingering, with boiling oil in it, I thought, paraphrasing a favorite line from Gilbert and Sullivan. Something humorous, but lingering, with either boiling oil or melted lead.

Poor Mildred wasn't alone. Many millions of dollars more had to swirl down the toilet before lawmakers began to sit up and take notice.

Congress could have done something, of course, by putting third-party viatical sales under the jurisdiction of the Securities and Exchange Commission. But, nooooh! They left it up to the states. And by the time individual states got around to exercising some control, the proverbial cows were well clear of the barn and had been dropping cow pies all over the country.

I clicked around and found a table: Laws Governing the Viatical Services Industry. Nearly forty states had laws of some sort on the books.

Maryland, unfortunately, didn't appear to be one of them.

I found that hard to believe. A few screens back I'd read that one of the nation's biggest cases of viatical investment fraud had originated in Baltimore, with coconspirators rounded up in Florida, Texas, California, Kentucky, and Ohio.

Maybe the table was out of date. I clicked over to http://mlis.state.md.us. The Maryland General Assembly had, for the second successive year, failed to pass a bill that would have put viatical brokers under the jurisdiction of the Maryland Insurance Administration. What were they thinking? In Maryland, it seems, life insurance can be bought and sold like houses, used cars, or season tickets to the Orioles. And anybody can do it, even the hot dog vendor at Camden Yards.

I thought about the last paycheck I'd received as a temp: $126.30, after taxes. Maybe I needed a change in career.

At noon the bells in the Naval Academy Chapel dome began to chime like Big Ben. I have a crotchety neighbor who complains about them, firing off indignant letters to the Naval Academy superintendent and *The Capital* on a regular basis. But I *like* the bells. They're steady and reliable, something you can count on in the howling chaos of this world. As the last note faded away, I found myself sitting there with my eyes closed, wondering: what happened to Valerie's policy after it left Jablonsky's hands? If Valerie's policy had been sold to an investor, I reasoned, every day that Valerie lived had cost that investor money. I wrapped both hands around my glass, and although it was easily 75 degrees in the shade, I shivered. Suppose, just suppose, that investor had grown impatient waiting for Valerie's policy to "mature"?

I drank the last of my tea, fished the lemon wedge out of the bottom and lobbed it in the direction of the compost heap. It plopped into the birdbath instead. I had just gotten up to retrieve it when the telephone rang. Leaving the sparrows to deal with the lemon, I hurried into the kitchen to answer the phone, nearly tripping over the neighbor's marmalade cat, Molly, who was basking in the sun on our back stoop.

It was Paul on his cell phone, calling from sea with a progress report. His voice faded in and out as it bounced from satellite to satellite, but it cheered me enormously just to hear him.

"Looks like you've got gorgeous weather," I said.

"Maybe where you are, sweetheart, but out here it's pretty crazy. Heading south on the bay we got caught by a couple of thunderstorms. Lightning struck the mast and fried our electronics, including my new GPS."

Paul loved his Global Positioning Satellite receiver almost as much has he loved his wireless PDA. "Lightning?" I said. "My gawd! What are you going to do without a GPS?"

"Well," he laughed, his voice a chain of echoes pulsating down the line, "we can always follow the other sails!"

"Be serious, Paul!" Although the crew of *Northern Lights* would probably accept it as a challenge, the thought of a bunch of guys in the middle of the Atlantic navigating by stars and a handheld compass didn't fill me with confidence.

"Don't worry, Hannah. We've got two spares," Paul said, reading my mind.

"And lots of batteries?"

"Lots." He sounded amused.

"You're having fun, aren't you?" I teased.

"Aaaaaaayaaayaaa-yaa-aaa-aaa-aaa!" It was a valiant effort, but Paul's Tarzan yell petered out at the end, as if my ape man had come to a sudden stop, like against a tree.

"Be careful out there," I warned. "The deck's bound to be slick with all that testosterone sloshing about."

Paul laughed, then got serious, asking me about the funeral and worrying aloud that he hadn't been there. I figured he had enough worries without burdening him with my suspicions about Valerie. So I told him the funeral was fine, I was fine, everything was fine, and that I'd be spending Sunday afternoon in Baltimore with my sister, Georgina.

But after we said good-bye I changed my plans. I called Georgina and told her something had come up.

What *had* happened to Valerie's life insurance policy?

I wasn't going to ask Gilbert Jablonsky, that was for sure. So there was only one other way I could find out. My famous turkey tetrazzini casserole and I would pay a condolence call on Brian Stone.

CHAPTER 10

Brian himself answered the door. He looked like hell. Dark stubble speckled his cheeks and covered his chin, his eyelids were at half mast, even his ponytail looked dejected, hanging limply down his back like a damp rope. He wore khaki shorts and a Grateful Dead dancing turtles T-shirt with a big coffee stain, as if the blue turtle hadn't made it to the Porta-Potty in time.

For a moment I just stood there, taking it all in, barely noticing that the casserole dish was freezing my hands off. I straightened my arms, thrusting it forward. "I thought you could use this, Brian."

He took the dish from me. "That's really thoughtful, Hannah. You didn't have to, you know."

"But I wanted to," I said stupidly. We stared at each other uncomfortably for a few moments while I tried to figure out how to wrangle an invitation inside. "It's not much. . . ."

"Wanna come in?" he asked.

"Thanks," I said, stepping over the threshold.

The foyer looked the same as the last time I visited, except now a matched set of suitcases was lined up neatly to the right of the door. I followed Brian and my casserole to the kitchen where a menagerie of foil-covered dishes and colorful Tupperware containers littered an expanse of countertop the length of a runway at BWI. Brian turned, *Help me* writ plain in his eyes.

"It's frozen," I prompted.

Brian blinked. Clearly, I wasn't getting through. I circumnavigated the kitchen island, took the casserole from his hands and set it down between a Corning Ware dish and a rectangular cake pan. "Look, Brian. Why don't you let me help you put some of this away?"

"No, that's okay," he said. "Val's mom is still here. She's out with Miranda now, buying her a swimsuit. We're leaving in the morning."

"Well, in that case, your mother-in-law needs all the help she can get," I said, turning up a corner of foil on a blue baking dish in order to check its contents. Green bean casserole. I popped it into the freezer. "So, you're going to New Jersey?" I asked. "I thought it was just Miranda." The next dish held a salad. I found a place for it easily. Valerie's refrigerator was the size of your average New York City apartment.

Brian leaned against the stove. "We're taking Valerie home," he said. "She'll be buried in the family plot."

"Oh." I couldn't think of anything else to say, and neither could Brian. He stared out the French doors, twisting his wedding ring round and round. Seeing him like that just about broke my heart.

"I'll be back in a couple of days," he said, suddenly snapping back from wherever it was he'd gone. "Miranda will stay on with her grandparents, for a few weeks, anyway. She's going to camp."

Camp? At age four? I couldn't believe what I was hearing. "Sleep-away camp?" I stammered.

"Oh, no!" Brian replied, his lips lifting in a tentative smile. "It's a mini day camp. Sports, creative arts . . . you know. They'll teach her to swim." The smile vanished as quickly as it had come. "Kat will make sure she gets there and back every day."

I was standing there, gawping, holding a foil-wrapped brick of something that looked suspiciously like pound cake, when Brian came to life again. "I mean it, Hannah. Kat is going to take care of this." He took the package from me. "If you want to be helpful, I could really use another cup of coffee." He pointed to the coffee maker, a sophisticated contraption with buttons and knobs that appeared, upon closer examination, to do everything for you, including grind the beans. The bean reservoir was empty.

"Coffee beans?" I asked.

Brian pointed to the cupboard over the coffee maker.

Valerie must have really loved her coffee. The cabinet held bags and bags of coffee beans arranged in two rows and neatly labeled: Mocha Java, Kenya, Tanzanian Peabury, Sumatra Mandheling, Kona, Brazilian Santos, Costa Rica, and—my heart flopped in my chest—Val's Blend. I quickly refilled the hopper with Val's Blend, crumpled the bag into a ball and tossed it in the trash. At least Brian wouldn't stumble across that sad reminder of his dead wife.

Meanwhile, Brian had unwrapped the pound cake, sliced off several pieces, and arranged them on little plates, adding a scoop of fresh-cut fruit from a bowl sitting out on the sideboard. The man wasn't as helpless as I'd thought. When the coffee was done, we poured it into mugs and took turns adding milk directly from the carton.

"Let's sit on the patio," he suggested, using his elbow to push open the door.

Outside, I set my cup on a honey-gold teakwood table, pulled out a chair and lounged back appreciatively. "What a view!" Over the vanishing edge of the Stone's in-ground swimming pool, sun sparkled on the gray-green water of the Chesapeake Bay. A windsurfer zipped past, his pink vinyl sail glistening. Because it was a Sunday, sailboats were out in force, too, scooting back and forth across the bay and in and out of the mouth of the South River like white-winged butterflies.

"It *is* wonderful, isn't it?" Using his fingers, Brian picked up a cube of pineapple, popped it into his mouth and chewed thoughtfully. "Valerie loved sitting out here."

"I can see why," I said. "If I lived here, you'd never get me off the patio."

Brian leaned back in his chair, propping his feet—flip-flops and all—up on the table. He stretched, laced his fingers behind his head and closed his eyes.

Out on the river the windsurfer had turned and was heading in our direction, skimming along at maybe twenty knots. Just feet from the shore, he jumped, spun and flipped the sail, heading across the river again, completely at one with his board.

"We talked about buying a boat," Brian said languidly, "but we never got around to it."

I reached over and gently squeezed his arm. "Valerie didn't have any regrets, Brian, and you shouldn't, either. Those last months? You made her so very happy."

Brian turned to me, his eyes moist. "You think so?"

"I know so."

"It's just that I feel like such a shit, sitting here, enjoying all this . . ." He waved an arm. ". . . when I know Valerie paid for it with her life."

"But Valerie was given the time to enjoy it, too. Surely that counts for something?"

Brian shrugged. "I suppose."

We sat in silence for a while, drinking coffee. At one point the telephone rang, but Brian ignored it, letting the answering machine pick up. "Brian?" I said after a bit.

"Ummm?"

"I went to see Gilbert Jablonsky yesterday."

Brian's head swiveled around until he was looking directly at me. "Did you like him? Isn't he great? Are you going to go with him?"

I raised both hands. "Whoa! One question at a time!"

Brian grimaced. "Sorry. I didn't mean to sound like an infomercial for the guy."

"That's okay." I grinned back, hoping to put him at ease. "Yes, yes, and no."

"Huh?"

"Yes, I liked him. Yes, I think he's great. And, no, I don't know whether I'll be selling my life insurance policy or not." I paused, letting those blatant falsehoods sink in before continuing. "It's just that Paul's away on a sailing trip and I'll need to talk it over with him first."

"What's not to like?" Brian swung his feet to the ground, rested his arms on the table and leaned toward me. "When Jablonsky called us, we jumped at the chance."

"Wait a minute! Jablonsky called *you*?"

Brian nodded.

"How did Jablonsky find out that Valerie was sick?"

Brian shrugged. "Who cares? It was a good deal and we took it."

If what Brian said was true, Jablonsky had to have someone—like at the doctor's office or at the hospital—on his payroll. My stomach lurched. I swallowed twice, trying to calm it.

"Do you mind if I ask you something about your deal, Brian?"

"Sure. Shoot."

"Jablonsky told me he's just a broker, that some other company actually buys the policies."

Brian nodded. "Right."

"So, do you know who bought Valerie's policy?"

"An outfit called ViatiPro, Inc."

I squirmed in my chair. "I don't know about you, Brian, but it makes me really uncomfortable thinking that there might be some investors out there wishing me dead."

Brian shook his head slowly. "I can see where you're going with that, Hannah, but you're way off base. Valerie died quietly in her sleep. ViatiPro had absolutely nothing to do with it." Brian's chair legs screeched on the concrete as he scooted it closer to mine. "Let me explain. ViatiPro buys hundreds and hundreds of policies. If somebody doesn't die as soon as they expected . . . ?" He shrugged. "They're a big company. One policy, more or less, wouldn't make the least bit of difference to their bottom line."

"How about the investors, then? What if one of them—?"

"Hannah," he said with exaggerated patience, "ViatiPro sells policies in packages. So, investors are buying shares in more than one policy; and the policies mature at different times."

Mature. There was that word again. The only way an investment like this could "mature" was when somebody died.

"Even so, just for the sake of argument, what if some investor . . . some desperate investor, say, got tired of waiting for his investment to, as you say, 'mature'?"

Brian stopped me. "I see what you're getting at, but let me assure you, ViatiPro erects pretty secure firewalls between policy holders and their investors."

"Okay. I can buy that. But I'm still puzzled. If they keep the names of the viators secret, then how do the investors know they're buying *legitimate* policies?" I remembered some of the articles I'd read, like "Scam Watch: Grim Reapers Target Deathbed Investors." "How do investors know that ViatiPro isn't just taking their money and buying imaginary policies with it? You know, ripping them off?"

Brian grinned. "Well, it was a little weird," he said, "but a ViatiPro rep used to call us up once a month to see how Valerie was doing, so they could report back to their investors."

"Ugh!" It just slipped out. I couldn't help myself. "What kind of report?" I asked.

"Every viator has a number. ViatiPro has a website where you can type in that number and track your investments . . ." He drew double quotes in the air with his fingers. ". . . on-line."

The cake I had just been nibbling turned to sawdust in my mouth. I washed it down with the last of Valerie's special coffee.

My husband watched the stock market go up and down on CNN or the Business Channel. What could possibly be going through the mind of an individual who logged onto the Internet each morning checking (hopefully!) to see if anybody in his investment portfolio had died!

"High tech," is what I said.

I was thinking, though, that financial speculation in the death of others didn't strike me as evidence that our species is advancing.

CHAPTER **11**

The whole viatical thing was giving me the creeps.

After my matter-of-fact conversation with Brian about Valerie, I went home and took a bath—a long, hot bath—hoping to soak the revulsion out of me beginning at some deep molecular level. It didn't work. Every time I leaned back in the tub and closed my eyes, vultures began to gather and circle beneath my eyelids, peering down with flame-red eyes at Valerie, sunning herself poolside, oblivious to the danger hovering overhead.

After I dried off and changed into pajamas, I tried to telephone Paul, but got switched to his voice message. *Northern Lights* must be out of cell phone range. I checked the itinerary tacked up on the bulletin board in the kitchen: they would be somewhere off the coast of New Jersey that night. If they were making good time, Montauk Light—110½ feet tall, with a beam that was visible for miles—would be flashing every five seconds on the horizon. If they weren't, well, let's be optimistic. Maybe somebody on the beach at Fire Island would be flashing.

I left a message for Paul to call me, then cobbled together a dinner: leftover tuna noodle casserole and what remained of a can of stewed tomatoes.

Then I did what anyone else would have done under the circumstances. I ate a half pint of Häagen-Dazs rum-raisin ice cream all by myself, crawled into bed, and fell asleep watching a rerun of *The X-Files*.

Our lives are defined by milestones. Graduations, weddings, the birth of our children. For me, life is either BC or AC—before cancer or after. Every day AC is a precious gift. I'm sure Valerie thought so, too.

Monday, June 15. My friend had been dead for a week. When I got out of bed that morning, I stared at my polished toes and thought that when I got that pedicure, Valerie Stone was still alive.

I didn't feel much like breakfast, but figured I'd better eat something, so I toasted a bagel.

As I sat at my kitchen table, munching thoughtfully, it bothered me that I still didn't know very much about Valerie's passing. *Peacefully in her sleep, of heart failure*. More than that, the newspaper hadn't said. And who had discovered Valerie's body? Brian would know, of course, but it would have been crass and insensitive of me to ask.

I wondered, too, if there had been an autopsy. I knew that the bodies of people who died under suspicious circumstances were sent to the Office of the Medical Examiner in Baltimore; that was the law. Yet, nobody seemed to think there was anything the least bit suspicious about Valerie's death. Nobody, that is, except me.

Paul would tell me I was overreacting. Maybe so. But rock a few boats, shake a few trees, and sometimes the truth falls out.

After a few minutes I trudged outside in my slippers to pick up the newspaper, tossed it, still in its blue plastic sleeve, on the kitchen table, and tucked my mug and dirty plate into the dishwasher. As I filled the little trapdoor with dishwashing detergent and snapped it shut, I remembered with a pang that ghastly day when my mother had a heart attack, collapsing right where I stood, on my kitchen floor. The paramedics had been amazing, and everyone, it seemed, worked in concert to save my mother's life, even the neighbors who poured out of their houses and stood on the sidewalk, praying she'd be okay. Police and emergency vehicles blocked the street, lights flashing, for nearly an hour. Valerie couldn't have passed on, I reasoned, without somebody in her neighborhood noticing something. The people living in the faux Tudor disaster across the street, for example, or the house I had taken for a toolshed just next door.

You never know until you ask.

Television's intrepid Jessica Fletcher might have gone trundling off to Hillsmere on her bicycle, but I went looking for a cover. That sent me back to the deep freeze for another of my rainy day casseroles. I set it carefully on the floorboard of my car and drove it to Hillsmere, hoping that the Stones weren't surrounded by commuting couples who couldn't tell you whether their siding was white or yellow because they so rarely saw it during daylight hours.

With my tires spitting gravel, I brought my LeBaron to what I hoped was a conspicuous, screeching halt in the Stone's driveway, then, carrying my casserole, I strolled casually up the walk and rang the bell. Nobody answered. Shading my eyes with one hand, I peered through the tall, narrow windows that flanked the door. The suitcases that had been there the day before were gone. A good sign.

I left my car parked in the Stones' driveway and carried my casserole out onto East Bay Drive. According to the mailbox, the house next door belonged to an R. Carpenter. It was much larger than a toolshed, of course. I could see that clearly as I rounded the hedge and strolled leisurely up a walk of round concrete slabs, each one decorated with a different fossilized plant. R. Carpenter and his missus—if there was a missus—shared a modest, sixties-style split foyer. The aluminum siding—in creamy vanilla—was complemented by dark green shutters. All of it looked brand new. A copy of the *Washington Post* lay on the lawn. A good omen. Someone must be home.

I tucked the newspaper under my free arm, rang the bell.

Just on the other side of the door, a dog barked. After a few seconds the door swung wide and I found myself gazing into a pair of pale blue eyes set in a plump, pleasantly round face, fresh-scrubbed and pretty, without a speck of makeup.

Even without her strand of fat pearls, I recognized her immediately: the woman in pink I'd seen talking to Brian at Valerie's funeral. Now she was dressed in a soft apricot warm-up suit the same color as her hair, and she'd clumped downstairs to greet me wearing a pair of white crepe sole creepers so clunky that I was amazed she could even pick up her feet. On the steps behind her a miniature poodle was yapping.

"Hi," I said, raising the casserole dish slightly for illustrative purposes. "I'm Hannah Ives, a friend of the Stones? I brought this casserole over for Brian, but I can't get anyone to answer the door."

The longer I talked, the faster the dog yapped. The little mutt must have been on speed.

Mrs. Carpenter covered her ears with both hands, turned her head and shouted, "Shut up, Yacky!"

"Yacky!" I had to laugh. "What an appropriate name for your dog."

Still holding the door open with one hand, she beamed out at me. "It is, isn't it? Didn't start out that way, of course. Yacky's short for Cognac. Sorry, you were saying?"

"Uh, I wanted to leave this casserole for Brian and Miranda, but nobody seems to be home."

Mrs. Carpenter joined me on the little porch, pulling the door closed behind her, probably to keep Yacky from escaping and terrorizing the neighborhood like Dogzilla. "Such a pity about Valerie, isn't it? She was the *sweetest* thing. . . ." Her voice trailed off.

"Valerie and I used to jog together," I told her, stretching the truth just a smidge. "I still can't get used to the idea that she's gone."

"We haven't been neighbors for long, but in that time I grew to love her like a daughter." She half leaned, half sat against the wrought-iron railing. "When the Stones were building their house—you should have seen the old place, it was such a dump!—Valerie used to come over and visit with me while Brian talked to the contractors." Her eyes glistened. "I feel so sorry for Miranda."

My casserole was melting. The foil had frosted over; water had condensed on the sides and sweated off, dripping on my toes, which stuck naked out of the ends of my sandals. "I guess I should take this home," I said.

"Oh, no. Don't do that. Why not leave it with me? I'll just pop it in my freezer and keep it until Brian gets back." She pushed open the door, stepped back into her foyer and motioned for me to follow. "They've gone to New Jersey, by the way. With Valerie's body."

I figured some sort of response was required, so I said, "Oh."

The instant I stepped over the threshold, Yacky went nuts.

"Just ignore him," Mrs. Carpenter said. Easy for her to say. She wasn't carrying a newspaper and balancing a casserole with a maniac dog nipping at her heels. "What is it?" she asked.

"What's what?" I said, puzzled.

"The casserole."

"Oh, eggplant parmesan."

"My my," said Mrs. Carpenter. "I'd better label it 'Tofu Delight' or Dick—that's my husband—will be all over it the minute our backs are turned." She waved an arm. "Come in, come in."

With Yacky dancing around my ankles, I followed her into the kitchen.

"Dick's off at a SPEBSQA convention," she said in way of explanation. "So it's just us girls."

Spebsqua? What the heck was a spebsqua?

Mrs. Carpenter grinned, apparently reading my mind. "S-P-E-B-S-Q-A," she spelled out. "It's the Society for the Preservation and Encouragement of Barbershop Quartet Singing in America. Dick sings in a quartet." She opened the door of her side-by-side, shuffled a few items around, then pushed my eggplant parmesan all the way into the freezer with the flat of her hand. "There! Now we can tell Brian to come over here the next time he needs a good dinner. I'll even heat it up for him."

"Thanks, Mrs. Carpenter. I really appreciate it."

She flapped a hand. "Pshaw! And call me Kathy, *please*. Would you like some coffee?" she asked, all in one breath. "It'll put hair on your chest, but it's hot."

Kathy's coffee was as different from the cup I shared with Brian the day before as Valerie's coffee was from instant. "Mmmm, robust," I said. We were sitting at the kitchen table. A picture window, hung with cheerful yellow curtains dotted with plump strawberries, overlooked the river, which sparkled in the mid-morning sun.

"Kathy," I said after a respectful silence during which I was supposedly savoring the full-bodied flavor and aroma of her coffee, "I keep worrying about something."

Kathy set her cup down in its saucer and gave me her full attention. "What is it, dear?"

"Well, the last time Valerie and I talked, she told me Brian was going to be out of town on Monday. He had some sort of assignment, she said. I know they don't have live-in help, so I worried . . ." I paused. "I worried that it was Miranda who found her mother's body."

Kathy nodded so vigorously that the half glasses that had been perched on her forehead slipped down to rest on the bridge of her nose. "I'm afraid so."

I shuddered, suddenly cold in spite of the scalding hot coffee and the sun streaming through the window. "Poor little thing! What did she do?"

"She came looking for me, thank goodness. I'll never forget that day as long as I live." Kathy fished around in her jacket pocket, withdrew a wad of Kleenex and used it to blow her nose. "Eight o'clock in the morning, and there she was, at my back door, wearing her Hello Kitty pajamas, carrying her Elmo doll and telling me, 'Mommy won't wake up.'" Kathy pressed a hand flat against her chest and took a deep breath. "I thought my heart would *break*." A fat tear slid down her cheek; she swiped at it with the wadded-up Kleenex. "I'm like a *grandmother* to that child. Brian's parents have been dead for years and, well, you've met Katherine and Fletcher. . . ."

For a split second I couldn't think who she was talking about, then I remembered—Valerie's parents, the Honorable Judge and missus. I set my coffee cup down on the table, narrowly missing the saucer. "Kathy, I'm so sorry. What on earth did you do?"

"I went next door with Miranda, of course, and sat her down in the kitchen with some cereal. Then I went upstairs to check on her mother." Kathy was crying openly now, the Kleenex ragged and useless. I got up, ripped a paper towel off the roll mounted over the sink and handed it to her. After a while she continued. "Valerie was cold as ice, Hannah. I don't have much experience with these things, thank goodness, but I suspect she had been dead for hours and hours."

"How awful for you."

"I dialed 911, as anyone would, and the paramedics came right away." She shook her head. "But there wasn't anything they could do." She spread the paper towel out on the table, smoothed out the creases, then pinched bits absentmindedly off the edges as she continued. "Then a policeman came, a nice young man, who stayed with us until we could get in touch with Brian."

"Where *was* Brian?" I asked.

She plowed on, ignoring my question. "It wasn't easy, I can tell you! I left three urgent messages on his cell phone. Three! It was over an hour before he called us back."

"I would hate to have been in your shoes, Kathy. How did you tell him? What on earth did you say?"

"Oh, I didn't talk to him, dear. I just couldn't! I let the policeman do it. I mean, it was private, family information, wasn't it? People to be notified. Decisions to be made. And Brian was *miles* away in Harpers Ferry."

"He must have been wild with grief."

"Oh, he was, he was. Brian was practically incoherent on the phone. Not much use to the police, I'm afraid. It was me who helped the officer find the telephone number of Valerie's doctor."

"Doctor?" I paused, swallowed, hoping she hadn't noticed that I'd practically yelped the word. "Didn't the police call the medical examiner?"

"The medical examiner? No, dear, why?"

"Well, I understood that all unattended deaths . . . you know."

She shook her head. "Everybody knew about the chemo and the risks Valerie took when she agreed to go through with it. Allen Kimmel's been her GP for years. He rushed right over and examined Valerie himself. If there had been even the slightest *hint* of something out of the ordinary, I'm sure Dr. Kimmel would have noticed."

"I'm sure," I said, but I wasn't sure at all.

"We should all be so lucky," Kathy Carpenter said, turning her cup round and round in its saucer.

"How so?"

"When my time comes, to go to sleep all peaceful like that, in my own bed with a comforter tucked up nice and neat under my chin."

Once again I froze. In the hospital, Valerie had tossed and turned until her bedding resembled a mixed salad. I decided to keep that information to myself. "I think Valerie deserved a few more years, don't you?"

Kathy's gaze shifted heavenward and she said, as if reading the words off the ceiling, " 'So teach us to number our days, that we may apply our hearts unto wisdom.' " Her eyes settled on me again, and she smiled. "Psalm Ninety."

"Oh, I do," I assured her. "I most certainly do."

At that moment, though, I wasn't applying my heart unto wisdom or anything else. My heart was aching, picturing Miranda, dressed in her footie pajamas, eating Cheerios in the kitchen while her mother lay dead in a bedroom upstairs. That image would haunt my dreams for a long, long time.

CHAPTER **12**

It's gotta be a law. When you need a shoulder to cry on, all the shoulders you know and love are bound to be out of town. Paul was at sea, Daddy wouldn't be back from Arizona until Wednesday, and the shoulder I ached for most—my mother's—had been lost to me forever.

I was well into my forties, Raggedy Ann was, well, raggedy, and I hadn't worn footie pajamas for years, but I had a lot in common with Miranda.

Something else I shared with Miranda was an honorary grandmother. Mine was Nadine Smith Gray, a.k.a. L. K. Bromley.

I telephoned Mrs. Bromley and, like all perfect grandmothers, she was at home. I invited myself for lunch, which, being a perfect grandmother and a perfect friend, didn't ruffle her feathers a bit.

I hadn't been to Ginger Cove for several months, so the construction took me by surprise. A contractor had begun working on the new assisted living center; construction trailers and piles of lumber and bricks made it necessary for traffic to be temporarily rerouted. I wound right, then left, then right again, then drove in a big circle before slotting my car into a parking space in front of Mrs. Bromley's building. When I got in range, I'd given her a ring on my cell phone. I found her waiting for me on the ground floor nearest the stairway leading to her apartment, holding the security door open.

I gave her a hug. "I'm so glad to see you, Mrs. Bromley."

"For heaven's sake," she said for about the twentieth time since we'd met. "When are you going to start calling me Naddie?"

Our relationship had begun on a professional level: she the famous mystery writer, I a lowly temp. I wondered if I'd ever feel comfortable calling L. K. Bromley by her given name. "I'll work on that," I promised.

"Come up. I've decided we'll eat in my apartment today. You could use a bit of cheering up, so, no sick people, no wheelchairs."

I was enormously grateful.

"Besides," she said, "If we eat *chez moi*, I won't have to change."

I'd never seen Mrs. Bromley wearing blue jeans before, but they flattered her slim figure. A bright pink long-sleeve T-shirt was tucked into her waistband. An Indian silver belt set with turquoise stones and Easy Spirit sandals completed the ensemble.

"I like your shirt," I said.

"It matches my eyes," she chuckled as she preceded me up the stairs.

"What?"

Mrs. Bromley stopped on the top step, turned, and her eyebrows shot toward her hairline. Her eyes grew wide. "Bloodshot," she said. "Too many late nights for an old lady."

"You? I thought you never stayed up past the eleven o'clock news."

"Not lately," she said. "Check this out." She opened the door to her apartment and waved an arm. "*Voilà!*"

Propped up on easels and lined up against the walls of her living room were dozens of paintings—still lifes, seascapes, and a few portraits, mostly of children. I recognized Annapolis Harbor and views of the Severn River and the Naval Academy. As for the still lifes, the fruit might be long gone, but the decorative plates and vases that had posed for their portraits had been returned to their places on Mrs. Bromley's built-in, Williamsburg-style bookshelves.

"This is lovely," I said, pausing in front of a portrait of a towheaded boy with his dog. The boy carried a fishing pole over one shoulder. A string of minnows dangled from his left hand. He stared out at the viewer, while the dog studied the minnows with large, luminous eyes.

"I worked from a photograph," she said, handing me one of two glasses of wine that were sitting ready on a side table. "But I always insist on taking the photo myself." She raised her glass. "Cheers!"

"Thanks," I said, taking a sip. The wine was cool, crisp, and slightly sweet. "I needed that."

I inched my way around the perimeter of the room, sipping wine and admiring Mrs. Bromley's work. "Everything's wonderful!" I enthused. "What's up? You having a sale?"

"As a matter of fact, I have a show in a couple of weeks at Markwood Gallery on Maryland Avenue. Do you know it?"

"I sure do. I live just around the corner, remember? Will I be invited to the opening?"

"Count on it." Mrs. Bromley had wandered from the living room into her pocket kitchen, where she pulled plates and glasses out of the cupboard. "Several of my students are exhibiting, too, so it should be quite interesting . . . if you have a taste for watercolors. Not everybody does."

I had planned to tell her after lunch, or wait until dessert, at least, before letting my hair down, but I blew it. Maybe it was Mrs. Bromley's Impressionistic portrait of a young mother and child that set me off, but whatever, the floodgates opened, and I told her about Valerie's untimely death, about my appointment with Jablonsky and everything I had learned to date about viaticals.

"It turns the whole notion of life insurance on its head!" I ranted. "How can it be a good idea to have strangers wishing me dead? A beneficiary should have a vested interest in my well-being, for heaven's sake, not hovering about waiting for me to die."

"I'm not familiar with the term 'viatical,'" Mrs. Bromley said thoughtfully after I'd stopped sputtering. "But what you're describing sounds a lot like senior settlements."

"Is that where a senior citizen sells the rights to his life insurance policy for some sort of percentage of its face value based on a sliding scale according to age?"

"Bingo." She twisted the cork out of the wine bottle and topped off my glass. I took another long swallow. If I didn't take it easy, I'd be too tipsy for the road, and I'd have to spend the afternoon sleeping it off on Mrs. Bromley's sofa.

While I continued sipping, observing through the pass-through, Mrs. Bromley bustled about her kitchen, hauling plastic deli containers out of the refrigerator and lining them up on the counter.

"Several months ago," she said, spooning some pasta salad onto a luncheon plate, "one of our residents invited me to a cocktail party. So I went." She put the lid back on the pasta container and opened one containing olives. "You know me," she chuckled. "Never turn down the chance for free hors d'oeuvres." She thrust the container in my direction. "Olive?"

I selected a fat green one stuffed with garlic and popped it into my mouth.

"Turns out," she continued, sliding an olive into her own mouth, "turns out to be like a glorified Tupperware party. There was an investment adviser who trotted out a little PowerPoint show and encouraged us to invest our money in blocks of used life insurance policies." She arranged some fresh fruit and sliced tomatoes on the plates. "I don't know about you, Hannah, but any time I feel like my arm's being twisted, I take a step back and say whoa! And this fellow was *real* hard-sell. Claimed it was a no-risk thing, better than CDs or stocks. As the young folks say: as if."

She handed me a plate. "A couple of the folks signed up right away. Let me tell you about Clark Gammel."

We carried our plates and the wine to a table in her breakfast room, a bright alcove with a bay window overlooking the woods. When we were settled, she handed me a red and yellow plaid napkin, spread one in her own lap, and continued with her story.

"As I was saying, my friend, Clark, told the adviser that it all sounded very good to him, but that he'd tied up most of his assets buying into Ginger Cove and just didn't have money lying around to invest."

"The guy probably had an answer for that, too," I commented around a mouthful of cantaloupe and pineapple chunks.

"*Mais oui.* He advised Clark that he could sell his *own* life insurance policy and use the proceeds from that sale to invest. He promised a return of twenty- to twenty-five percent."

"In other words, your friend Clark would be investing in secondhand life insurance policies of people who were older and/or sicker than he was."

She nodded. "Morbid, isn't it?"

I had to agree.

"And then do you know what happened?"

I shook my head.

"Clark up and died. He didn't even outlive his investments."

First Valerie, now Clark. Coincidence? I thought not. "What was this guy's name, do you remember?"

Mrs. Bromley squinted out the window. "Not offhand. But I think I saved the brochure he gave us." She laid down her fork. "Let me go look for it."

I raised a hand to stop her. "After lunch is fine."

"At my age, if I don't do something while I'm thinking about it, I'm sure to forget." She bustled off in the direction of the bedroom.

I was thinking that age had nothing to do with it—I had visited my office twice that morning before I remembered that I'd gone down there looking for a stapler—when from deep within the recesses of my purse, my cell phone began to ring.

At first warble I thought it might be Paul, but I'd set his ring tone to play the Monty Python theme song. I let it ring a few more seconds. It wasn't Emily, either. Her signature tune was the theme from *Star Wars*. I was going to ignore the call, but Mrs. Bromley was still in the bedroom, so I wrestled the cell phone from its pocket and pushed the talk button, silencing it in the middle of a spirited rendition of Beethoven's Ninth, the ring tone I'd assigned to unknown numbers.

"Mrs. Ives? This is Gail Parrish. Mr. Jablonsky's receptionist? We met when you came into the office the other day?"

"Oh, yes?"

"Mr. Jablonsky would like to speak with you? Is this a good time?"

It wasn't, really, but I was dying—so to speak—to hear what the man had to say.

When Jablonsky came on the line, his tone was casual and upbeat, as if I'd just won an all-expenses paid trip to Bermuda. "Mrs. Ives. *Hannah*. Well, I have some good news for you and some bad news."

I was glad to have visited his office, because I could picture him delivering this news: shirtsleeves rolled up, leaning back in his chair, size 10½ Johnston & Murphys propped up on his desktop. "The good news is that according to our experts, your life expectancy is at least five years."

"Oh, goody," I said. "My husband will be glad to hear it. So, what's the bad news?"

"The bad news is that this cuts back considerably on the amount of money we're able to offer for your policy."

"How bad is it?" I said, expecting Johnny Carson to pop out from behind the curtain any second.

"With a life expectancy of five years and a face value of $250,000, the most we can get for you is sixty percent. That's $150,000."

"Better than a sharp stick in the eye, as my mother used to say."

Jablonsky chuckled at my little joke. He even made it sound sincere. "Exactly."

"So, what do you think I should do, Gil?"

"Oh, I'd take it," he said. "Definitely. ViatiPro is an excellent company!"

ViatiPro. If I had had antennae, they would have shot straight up out of my head like *My Favorite Martian*.

That said, I was tempted, I really was. With $150,000, I could set aside $5,000 for my funeral. No, $6,000. Why be chintzy? I could put $50,000 each in college funds for Chloe and Jake and still have $44,000 left to blow on whatever I damn well pleased.

"Frankly, *Gil*," I said, pushing a little harder on the man's buttons, "I'll have to talk it over with my husband first. When I brought up the subject the other day, just to test the water, you know, I think it's fair to say he wasn't very enthusiastic."

"Not enthusiastic in what way, Hannah?"

"In point of fact," I said, embroidering as fast as I could, "he absolutely blew his top."

"I see," said Jablonsky. "Well, perhaps if you brought your husband in? What's his name, by the way?"

"Paul."

"Well, perhaps if you and Paul were to come in where I could lay out all the facts and figures in front of him, you and I could help him change his mind. I can be very persuasive."

"If it were for just a *bit* more money," I hinted broadly, "maybe he'd go for it."

"I'm afraid $150,000 is the best we can do for you, Hannah, under the circumstances." There was a long pause. I spent it filling in the blank. *If your cancer recurs, of course, and it looks like you're going to croak, that'd be a different matter entirely.*

"You know," Jablonsky said after a few more ticks of the clock, "we have some other plans that may interest you. And it wouldn't involve selling policies you already have."

"That's sounds intriguing," I said. "Very intriguing."

"And if we set it up right," he continued, "you needn't even tell your husband about it."

"That's even better," I purred.

"Let's not go into it over the phone," he said. "Can you stop in sometime midweek?"

Like a good little sucker, I agreed. Jablonsky switched me back to Gail, who inked me in for 11:00 A.M. on Wednesday. She seemed in a much cheerier mood than when I'd met her the previous Saturday.

"Do you work six days a week, Gail?"

"Oh, yeah," she said. "Saturday's usually a half day, though."

"Slave driver," I quipped, referring to her boss, Jablonsky.

"I don't mind, actually," she said. "I can use the money."

"Can't we all?"

Just about the time Jablonsky was handing me back to Gail, Mrs. Bromley rejoined me in the breakfast room, waving a brochure. She waited for me to finish my conversation with Gail, then plopped the brochure down on the table next to my plate.

Smiling out at me from the front page of the full-color trifold, impeccably dressed, well-coiffed, gray-haired septuagenarian couples fished, swam, golfed, and otherwise were living large on the tragedies of others.

The brochure was sprinkled with mini-testimonials. *Thanks for the wonderful service!!! You told me to expect 18 to 24 months for my investment to mature!!! Imagine my delight when my $50,000 investment turned into $62,000 in just five (5) weeks!!! That's a whopping 249.6% APR!!!*

It wasn't just all the exclamation points that made me want to barf.

"It's from MBFSG," Mrs. Bromley said, pointing to the investment firm's logo printed on a little gold address label stuck to the bottom of the last panel. MBFSG, I read, was offering one to five year "programs," with six, eighteen, thirty, and forty-two month contracts available "upon request." It didn't take a mental giant to figure out what the months meant.

"Do you know them?" Mrs. Bromley asked.

"Oh, yes, I know them." I looked up. "Do you remember the name of the investment adviser you spoke to?"

"The name's on the tip of my tongue. Czech, I think. Or Polish. Hungarian, maybe."

I took a wild stab. "Jablonsky?"

"Yes! That's it. Jablonsky." Her eyes narrowed and she studied my face intently, as if searching it for clues. "Oh, dear. He's the one, isn't he? The snake oil salesman you talked to?"

I nodded. "Be afraid," I said. "Be very afraid."

CHAPTER 13

I like to think I've got an all-occasion wardrobe. As I stood in the doorway of my closet wearing my NO SHIRTS, NO SHOES, NO WORRIES T-shirt from Cooper Island Beach Club, nothing seemed appropriate for visiting somebody as shady as Jablonsky.

Hanging on the rod to my right were the slacks, blouses, colorful tops, and casual jackets that had, over the past few years, become my uniform.

On the far back wall hung the business suits I abandoned along with the commute when I quit working in Washington, D.C. I knew I should send them to Goodwill, but some of those suits had sentimental value—the gray, double-breasted pinstripe I wore when I successfully interviewed for the job at Whitworth and Sullivan, for example. Or the red plaid jacket I had on when they told me I'd won the Drew Award for Excellence in Management: $10,000 plus a crystal paperweight with my name on it, shaped like an owl. Paul thinks I should chuck it all out. If you want to remember things, he says, buy yourself a charm bracelet.

We have arguments about my closet. Why Paul should care about something he can't even see when the door's closed, I fail to understand. In his closet, the hangers are three inches apart, precisely, like one of those New York boutiques, where they have one salesclerk for every garment.

I continued to rummage, shoving clothing back and forth, separating empty hangers that clung stubbornly together; they would resume their romantic entanglements down in my laundry room. In the process, I found a jacket I'd forgotten—a perfect match for the slacks I'd recently purchased at Chico's. I located the slacks and draped the jacket over the same hanger, then went prospecting for a lavender blouse I vaguely remembered that might complete the outfit.

Wait a minute! I paused, three hangers and two belts in hand, a pair of shoes tucked under one arm. If I didn't watch it, the situation could escalate into a full-fledged spring cleaning. *Focus!* Cluttered closets and messy drawers had always been my nemesis, but right then, I reminded myself, Jablonsky was my business, my only business.

I dropped the items I was holding onto a nearby chair, stared into the depths of my closet and got serious. In my previous visit to Jablonsky's office, I had come off as a bit of a dingbat. What would a dingbat wear?

Way in the back, barely illuminated by the overhead bulb, was a small section of closet I laughingly reserved for resort wear. I hauled out a halter-top Hawaiian print sundress I hadn't laid eyes on since 1986 and a hot pink cotton cardigan. I considered them critically. Might do. I had a Wonder Bra somewhere—Jablonsky seemed like the type who'd appreciate the effort—but, alas, it wouldn't work with the sundress: my straps would show, and I was well past the age where exposed bra straps could be viewed as a fashion statement.

I had laid my outfit on the bed and was looking around for an appropriate pair of shoes when the telephone on the bedside table rang. It was Daddy, reporting that he'd arrived home safely from Arizona.

"Want to come over for dinner?" I asked. "Paul's still in Newport. I could use the company."

"Are you sure?" he teased. "I'll bring pictures."

"Promise?" I was possibly the only person in the world who actually *enjoyed* looking at other people's vacation slides. Daddy loved photographing sunsets, but some of his snapshots, I knew, would feature Cornelia Gibbs, the widow who was Daddy's off-and-on traveling companion.

"You and Neelie have a good time?"

"I'll never tell." He crooned, using his Cary Grant voice. That got my attention. Up until now, Neelie had always insisted on separate rooms, or cabins, as the case might be. I found myself wondering if the situation had changed.

I would pull a couple of steaks out of the freezer before I left for Glen Burnie, I decided. Bribe him with a thick, juicy steak and Daddy was putty in my hands. Add square-cut french fries and he'd tell me anything. "I think I'm out of club soda," I added. A recovering alcoholic, my father didn't drink. "Could you stop by Graul's and pick some up?"

"No problem."

"It'll be good to see you," I said. "I have a lot to tell you."

"Me, too," he said cryptically.

I opened my mouth to beg for a hint, but the charming rascal had already hung up.

Still holding the receiver, I plopped down on the bed and considered calling my father back. Then I smiled. Let him keep his secret for a few hours. I had more than enough to worry about that afternoon. I cradled the phone and padded off to take a long, hot shower. I had the feeling I'd need it.

Still smelling like lavender soap, I arrived at MBFSG a few minutes early and rode the elevator to the fourth floor, where Gail greeted me like a long-lost friend. Jablonsky probably paid her extra for that. "He just called," the young woman said, emerging from behind the reception desk. "He's been delayed in traffic, but hopes you won't mind waiting. Coffee?"

"A Coke, if you have one."

"Sure." I followed Gail into a kitchenette, where a coffee machine, microwave oven, and a small refrigerator vied for limited space on a butcher block counter.

She opened the fridge. "Diet?"

I shook my head. "Regular, please."

Gail handed me a Coke and selected a ginger ale for herself. "Let's sit," she said, gesturing with her can toward a small round table.

I sat opposite her in one of two chairs. "Have you worked here long?" I popped the tab on my Coke.

"Two years." She took a sip of her drink, held it in her mouth a moment, then swallowed. "I started out with Gil at Allstate. When he left Allstate to start up MBFSG, he brought me along."

"You like it here?"

She shrugged. "It's okay. What I really love is Annapolis."

"Where do you live, Gail?"

"I lucked out on a house over in Eastport. The couple who owns it? They're sailing around the world. So I'm house-sitting."

"Wow," I said, genuinely impressed. "Rent free?"

She snorted softly. "Practically. I'm getting it dirt cheap because I'm looking after Nitro. That's their cat."

Gail stood, walked to the door and peeked into the reception area, presumably checking to see if her boss had returned. "The money I'm saving, I'm putting in a boat fund," she continued, resting her back against the jamb. "Maybe in a few years . . ." She shrugged again.

"Have you ever been to the sailboat show?" I asked, referring to the event each October that brought hundreds of sailboats and thousands of sailing enthusiasts to Annapolis Harbor.

Her face lit up. "Tons of times. My boyfriend . . ." She blushed. ". . . I guess I should say my *ex*-boyfriend, used to refer to the show as 'Gail's boat porn.'"

I laughed, as she probably intended me to. But the hurt was still fresh in Gail's eyes. Sad, I thought, when one half of a relationship had a passion for something that the other half didn't share. "I've been," I told her. "All those boats. All that nifty equipment. It blew me away."

We'd been to the boat show more than a dozen times, Paul and I, drooling over sailboats we couldn't afford even if we set up housekeeping in a cave, gave up eating, and saved every penny for a million years. "Maybe if I sell my policy . . ." I let my voice trail off and I stared into space dreamily.

"Ooops, gotta go." Gail shot out the door. "Gil's coming."

Thanks to Gail's infallible Gil-dar, she was back behind the reception desk and I was sitting in the waiting room calmly paging through a *New Yorker* when Gilbert Jablonsky breezed into the office. "Hannah! So *sorry* I'm late! Thank you for waiting."

"That's okay," I said, pointing at my soft drink can. "Gail took good care of me."

Jablonsky shot an exaggerated wink in his receptionist's direction. "That's my girl!"

When he turned his attention back to me, Gail crossed her eyes and stuck out her tongue, and I had to bite down hard on my lower lip to keep from laughing. I was beginning to like the woman.

"Thanks for seeing me, Gil." I eased myself out of the chair and gave him my hand.

He clasped mine in both of his and pumped it up and down. "My pleasure. Let's go back to my office, shall we?"

Jablonsky preceded me down the hall, shucking his

sport coat as he went. "Hold my calls, please, Gail," he called over his shoulder. When we reached his office, he nodded to the chair I'd previously occupied. "Have a seat."

"So," he continued, once we'd gotten settled. "Have you thought about my offer?"

I nodded. "Yes, but I'm afraid my husband is dead set against it. It's really kind of *sweet*," I said, leaning forward and resting an elbow on his desk. "When I asked Paul about it, he went all *gooey* on me, saying I was absolutely *not* going to die, and we weren't going to sell that policy no matter what. End. Of. Story."

"The man loves you," he said.

I aimed a thousand watt smile at the guy. "I guess so!"

Jablonsky leaned back in his chair, hooking his thumbs in his belt. "So, Hannah, tell me. How would you feel about acquiring additional insurance?"

I wagged my head back and forth, my hoop earrings bouncing against my neck. "I don't think so, Gil. The premiums on the policy I already have are expensive enough."

A slow smile crept across his face. "It wouldn't cost you a thing."

"Now, Gil, I don't pretend to know very much about the life insurance business, but even *I* know you can't get insurance policies for *nothing*."

"Under special circumstances you can."

"I find that *real* hard to believe."

"It's easy. Let me explain." As he spoke, he ticked the points off on his fingers. "First, you apply for the policy. Then, we'll hold it for a couple of years, pay the premiums for you, and, after a suitable amount of time has passed . . ." He held out his hand as if something small and valuable were sitting on it. "We viaticate it for you."

I raised an eyebrow. "Why would I want to do that?"

"There'd be compensation," he said.

"Compensation? What sort of compensation?"

"For each policy you sign up for, we can pay you twelve thousand dollars."

I gasped. "You're kidding. Right?"

He shook his head. "I'm dead serious."

I continued to stare at him, slack-jawed. "Oh, wow!"

Jablonsky opened a file drawer, extracted several forms, and laid them one at a time—carefully, almost tenderly—on the desk in front of me. "Take a moment to look these over," he said.

I scooted my chair forward a few inches, to demonstrate how seriously I was considering his offer. I picked up the first application, attracted by its stylized logo and the words *Victory Mutual Life Assurance Company* printed in Goudy Old Style. The rest of the document was set in Times New Roman. If there's ever a demand for people who can identify typeface styles in their sleep, I'm your woman, and whatever their faults, I'd have the editorial work I did for Whitworth and Sullivan to thank for it.

Victory Mutual's application form had six pages, both sides, and was fastened together at the top. The other two applications were of similar length, but less attractively formatted. I studied them critically.

I'm sure the folks at Sun Securities of N.A. intended to symbolize rock-solid, strong-as-the-dollar security the way they scattered suns and obelisks all over the cover page, but if so, their art department had made a hash of it. The sunbursts were ragged and sickly yellow, hardly confidence-building. And I lost my way completely in Sun's maze of teeny-tiny print (New Zurica, sans serif, six points max). After several frustrating minutes, I put their application down.

The questions on the application from New Century Auto and Life were printed in fourteen point, light blue, GalexicaMono. What were they thinking? Easy on the eyes, maybe, but didn't New Century know that blue print doesn't photocopy well?

From the grunts and under-his-breath muttering, I assumed Jablonsky was busying himself with his e-mail. While he clacked away on his computer keyboard, I leafed through each application, reading carefully.

After fifteen minutes I spoke up. "Gil, this is so *confusing*! All these paragraphs and subparagraphs and words I don't understand? How can I possibly choose?"

He lifted his fingers from the keyboard, slowly, like a pianist after the last note of a sonata. "You don't have to choose," he said. "Perhaps I haven't been clear. I'm recommending that you apply for *all* of them."

A hot shot of adrenaline surged up my neck. My ears hummed. I'd read about it on the Internet, and there it was, up close and personal: wet inking. My signature would be barely dry before Jablonsky turned these policies around.

I stared at Jablonsky, who stared back at me, unblinking, while I processed that information. Three applications times $12,000. That was $36,000. It was a luxury vacation. A sunroom with a hot tub. A previously owned 450SL parked outside my door.

"That's legal?" I asked.

Jablonsky loosened his tie. "Absolutely legal."

I picked up the application from Victory Mutual and flipped through the pages, skimming the text. "You know, this isn't going to work," I said. I turned the form in his direction and tapped page six with the pen he had given me. "In this block it asks if I've ever been advised of, treated for, or had any known indication of a whole lot of things. Like cancer." I looked up to judge his reaction. "And over here." I flipped to the next page. "Here it wants to know if any of my parents or siblings had cardiovascular disease. My mom died of congestive heart failure. I'm sorry to disappoint you, Gil," I said, closing the application, "but there's no way I could pass a physical examination."

"That's the beauty of it," Jablonsky oozed. "A physical isn't required for policies in amounts under $100,000."

"Oh." I stared at him, blinking rapidly. So that was the path he was leading me down! About time that I rattled his cage. I turned back to page one and waved the pen over the block labeled CLIENT. I deliberately hesitated, sucking thoughtfully on the pen's retractor button.

The man had stopped breathing, I swear. Before he could pass out from lack of oxygen, I wrote *Ives* in the first space, *Hannah* in the second, and *A* in the third, then proceeded rapidly through the application form, checking some boxes and leaving others blank. On page five I paused. "Wait a minute! It asks here if this life insurance is for the benefit of a viatical company, or if there are plans to viaticate it, or if it replaces a policy that was already viaticated."

Jablonsky tented his fingers. "I can't tell you how to fill out the form, Hannah, but I *can* tell you if you have a wrong answer."

"Okay." I checked no and moved on. Had I ever been accused of a felony? No. Was I a pilot? No. Had I ever been charged with drunken driving? Never. Do I enjoy skydiving? As if.

Inevitably I arrived back at page six: medical history. "It asks about cancer, Gil," I reminded him, "and breast disease. Should I check 'Yes'?"

Jablonsky smirked. "That's not a good answer."

I'd read about that, too. Clean sheeting. Swearing on an application that you're healthy when you're not.

The man had gone too far, too far even for Hannah-the-Dingbat. I felt sick to my stomach, thinking of Valerie sitting in Jablonsky's office, in the same chair I was, listening to the same sales pitch, maybe even filling out the same damn form. And look where it had gotten her.

"I'm sorry, Gil, but I just don't feel comfortable lying to an insurance company." I stood up, laying the pen on top of the Victory Mutual packet.

"No one will ever know."

"*I'll* know," I said.

Jablonsky shrugged. "Thirty-six thousand dollars?"

"It's tempting, *really* tempting." I scooped up my handbag. "Tell you what. Let me go home and think about it for a couple of days. Okay?"

"I'll look forward to seeing you, then. You won't be sorry." He held out his hand.

I didn't want to, but I shook it. It felt hot, and damp. Good. I'd made the outlaw sweat!

"Call me if you have any questions." He was talking to my back.

I waved vaguely, then hustled down the hall, wiping my hand on the front of my sweater as I went, stopping only long enough to say good-bye to Gail Parrish.

"See ya," she chirped.

"I hope so," I said, meaning it. June was prime sailing season on the Chesapeake Bay. The next time Connie and Dennis called looking for crew, maybe I'd suggest Gail.

All the way down in the elevator, though, I worried about the receptionist. Did she know what her boss was up to? If he got sent to the slammer, would she have to go, too?

Yet if Gail were in on it up to her charming, tip-tilted nose, if she were helping Jablonsky rake in money hand over fist, would she spend her leisure hours cat-sitting? Scrimping on the rent in order to buy a boat? I doubted it.

As I crossed the parking lot to my car, I itched to blow the whistle on the weasel. Yet, if what Valerie had told me was true, Jablonsky's business with her had been completely legitimate. And if I'd sold him my *existing* life insurance policy, that would have been completely legitimate, too.

As for the clean-sheeting, what was there for me to report? I hadn't signed any forms and no money had exchanged hands, so as far as I knew, no laws had been broken. Hell, even if I'd had a secret microphone tucked into my bra, I couldn't remember a single thing Jablonsky had said to me during our meeting that might actually have landed the man in a court of law.

After the darkness of the lobby, it took a few seconds for my eyes to adjust to the afternoon sunshine. I stood in the parking lot, blinking, trying to remember where I'd parked my car. Fortunately, I had one of those remote keyless gizmos. I pushed the unlock button and an orchid LeBaron parked near Manny's Auto Body flashed its lights at me and beeped. Ah, yes. I'd parked in the low rent district. I trudged off in that direction.

Judging from the cars surrounding mine, Manny's clients had a weakness for vanity plates. I had a vanity plate once: SIR5ER. Recently, though, I'd switched from the "Survivor" plate to one featuring a heron, to help Save the Bay.

I stopped and looked around. I12HUGU on a Taurus with a crushed fender. PB4UGO. I had to laugh. Even if the Subaru wearing that plate didn't have stuffed animals strewn about the backseat, you had to know the owner had kids.

Parked between the Subaru and me was a gold BMW, its license plate—N4SIR—enclosed in a decorative frame. I had to say it out loud—"Enforcer"—before I got it. Manny, it seemed, did body work for a dangerous crowd. I opened my door carefully. Wouldn't want to ding the paint of *that* dude.

I slid into the seat and slotted my key into the ignition. When I started the car, both the air conditioner and the radio came on, full-blast. I leaned my head against the headrest, closed my eyes and let Mozart and the cool air wash over me.

Jablonsky was defrauding insurance companies. That much I knew for sure. I also knew the names of three of them. That would be as good a place as any to start.

Maybe Jablonsky hadn't been *directly* responsible for

Valerie's death. But I knew as surely as I knew that I was sitting in a car parked in Glen Burnie, Maryland, US of A that it had all started here. And if I picked up the string and began to follow it, I might eventually learn the truth about how Valerie had died.

CHAPTER 14

We'd had a wet spring in Annapolis and the mosquitoes were plump and vicious. When I stepped onto the patio early Thursday morning, they swarmed around me with tiny buzzing cries of "fresh meat."

I plunked down the coffee cup and telephone book I was carrying on the patio table and returned to the utility room, where I kept an emergency bottle of Skin-So-Soft bath oil slash mosquito repellent. I slathered it on, paying particular attention to my ears. Then I went back out to the patio to enjoy the sunshine and try to ignore the humming.

Molly the cat was lying on my picnic table in a patch of sun. She didn't seem to mind that I smelled like I'd swum through a perfume spill the size of the Exxon Valdez. I stroked her fur and she stretched leisurely, turning slowly to expose her belly for additional scratching. She purred like a motorboat. "Little slut," I purred back.

Daddy's news at dinner had been surprising, and not the least what I expected. Daddy and Neelie had become an item. She'd been a widow for six years, he a widower for four. So, when he joined me for dinner the previous evening, I was certain he'd bring news of an engagement.

But no.

After a full career in the Navy followed by a decade of work for the aerospace industry, Daddy was being lured out of retirement. A contractor doing work for the Naval

Air Warfare Center at Wallops Island on Virginia's Eastern Shore wanted to tap Daddy's considerable expertise and plug him in as project manager on a contract at NASA's Wallops Flight Facility—one of the oldest launch sites in the world. Daddy was considering the offer seriously. But it would mean a move to southern Virginia, he said, or Maryland's Eastern Shore, to a town like Snow Hill or Athol.

I'd nearly choked on my steak. I'd sat, stone-faced, chewing without tasting. "When they ask if you like living in Athol," I'd muttered at last, "the only legitimate response is 'Yeth.'"

Daddy had three weeks to make up his mind, so that gave me plenty of time to stew about it. I'd lost my mother, and even though Snow Hill, Maryland, was a beautiful colonial village only two and a half hours drive from Annapolis, I felt like I'd be losing my father, too. Of what importance was an insurance scam when you were about to become an orphan?

On the other hand, fretting about Jablonsky would be a distraction. Money had gone into furnishing his office, that was for sure, and considering the newness of the building, the rent had to be high, in spite of the neighborhood.

I wondered where the guy lived.

I eased Molly's tail off the cover of the phone book and turned to the J's. Gilbert and Irene Jablonsky shared an address on Cherry Tree Cove, a street that I recognized as being in Fishing Creek Farm, an upscale Annapolis waterfront community where the homes cost more than the gross national product of some third-world countries. Must be nice. I was more convinced than ever that Jablonsky had to be supporting his expensive office and residence habits by defrauding insurance companies.

Didn't Maryland have some sort of state insurance commission I could report him to? I made a note to check the Internet about that.

Should I contact the insurance companies I knew about

for sure and warn them about Jablonsky? If he'd been operating his scam long enough to afford a home in Fishing Creek Farm, I reasoned, a lot of bogus policies must have passed through his hands.

I turned to the Insurance section in the yellow pages and learned that Victory Mutual had an office on Riva Road, not far from the mall in nearby Parole. Sun Securities seemed to be handled by an independent insurance agent with an office in Bowie, Maryland, but there was no listing for New Century. The company must be out of state. I'd have to look it up on the Internet, too.

I sat back and thought about Jablonsky for a long time, while idly stroking Molly's fur.

Supposing I did contact Victory Mutual, Sun Securities, and New Century? Exactly what was I going to tell them? Let's assume I *had* completed that insurance application, checking no when it asked me about the cancer. Supposing further that Jablonsky had sent it in. Even if the insurance company had wised up and called him on it, Jablonsky could always feign shock and surprise, throw up his hands and say, "How was I to know? It was that wretched Ives woman who falsified the application, not me!"

A beautiful scam, especially if you're a crook.

I sighed, closed my eyes and turned my face toward the sun, hoping for inspiration. I was still sitting there five minutes later, either courting melanoma or enriching myself with vitamin D, depending upon your point of view, when a fat, green garbage bag sailed over the fence, landing with a rustle and a splat in my garden, flattening a bed of impatiens that had never harmed a living soul.

Molly started, leaped from the table, trampolined off my lap and streaked away under a bush.

Hoo-boy! Old Mrs. Perry was at it again. Second time this week.

I sighed, gathered up the bag and, leaving the phone book pages to turn themselves quietly in the morning breeze, dragged it next door and onto the Perry porch, cans rattling.

I rang the bell.

To my surprise, it wasn't Mrs. Perry's caregiver who answered the door but Bradford himself, his tie dangling loose from his collar and a portable phone clamped to his ear.

I raised the garbage bag.

Brad rolled his eyes. "Shit!" With his free hand, he motioned me inside the entrance hall. "I'm on hold," he said.

"It's okay," I said, "really," referring to the garbage bag. "I could have just thrown it away, but you said you wanted to know."

He raised a finger. "Yes, Linda," he said into the telephone. "This is Brad Perry. Judy Warren called in sick today, so I'll need you to send someone else to look after Mother."

While he talked, I held onto the green plastic bag, admiring Brad's impeccably decorated living room, full of exquisite rugs and fine, Asian antiques that had once furnished his parent's gracious home outside of Nashville, Tennessee.

"Noon?" He frowned. "Well, if that's the best you can do, then." He punched the off button and motioned for me to follow him.

Once we reached the kitchen, he relieved me of the bag, opened the back door and tossed it unceremoniously onto the concrete landing. "I keep thinking if I tell Mother often enough that we're in Annapolis, not Thomasboro, it'll eventually sink in.

"Maybe it was a mistake bringing her furniture here," he continued, pulling the door shut behind him. "I thought it would make her feel at home, but the problem is, now she thinks she *is* home. That she's still in Thomasboro. I can point out the Naval Academy chapel dome and she'll agree, yes, that chapel dome is in Annapolis, and then she wonders how I did it."

"Did what?"

"Move Thomasboro all the way from Tennessee to Annapolis, Maryland."

"My, you are a clever boy!"

Brad grinned. "So Mother tells me."

I had a brainstorm. "Brad, I don't have anything in particular on my agenda this morning. I'll be happy to sit with your mother until the nurse gets here."

"Thanks, Hannah, but I've already told the office that I'll be late. It's an excuse, really. There's this extracurricular project I've got going."

"I don't mind, really. I'd like to help."

"It's no problem. Mom's had breakfast. I've just got her settled up in her bedroom. She's watching *Parenthood* for the umpteenth time." He grinned. "Love that movie!"

"You sure?"

He nodded. "If you really want to help me with something, though . . ." He gestured toward the swinging door that I knew led into the dining room. "In some insane moment, I agreed to help with my high school reunion next month." He spread his arms wide. "You're looking at the yearbook committee."

"Lucky you!"

I followed Brad into the dining room, where piles of photocopies that were soon to become "The Tiger Rag" were neatly arranged on the long, highly polished mahogany table. "There's a pile for every page," he said. "Thank goodness there were only forty in my graduating class at Thomasboro High."

I made a circuit of the table, stopping for no particular reason at the M's. From the page on top of the pile, a high school yearbook photo of Anna Sally Miller smiled back at me. Anna Sally had been a perky, blond, ponytailed cheerleader, sang in the Glee Club, belonged to the future Homemakers of America, and, if the "Look at Me Today" picture was any indication, had packed on 150 pounds since graduation.

Brad stared at Anna Sally over my shoulder. "Sad, isn't it?"

"Oh, I don't know," I said, picking up the page and closely examining Anna Sally's recent photo. She was dressed for tennis and cradled a racquet in the crook of one elbow. "She looks happy, at least. There's a lot to be said for happy."

I smiled over my shoulder at Brad. "So, where are you, Mr. Bradford Perry, Esquire?"

I moseyed around the table until I came to the P's. In 1973, Brad had floppy hair and wore aviator glasses with photo gray lenses: in the flash from the photographer's camera they had instantly darkened. Young Brad as a blind man.

Brad tapped his temple with a forefinger, as if reading my mind. "Contacts," he said. "Never would have gotten a date without them."

Brad showed me how he was arranging the pages into notebooks, and I began circumnavigating the table behind him, picking up pages and putting them in order. All work should be so mindless. "Brad?" I asked on my second time around. "You're an attorney. What do you know about viatical settlements?"

"A minefield," he said. "Why do you ask?"

I shrugged and placed a copy of Sandy Starbuck's page on top of Charlene Wang's. "Just wondering." Oliver Smoot went on top of Carmen Stansbury. "I have this friend," I began.

Brad paused and laughed out loud. "My gawd, that's an old one!"

I stopped collating and looked at him. "No, seriously! I'd never even heard of viaticals until this friend of mine sold her life insurance policy to a broker. Frankly," I told him, "the whole idea gives me the heebie-jeebies."

"You and me both," he said. "The insurance companies I represent have been trying to get a law passed in Maryland for several years, but they always run out of time."

"Figures," I grumped. The Maryland legislature meets for only ninety days between January and April. It's a wonder they got anything done.

"The bill died in the House," Brad complained. "In spite of all the bad publicity following a major bust for fraud up in Baltimore. You'd think the Answer Care case would have been a wake-up call. Investors lost more than two million dollars in that fiasco."

"I've heard of that case," I said, "but I didn't make the connection until now."

I started around the table again, placing Jack Popham on top of Oliver Smoot. "But here's something I don't understand, Brad. What's to keep me from buying life insurance policies on everyone on Prince George Street?"

Brad glanced up at me sideways. "Well, even assuming you could afford to pay the premiums on all those policies, the life insurance companies have thought of that. A key insurance principle is insurable interest. What that means is the person buying the insurance has to have a vested interested in the insured person's well-being."

"Like a husband."

"Exactly. The beneficiary has to be a husband or wife or, nowadays, a domestic partner. Someone with a close relationship to the insured. Business relationships count, too, but not your second cousin twice removed.

"But," he continued, "you generally don't need an in-surable interest to buy an *existing* life insurance policy. The policy is considered personal property and can be sold pretty much at will."

"If that's the case, why can't they regulate the resale of life insurance policies like they do securities? People are investing in them, aren't they? You'd think the Securities and Exchange Commission would have something to say about it." I shivered, and began working my way around the table again. Chip Pickett on top of Jack Popham, and Ann Ogden on top of Chip. "Death futures," I muttered.

"Shouldn't be different than any other kind of futures, from the SEC's point of view."

"You know the sad part?" Brad said, moving around the table two piles ahead of me. "Most policyholders aren't aware that there are better ways to get money out of their insurance policies."

"Like?" A copy of Stuart Lollis's page slipped from my fingers. I bent down to retrieve it from under the table.

"You can borrow money on the cash value of your policy," Brad was saying when I surfaced. "You can use the policy as collateral. Or take advantage of accelerated death benefits, 'ADBs' for short. There are provisions for ADBs already written into most life insurance policies."

"Most people don't read their policies very well, I guess."

"You got it."

I laid an introduction and a title page on top of Pat Berry's beaming face, then evened up the yearbook I had just completed by tapping its edges against the table. I set it crosswise on top of a pile of others. "I need your advice, Brad."

Brad clipped a photo name tag to the front of the yearbook he'd been working on, laid it down on the sideboard behind him and gave me his full attention. "Shoot."

"I was curious about viaticals, so I visited this guy my friend recommended up in Glen Burnie." I told Brad about my visit to MBFSG, Jablonsky's offer to buy my life insurance policy for $150,000, and about the other policies he wanted me to apply for. "I'm not going to do it, of course, but I figure if he's tried it out on me, he must have done it successfully with others."

A furrow deepened between Brad's eyebrows. He grunted.

"When your mom tossed the garbage over the fence," I continued, "I was sitting in the backyard, worrying about it. Wondering who I should report it to. Jablonsky had a whole bunch of forms, but the ones I remember were Victory Mutual, Sun Securities, and New Century."

"Oh, man!" Brad fell back against the chair rail that divided the white-painted wainscoting from the blue and white striped wallpaper of his dining room. "You're not going to believe this, but Victory Mutual is one of my clients!" He swiped his fingers through his hair. "Tell you what. As soon as the nurse gets here, let me take you to meet Harrison Garvin. He's CEO of Victory Mutual. I think he'll be very interested in what you have to say."

After I okayed his plan, Brad seemed to lose all interest in putting together yearbooks. "I'm putting a kettle on for tea," he announced.

I gave the pile with a photo of Jan Falls doing cartwheels a friendly pat. Who am I to argue with a lawyer? "I second the motion," I said.

Just five hours later, at three in the afternoon, Brad Perry and I were ushered into Harrison Garvin's corner office on the top floor of the Garrett Building adjoining the nearly derelict Parole Plaza. Garvin's office afforded him a panoramic view of Annapolis Mall's vast, meandering architecture, as well as a bird's-eye view of the restaurant park on Jennifer Road, which had its advantages, I suppose, if one didn't feel like waiting in line at Red Lobster.

With a first name like Harrison, I expected Garvin to be tall and movie-idol handsome, but the man who rose to greet us was short—no more than five-foot-six or -seven—and stocky. His hazel eyes were enormous behind thick-lensed tortoiseshell glasses.

I told my story for the second time that morning, interrupted occasionally by Brad, who made an important point or two, while Garvin listened silently, his arms folded across his chest. "So," I said, winding it up, "I asked Brad what to do, and he brought me to you."

"I have half a mind," Garvin said, "to send you back to

MBFSG, have you sign up for the policy and see where it goes once it reaches us. Those other two companies you mentioned." He flapped a hand. "Big red flag. Sun is incorporated in both Texas and Arizona, where the laws on viaticals are very lax."

Brad was nodding in agreement.

"When Victory Mutual was young and aggressive," Garvin continued, "we might have been willing to overlook such details as physical exams, especially for the smaller policies, but not anymore. We've recently taken steps to minimize our risk—requiring blood and urine tests, for example—but it's not foolproof. Nothing ever is."

Garvin turned to Brad. "I wonder how these policies are getting in under the radar? I'd hate to think one of our underwriters was in on this scam."

Brad shrugged.

Garvin picked up his telephone and pushed a button. "Lisa, will you track down Donna Hudgins and ask her to come up here, please? Thanks." Garvin turned to me. "Donna's our head of Policyholder Services," he explained.

I was certain Donna Hudgins would be less than pleased at being tracked down and summoned to the principal's office, and I was right. When she arrived a few minutes later, Donna turned out to be an attractive woman in her late fifties or early sixties with short, stylishly cut gray hair. She wore a navy blue pants suit—any larger than a size two and I'd eat the brass barometer sitting on Garvin's credenza—rimless eyeglasses, and a prize-winning scowl.

Donna Hudgins managed to dredge up a smile from somewhere for Harrison Garvin, then turned her cool, ice blue gaze first on me, and then on Brad. I'd seen that look before. Someone's complained to the boss about some stupid-ass thing, and now, boy-oh-boy, the shit is going to hit the fan.

"Sit down, Donna," Garvin said.

Donna sat.

Garvin summarized for Donna what I'd just told him about Jablonsky. I was grateful. In the course of the day, I'd gone from wondering whether I should even mention Gilbert Jablonsky to thinking I should do my vocal cords a favor and tape record my story.

"Do we have a large number of policies that have changed hands recently?" Garvin wondered.

Donna, I noticed, had visibly relaxed. At least she'd stopped wringing her hands. "What with the reorganization and everything, I'm afraid I've been way too busy to notice."

Garvin frowned. "Donna, you are not the problem here, I assure you. I'm looking to you for a solution."

"I'm sure we can massage the software to get at that information eventually, but my God, Harrison, I simply don't have the time if we're going to meet our July first deadline! I'm swamped as it is."

"Allow me to make a suggestion." Brad rose from his chair and stood with his thigh touching Garvin's desk. "Hannah, here, isn't just my neighbor. She was, until quite recently, records manager at Whitworth and Sullivan."

Garvin's eyes darted from Brad's face to mine. "I've heard of them, of course."

"There's not much Hannah doesn't know about databases," Brad continued.

I felt my face grow hot. "My skills may be a tad out of date."

Garvin laughed out loud. "Not with the software we've been using! Do you know SQL?"

It all came back to me in a blinding flash. The long hours I'd spent writing *SELECT column_name FROM table_name WHERE column_name BETWEEN value1 AND value2 ORDER BY* . . . "Oh, yes," I assured him. "Quite well."

Garvin twiddled a pen between his middle and index finger while he considered me silently. "So, Hannah, would you have the time to help us out?"

"Oh, I'm sure Hannah is far too busy—" Donna Hudgins began, before Garvin cut her off with a flip of the retractor end of his pen.

"How long do you think it will take?" he inquired.

Donna shrugged. "I'm just guessing, of course, because I don't know what we'll find when we actually get into the database, but . . ." She squinted thoughtfully at the ceiling. "Three to four days."

Garvin grunted. "Sounds reasonable." He turned to me again. "How about it, Hannah? Do you have any time to devote to this?"

I nodded, already mentally rearranging my schedule for the next week. I'd start looking like a sheepdog, but I'd call Karen James and reschedule my haircut. The farmers' market could wait. I needed to pick up the dry cleaning and return books to the library, but nothing more urgent than that. "No problem," I said.

Garvin slapped his desk. "Okay, then Donna, have somebody clear out a cubicle, give Hannah a computer and the information she needs to get going." He turned to look at me. "You'll be identifying viaticated policies, singling them out for a closer look."

Donna gulped. "What about HIPAA?"

Garvin turned his owl-like eyes on me. "Donna means the Health Insurance Portability and Accountability Act of 1996, or HIPAA. By law, our records have to be kept confidential."

Brad raised a finger, but Garvin, it seemed, had anticipated him. "Take Hannah down to Personnel," he instructed. "Tell them to sign her up as a consultant through our contract with PeoplePlus. That should take care of it."

"Now?" asked Donna.

"Absolutely. Now."

"How much do you charge?" Garvin asked suddenly, taking me completely off guard.

I named a ridiculous sum, nearly twice what my hourly rate had been at Whitworth and Sullivan.

Garvin didn't even flinch. "Fine."

"And I can set my own hours?" I inquired.

"Absolutely. We'll give you a security pass so you can get in and out of the building. Just let Donna know, more or less, when she can expect to see you."

Donna's gaze was icy. "I'd appreciate that."

Garvin flipped a couple of pages forward on his desk calendar. "Today's Thursday." He glanced up from the calendar to me. "Can you start on Monday?"

I nodded.

"Good." He leaned back in his chair, fingers tented at chin level. "You'll write a report, of course."

"Of course."

"Then we'll talk."

I nodded.

"Good!" His smile broadened. "Thanks for bringing this to my attention, Brad."

Brad touched his forehead in mock salute. "I knew you'd want to know."

Garvin shook head slowly from side to side. "You get up in the morning. You think you know what you're going to be doing. Damn!"

Donna Hudgins stood, adjusting the cuffs of her jacket. "Will that be all, Harrison?"

It was. In less than thirty seconds we'd said our thank-yous and good-byes. In the hallway outside Garvin's office, Brad shook my hand and asked me to keep him in the loop.

A few minutes later I was trailing off to Personnel with Donna. Even from behind, I could tell her jaw was clenched. It would take a miracle for me to get on the good side of Victory Mutual's head of Policyholder Services.

When we stepped off the elevator on three, she spun around to face me. "You know I'm only doing this because Garvin ordered me to."

I grinned toothily. "I suppose this means we won't be sharing fashion tips over turkey roll-up sandwiches any time soon?"

As I turned and pushed my way through the door marked HUMAN RESOURCES, I thought I caught her smiling, too.

CHAPTER 15

Over the next few days I didn't have time to worry much about strategies for softening up Donna Hudgins. Paul came home early on Friday evening with lust in his heart and his head full of sea stories. First, we took care of the lust.

On Saturday evening Daddy invited us over after dinner to see the slide show he'd rigged up on his computer, so between Paul and my father, I was ODing on pictures of mountains, cacti, sand, sea, and sky. If you've seen one cactus, you've seen them all. Ditto seagulls.

On Monday, I reported to Victory Mutual bright and early—stepping off on the right foot, I hoped—and was through security and waiting for Donna next to the potted palm outside her office when she arrived promptly at eight.

"You're early," she said, fumbling for her keys.

"I didn't want to waste your time, Ms. Hudgins."

"I appreciate that," she said, pocketing her keys. "And please, call me Donna."

Donna opened a drawer on her filing cabinet, tucked her purse inside, then slid the drawer shut. "Mr. Garvin means well, Hannah, but I don't think he truly appreciates how much work there is. Coffee?"

I nodded, pleased at the apparent thaw in our relationship.

Donna showed me where to find the mugs, waited until I'd filled mine with coffee from a large urn, then filled a mug for herself. She opened the fridge and took out a pint carton of half and half. "Cream?"

"Thank goodness! I thought I'd have to use *this* stuff," I said, picking up a cardboard container of nondairy creamer and rotating it until I could read the ingredients. "Soybean oil, mono and diglycerides, dipotassium phosphate . . . yum yum."

Donna smiled. "This is my private stash." She poured cream into my mug until I held up my hand, then returned the carton to the fridge. "Next time," she said, "just help yourself."

"Thanks, I will." I added sugar to my mug and stirred. Perhaps a future biographer would write that our friendship had been cemented over a carton of half and half.

Soon my coffee and I were installed in a cubicle that belonged, if the decorations on the walls were any indication, to someone named Mindy who enjoyed trading recipes, had a thing for Brad Pitt, and occasionally rode motorcycles.

"Mindy's on maternity leave," Donna explained. She sat in Mindy's chair, powered up the computer, assigned me a logon and a password, then left the cubicle for a moment. When she returned, she carried an oversized, fat printout spring-bound in black plastic, which she plopped onto the desk to the right of the monitor. "Data fields," she said. "More than you ever wanted to know."

"Thanks," I said.

"Call me if you need anything. My extension is 1412."

"I'll do that."

I spent the first several hours perusing the printout, familiarizing myself with Victory Mutual's databases and trying to determine what information I would be able to extract from them.

Around ten I took a break and went for more coffee.

Since my last visit to the staff lounge, some angel had set a plate of chocolate chip cookies on the table with a sign reading "Help Yourself." As I wound my way back to the cubicle balancing a homemade cookie on top of the steaming mug, I thought I could get used to this (again!) I was enjoying being back in an office environment: the clack of computer keyboards, the intermittent warble of office telephones, the low hum of business conversations punctuated by laughter drifting out over the sound of a radio, turned low, playing soft rock several cubicles away. I even savored the smell of Magic Marker and the way the Xerox toner stung my nose. It was like being back at Whitworth and Sullivan in the halcyon days precancer, pre-RIF, but without the commute.

Reenergized, I returned to my desk and dove back into the printouts. I decided to limit my search to the last five years and to look for changes in the field having to do with reassignment of ownership. Among those, I'd look for ownership changes that went to a business or organizational name. Once I sorted those results, it would be easy to see if one particular organization name stood out.

I was jotting down my search strategy on a pad of paper and was about to try it out when Mrs. Bromley surprised me by ringing through on my cell phone.

"Hannah, could you meet me for lunch?"

I checked my watch. Eleven o'clock. I'd forgotten to ask Donna how much time Victory Mutual allowed their employees for lunch. Forty-five minutes? An hour? As a consultant, I wasn't exactly punching a time clock, but still, I didn't want to create a bad impression, especially on my first day.

I was about to beg off, but some urgency in Mrs. Bromley's voice made me hesitate. *Could you* meet me, is how she phrased it, not *would you like to* meet me. "I've just started a new project," I explained, "but I suppose they'll let me take a break." I suggested we meet at Macaroni's, a local branch of the popular Italian restaurant chain. It was just across the road, on the fringes of Annapolis Mall. "I can be there at noon."

"Wonderful!" She sounded so relieved I felt guilty about my initial lack of enthusiasm. "What's your new project, Hannah?"

"It's related to that insurance thing," I told her. "I'll fill you in over the linguini."

Perhaps it was just my cell phone, but her laughter rang hollow. "See you soon, then. And, thanks, Hannah."

At 11:55, I took my life into my hands and dashed, on foot, across six lanes of traffic on Jennifer Road, weaving my way through a long line of vehicles waiting to turn left into Sears. From there it was just a short walk across the parking lot to Macaroni's Grill.

Mrs. Bromley was waiting for me inside, near one of the deli cases that flanked the door, where fresh meat and vegetables were displayed in orderly rows. She was gazing into the case intently, as if she expected the sausages to leap up and start dancing, like the Radio City Rockettes. When I touched her shoulder, she flinched. "Hannah!"

"The very same," I said, kissing her cheek. "You look nice," I said, and she did, wearing black slacks and a peach-colored short sleeve blouse, open at the neck. "I hope you haven't been waiting long."

"No, no. I just got here."

We presented ourselves to the hostess, who grabbed a couple of menus and escorted us past the wine and dessert islands to a table for four, covered with white paper, near a louvered window at the back of the restaurant. We had just settled into our seats and were reading the plastic tent card detailing the specials when our waiter appeared.

"Hello, my name is Davon and I'll be your server today." Using two crayons held closely together—a red and a blue—he printed his name upside down on the tablecloth.

"Very good," I said.

"Thank you." He grinned. "Wine?"

"No thanks, I'm actually working. Mrs. Bromley?" I asked, just to be polite. Mrs. Bromley rarely drank before four in the afternoon, especially outside the home.

To my surprise, she nodded. "I do believe I will. A chardonnay, I think."

Davon brought a gallon jug of wine to the table and plunked it down. Using the blue crayon, he made a hatch mark on the paper tablecloth. "We're on the honor system here," he explained. "That's one glass. Just keep track and let me know."

Mrs. Bromley eyed the gigantic bottle, then looked at me. "Sure you can't help me with that?"

"Well," I said, signaling to Davon. "Maybe half a glass."

Davon returned with a glass for me and a round loaf of herb bread. "Hot from the oven," he said. I watched, stomach rumbling, as he drizzled olive oil onto an empty plate and grated fresh pepper and parmesan cheese into it.

When Davon left with our order—linguini with clam sauce and a Caesar salad to share—I tore off a portion of bread and dipped it into the olive oil mixture. "So, how's your art show progressing?" I inquired.

"Fine," she said.

"Need any help?" I asked around a savory mouthful of bread.

"No, my students are doing most of that."

Two tables over somebody named Tom was being serenaded by a dark-haired waitresses in a clear, high soprano. Happy Birthday, she sang, to the tune of "Ridi, Pagliaccio." A single candle stood in a piece of cheesecake on the table in front of the honoree. The flame wavered as the soprano really got into it, belting out the last *il cor* with such enthusiasm that I thought she'd beat the birthday boy to the punch and blow the darn thing out.

"She's so skinny," I commented, sotto voce, to Mrs. Bromley, "that if she turned sideways she'd disappear."

Mrs. Bromley looked up from her wine. "What was that, dear?"

"I said . . . never mind. It wasn't important." I reached out and touched her hand. "You seem distracted today, Mrs. B. Is everything okay?"

"Everything's fine," she said. She set her glass down on the table and pinched off a piece of bread. "So, tell me about your new project, Hannah."

Unless I'd completely misread her, everything was not "fine." I'd never seen Mrs. Bromley acting so squirrelly.

Davon brought our linguini, and while we dug into it, I explained about my undercover assignment at Victory Mutual and my relationship with Donna Hudgins. "What I'm hoping to find, in the final sort, is a high number of policies that have changed from private ownership to corporate ownership, to companies like ViatiPro."

"What then?" she asked.

"Then I turn the information over to Donna Hudgins and her claims review people. They'll dig up the actual policies, look at the death certificates, and compare the time that elapsed between the signing of the policy and the death of the insured person."

Mrs. Bromley laid her fork and spoon across her dish and pushed her linguini, half eaten, to the center of the table. "I'm embarrassed to tell you that I wasn't entirely truthful with you the other day." Tears shimmered in her eyes. "I've been agonizing over whether to tell you or not."

"Tell me what?"

She picked up a green crayon and doodled little circles on the tablecloth. "I'm just a foolish old woman."

"That's the silliest thing you've ever said to me, Mrs. Bromley."

"It's true, I'm afraid. Why else would I have fallen for the sales pitch of that dreadful man?"

I had been leaning forward over my linguini, but I fell back into my chair. "Jablonsky?"

My friend laid down her crayon and nodded.

I couldn't believe it. If someone as level-headed as Mrs. Bromley had snapped up the bait, what hope was there for the average senior citizen when the likes of Jablonsky oozed under the door?

"I had two policies," she said, "so I sold one of them." She looked away from me, out the narrow slats in the window and into the parking lot. "I'm not going to tell you what I invested the proceeds in."

Now it was my turn to feel embarrassed. Here I'd spent days rattling on and on about the evils of buying and selling viaticals. It was as if I'd spent hours complaining about what a lemon my new car was, only to find out that Mrs. Bromley'd gone out and bought exactly the same model.

Mrs. Bromley looked so stricken that I moved quickly to soften the blow. "I'm sure it made sense at the time, Mrs. B. It's not like you're disinheriting your children or anything."

She turned to face me again, and I noticed for the first time a slight puffiness in her eyelids. She *had* been crying. "Now I'm either paranoid or losing my mind," she whispered. "A few months ago, I was playing croquet on the green at Ginger Cove."

"Yes?" Ginger Cove residents played an annual match with the students from St. John's College. St. John's usually got trounced.

"While I was lining up a shot," Mrs. Bromley continued, "I noticed this cable TV installer coming out of Clark Gammel's building." She lowered her voice to a whisper. "That was the same day they found Clark's body. I didn't make a connection between the two events at the time. But then, just last week, I could have sworn I saw the same man delivering an armchair to Building 8100." She paused and took a deep breath, letting it out slowly. "Tim Burns lived in 8100, Hannah, and he died, too. He died the same day I saw that chair being delivered. And yesterday," she continued, her words tumbling rapidly over one another, "I saw a gardener working on the tulip beds just outside my building, and he looked a lot like that cable guy, too."

I'd never seen Mrs. Bromley so rattled, and it worried me. When my mother died, she'd been there for me. When my father disappeared into a bizarre alcohol rehabilitation program without telling anybody, she'd been my rock. I found myself a bit bewildered by the role reversal.

I watched a tear roll down her pale cheek. Nobody really notices the faces of people in uniform, I thought. Nobody, that is, except my friend, Mrs. Bromley, who in nearly half a century as a mystery novelist tended to notice everything. It would be a mistake to minimize her concerns.

Mrs. Bromley extracted her hand—I'd been holding it tightly—and bent to retrieve her handbag from the floor. She set the bag on her lap and slipped two photographs out of an envelope in the outside pouch. She laid the photos on the table in front of me. "I took these with my digital camera when I thought he wasn't looking."

The color was slightly off and the photos were grainy; they'd obviously been printed out on Mrs. Bromley's home computer. Although taken from a distance, they showed a lanky, broad-shouldered man wearing khaki pants and a dark green polo shirt, exactly what one might expect on a lawn care professional. In the first picture, the gardener was bent over, one foot on a shovel, frozen forever in the act of pushing the shovel into the ground. A ball cap obscured his face. In the second picture, the man had turned sideways but the photo was too fuzzy to make any sort of positive identification. He could have been any white male of that general height and build—Paul, or my father, even.

"Looks like a gardener to me, Mrs. B."

"But what if he *isn't* just a gardener? Residents have died at Ginger Cove recently, many more than one might expect. We were talking about it at dinner the other day."

"It could be a coincidence," I said without much conviction.

"Coincidence my foot! Clark sold his life insurance policy to Jablonsky. Tim Burns told me he was going to do the same. I know *I* sold the wretched man my policy." Her eyes flashed. The Mrs. Bromley I knew and loved was back. "What if," she murmured, so softly I had to strain to hear her over the hoots of Birthday Boy and Co. still celebrating at the next table, "what if Jablonsky is hurrying things along a bit?"

I tapped one of the photos. "This is *not* a picture of Gilbert Jablonsky."

"One of his henchmen, then."

Mrs. Bromley had an excellent point. What did Valerie Stone, Clark Gammel, and Tim Burns have in common? They'd viaticated their life insurance policies through Gilbert Jablonsky, that's what. And now all three were dead. No wonder Mrs. Bromley was freaked. If her suspicions were correct, she could be next on the list.

I began thinking out loud. "I wonder if there's a way to find out how many residents of Ginger Cove—besides you, Clark, and Tim—have viaticated their policies through MBFSG?" And then I remembered something. "That party you told me about, where Jablonsky came and talked to you? Do you remember who attended?"

She shook her head. "I've already thought of that. It was an open house, so people were coming and going the whole evening, picking up brochures, filling out forms to request more information. Like that. If they actually *sold* their policies, it would have been when Jablonsky contacted them later, one-on-one." She paused to sip at her wine. "Like he did me."

"I'll figure out something," I said, although other than breaking into Jablonsky's office after hours and rummaging through his files, I didn't have a clue how I might go about it.

"Perhaps this will help." Mrs. Bromley hauled another piece of paper out of her purse and laid it on top of the photographs. It was a handwritten list of ten names, headed by Clark Gammel and Tim Burns. "These are the folks at Ginger Cove who have died during the past year," she told me. "See if you can find out how many of *these* people are Jablonsky's customers."

She reached out and squeezed my arm. "I'm frightened, Hannah. I honestly think that gardener is stalking me."

CHAPTER **16**

First thing the following morning, I telephoned Jablonsky's office.

"Mutually Beneficial Financial Services Group, Gail Parrish speaking, how may I direct your call?"

"Congratulations!" I said. "That was flawless."

Gail giggled into her end of the phone. "Who is this?"

"This is Hannah Ives. Remember me? I was there last week."

"Oh, hi, Hannah. Sure, I remember. Gil thought you might be calling back."

I'll bet, I thought. Cheeky S.O.B.

What I said was: "Well, I don't know why he'd be expecting me to call back because I've been going so wishy-washy on him. If it were just up to me, you know, I'd sign up in a second, but my husband is dead set against it. Gil said I wouldn't exactly have to tell him. But Paul and me? Our marriage has always been based on trust, and I don't feel comfortable hiding stuff from him. You know what I mean?"

"Uh-huh."

"But here's the thing," I dithered on. "I've been talking to my dad about this viatical opportunity and I think *he* might be interested. Mom's been gone for a couple of years and Dad's been paying premiums on this policy he really doesn't need anymore.

"As it stands now, of course, I'll get something when he dies, but I don't want to be *selfish*. You know? He's eighty-seven," I told her, adding a couple of decades to my father's actual age. "He could go somewhere! Take a cruise!" I paused to take a breath. "Would Mr. Jablonsky be interested, do you think?"

"Gil would be interested if your *parakeet* wanted to sell its life insurance policy," Gail deadpanned.

"You are a hoot!" I screamed.

"Don't quote me," Gail said.

"Trust me, I won't. Parakeets!" I giggled. "Well, anyway," I forged on, like a telemarketer on commission. "My dad lives out at Ginger Cove, that retirement community off Riva Road? So, I was wondering. Are there any Ginger Cove residents Dad can talk to for references?"

Apparently Gail had never heard of HIPAA because she agreed to help me right away. "They're not organized like that in our database," she told me. "I'll have to check the contact files in Gil's office. It'll take a few minutes. Can I call you back?"

"Sure," I said, and gave her my number.

When I hung up, I felt guilty. Gail was a nice young woman. I hated lying to her. When all this was over, maybe I would be able to do something for her. Take her out for lunch or something. Try to explain.

The next thirty minutes crawled by. I loaded the dishwasher, watered my houseplants, and watched ten minutes of the *Today* show.

The phone sat silent.

I paced for a while, then went off in search of my knitting bag, which contained a partially completed cable-knit sweater I'd been working on since the last Winter Olympics. I plopped down on the living room sofa next to the portable phone and lengthened the back of the sweater by two rows—knit, purl, cheaper than Prozac, purl, knit—and was working in a cable when the phone finally rang. I could tell by the Caller ID it was Gail.

"Hey hey!" I said.

"Hi, it's me. Gail. As if you didn't know," she said.

"I just *love* Caller ID."

"I got some references for your dad," Gail said. "Got a pencil?"

"Shoot."

As Gail read, I jotted down the names. Gammel and Burns were no surprise, nor was Nadine Smith Gray, the name Mrs. Bromley's mother gave her at birth. By the time Gail was done, though, I was hardly breathing. Of the nine potential references Gail read out to me, six would never be referring anybody to anything ever again. They were numbers one, two, four, six, seven, and nine on Mrs. Bromley's obituary list.

I'd gone pretty far, but the adrenaline was pounding in my ears, and I decided, perhaps recklessly, to push it. "Gee, thanks, Gail," I gushed, "That'll help me a lot." Then added, hoping that it might sound like an afterthought, "Say, Mr. Jablonsky was telling me about the zillions of companies he was dealing with and how some were better than others. Can you tell me what companies bought these policies?"

"I'm not supposed to," Gail whispered, "but Gil almost always goes with ViatiPro, especially for the seniors."

I heard the clack of her computer keys. "Let's see now. Wyetha Hodge. That's ViatiPro. *Clack-clack*. Timothy Burns. ViatiPro. *Clackety-clack*. Parker, ditto . . ."

I was beginning to wonder if Gilbert Jablonsky ever did business with any companies other than ViatiPro.

Gail paused. I could hear her breathing. "Gammel, ViatiPro." Her keys clacked a few more times, then she muttered, "Say, this is odd. Let me call you back."

The telephone went dead in my ear.

I sat there on my sofa, staring at the receiver, feeling cheated. "Gail, come back!" I wailed. Nothing.

I cradled the receiver, stuffed my knitting back into the bag and set it aside.

Valerie's policy had been sold to ViatiPro. Now I knew for sure that Clark Gammel had sold his policy to ViatiPro, too. As had the late Mr. Timothy Burns.

Barbara Parker, number three on Mrs. Bromley's list, hadn't croaked—yet—but James McGowan had, and he was lucky policy holder number six.

Maybe Gilbert Jablonsky wasn't the common denominator at all, I thought. Maybe it was the folks at ViatiPro who were, in Mrs. Bromley's words, helping things along.

There's a clock mounted on the ceiling as you head down to our basement. Nobody knows why. It was there when we moved in ten years ago, and as far as I knew, nobody'd ever changed the battery, yet it continued to run, regular as, well, clockwork. As I headed down to my office to check out ViatiPro on the Internet, the clock glared at me accusingly: 8:45. I'd promised Donna I'd be in by nine. I was a professional. If I didn't hurry it up, I'd be late for work.

By taking the back roads—through West Annapolis, out Ridgely to Bestgate, I made it to Victory Mutual and was sitting in Mindy's cubicle, typing away, only seconds before Donna passed by on her way to the coffee urn.

She waved.

I waved back.

After she turned the corner, I clicked out of the Victory Mutual database and logged onto the Internet.

ViatiPro's website was slick and professional, last updated, I noticed, only the day before. Headquartered in Greenbelt, Maryland, they had offices in Frederick, Salisbury, and St. Mary's City, geographically situated to serve the entire state of Maryland, "Proudly," I noted, "since 1994."

In additional to viatical settlements, ViatiPro offered investment opportunities that included the usual stocks, bonds, mutual funds, REITs, and limited partnerships (whatever the hell they were!), as well as opportunities to invest in a proposed resort out western Maryland way at Deep Creek Lake and in an upscale restaurant in Rockville, just outside of Washington, D.C.

Investment advisers were available to talk with me from 10:00 A.M. to 7:00 P.M. daily, or I could fill out the blanks in their handy online form, click Send, and information would soon be winging my way. No cost, no obligation.

For sure.

I clicked around some more and located a picture of C. Alexander Steele, founder and CEO of ViatiPro. Steele smiled out from the screen with the teeth, hairdo, and guileless blue eyes of a television evangelist. He wore a blue suit, white shirt, and red tie, and looked so patriotic, I felt like saluting.

With my mouse, I circled my pointer around the CEO's face. "C. Alexander Steele," I said to his computerized image. "Look out, because I've got your number."

I picked up my cell phone and dialed.

CHAPTER 17

"Hannah, you are out of your ever-loving mind!"

By that remark, I guessed my husband wasn't exactly giving a stamp of approval to my plan.

"She's your daughter, George. Can't you talk some sense into her?"

We were sitting in my father's spacious kitchen around a table strewn with the remains of an excellent five-course Chinese carry-out dinner.

Daddy polished off a dumpling. "I don't know, Paul. It sounds like fun."

"Fun?" Paul jabbed his chopsticks into a container of mushi pork, where they stood up straight and quivered. "It's plain crazy."

Daddy grinned. "I agree with Hannah. I think we need to see what this guy Steele's game is."

Paul's face wore that troubled expression where his eyebrows nearly met. "You really think he's snuffing people for the insurance money?"

"I think *somebody* is," I said. "Besides," I added. "It's too late. I've already called for an appointment. I'm on at ViatiPro for three-thirty tomorrow afternoon, so if you won't play along . . ." I pointed to Paul. ". . . then eenie-meenie-miney-moe, I choose you!" My finger stopped, pointing to my father.

Daddy rotated his shoulders and stretched his neck,

preening like a peacock. "Who shall I be, then? A Texas oilman? A wealthy industrialist? The owner of a small, but successful, chain of jewelry stores?" His eyes sparkled. Daddy was just getting warmed up.

"Just come as you are," I suggested with a smile.

"Under what name?"

"Lord, give me strength!" Paul lifted his eyes heavenward. "They're using aliases, now!"

"I always fancied being a Herbert," Daddy mused. "Or a Jerome."

"Cool your jets, Daddy. They have databases these days. They can look you up and know everything about you by close of business today, including your shoe size and brand of deodorant. Sorry, you're just plain old Captain George D. Alexander, U.S. Navy, Retired."

"Cuthbert?" Daddy raised an eyebrow hopefully.

"Behave yourself!" I picked a stray curried rice noodle off his shirt. "If you want to be creative . . ." I paused to think. "You know that string tie you brought home from Arizona?"

"The one with the silver dollar?"

Paul's eyes widened. "There's more than one?"

I ignored him. "That's the one. Wear that."

Daddy pinched my cheek. "Sho nuff, sweet thang."

I hardly recognized the dashing elder statesman who came to pick me up on Wednesday afternoon. Since retirement, Daddy had taken to favoring chinos and loose pullover sweaters. If he wore shoes at all, they'd be Docksiders or sandals.

This time, though, he'd spent some time cultivating his look. My "date" wore black leather, panel toe low-rise boots, and a light blue shirt with his dark gray, Sunday-go-to-meeting suit. The string tie had been an inspiration, adding a certain *je ne sais quoi* to his ensemble. His curly gray hair was freshly washed, and with the help, I suspect, of a little gel, combed straight back. If Neelie Gibbs could see Daddy now, she'd forget all that nonsense about separate hotel rooms and jump his bones for sure.

"How do I look?" he asked me.

"I'm speechless."

"Is that good or bad?"

I kissed his cheek. "It's good. Very good."

Daddy spread his arms wide. "I thought I'd hint at old Texas money gone East." He winked. "That's why I left the Stetson at home."

"Thank goodness for small favors."

"Wanna know something, sweetheart?" He grinned. "I haven't had so much fun since I played Bunthorne in high school."

I stopped to think. "Bunthorne?"

"You remember. The effete poet in Gilbert and Sullivan's operetta *Patience*."

"Oh, right! The Oscar Wilde character." I had to chuckle, picturing my father wearing a velvet smock and a floppy beret and carrying, as Bunthorne did, a limp lily. I hoped this role wouldn't prove more demanding; at least he wouldn't be required to sing.

"So." Daddy took me by the shoulders and held me at arm's length. "What are you supposed to be?"

"Trophy wife," I said.

Indeed, I looked like I'd walked straight out of Talbot's red door, in a beige linen suit with matching hose and high-heeled sandals I'd recently bought for a wedding. I'd accessorized with a Hermès scarf and a bit of gold jewelry, but the pièce de résistance was the ring, a two carat cubic zirconium Paul'd once given me as a joke. I'd dug the CZ out of my jewelry box and slipped it on my right hand, hoping Steele wouldn't get close enough to notice that my diamond had come from JC Penney rather than Bailey, Banks and Biddle.

"I like your hair," Daddy said.

"Thanks." My bangs had grown too long, so I'd tamed them by sweeping them to one side and clipping them in place with a rhinestone-encrusted gold butterfly.

Daddy licked an index finger and pressed it into my shoulder. "Ssssssst," he teased. "Hot stuff."

I slapped his hand. "Save it for your other girlfriends," I teased.

As we sped down Route 50 toward the Washington beltway, I switched the car radio off and filled my father in. "I'm not exactly sure what we're looking for," I said, "but I've been sticking my nose into this business long enough that I think I'll know it when I see it.

"At first, I thought Jablonsky was the lowest common denominator," I continued. "But now I think he only serves as a middleman. He simply arranges the sale of the policies—presumably to the highest bidder—and takes a percentage of the sale up front."

Daddy eased his Chrysler out into the fast lane to pass a slow-moving truck. "Was it Deep Throat who advised Woodward—or was it Bernstein?—to 'Follow the money'?"

"Well, exactly," I agreed. "Jablonsky's already been paid, so I can't figure out what he'd have to gain by bumping anybody off."

"What's Steele's role, then? He's next in the food chain, right?"

"Yes, and that's where it gets a little murky. In a basic scenario, Steele—or rather, ViatiPro—would buy a policy at a percentage of its face value, hold on to it until the person died, at which point the insurance company would pay Steele, as beneficiary, the full face value of the policy. If the person dies quickly enough, Steele stands to make a handsome profit."

"And, as you say, have a fine motive for murder if the person doesn't oblige by dying on schedule."

"But that's just it," I complained. "Steele doesn't take

any chances. He turns right around and sells the policies he's just bought to investors." I poked my father in the arm with my finger. "I.e., you."

"So the only person with a motive for hastening the death of the—what's the word?—viator, would be the person whose name appears as the beneficiary on the policy."

"Yes."

"And that would be ViatiPro or a ViatiPro investor."

"Right."

"But you'd have to know who the viator was before you could help him pack his bags for a one-way trip to heaven on the gospel train."

"Uh-huh."

Daddy steered the Chrysler onto the exit ramp and eased into the heavy traffic moving west on I-495. "ViatiPro would have the names of the viators on file, of course, but how would I, as an investor, get this kind of personal information? Surely the viators are assured of privacy?"

"One would assume so."

"So, again, if you're not considerate enough to die and make me richer, how do I find out who you are and make it so?"

"That's what I hope we're about to find out."

I'd been spending a lot of time in offices lately, but Steele's was the handsomest of the lot, occupying a suite on the top floor of a glass and steel building overlooking Route 450 and the Washington beltway.

When the elevator doors slid open and deposited us into the lobby at the stroke of three-thirty, we could see, even through the double glass doors to our right, that Steele and his staff went about their business with the hum of commerce tastefully absorbed by plush plum carpeting, dark wood paneling, and handsome, custom-upholstered over-stuffed furniture.

The receptionist, a clean-cut young man who looked

like he should be selling Bibles door-to-door, buzzed us in. "Mr. Steele's expecting you," he said. "Please have a seat."

I settled comfortably into a leather wingback chair that would have looked quite at home in a men's club. If I worked there, I thought, I'd spend half my time curled up in the furniture, fast asleep.

Daddy picked up a copy of *Field & Stream* and began leafing through it. I grabbed a *National Geographic* with a dinosaur on the cover and began reading about islands in the South Pacific.

On the wall behind the receptionist's head the big hand of a bronze Art Deco clock clicked slowly from VI to VII. I coughed.

The receptionist looked up.

I pointed to the clock.

He made a Y with his thumb and little finger and tapped his ear: Steele was on the telephone.

I went back to drooling over pictures of Pacific atolls.

The big hand had clicked onto the IX when the elevator doors slid open and a stocky, balding man erupted from them. When the receptionist buzzed him in, the guy—a symphony in brown with tie ends flapping—straight-armed his way through the glass doors. He brushed past without even looking our way, and loomed over the reception desk like a malevolent mushroom.

"He in?"

"He's on the phone, sir."

"I gotta see him, Matt. Now."

"If you'll just wait a minute, sir." The receptionist picked up the phone and was punching buttons as if his life depended on it. Maybe it did.

"Can't wait." The guy turned and chugged down the hall.

The receptionist leaped up with the telephone still pressed to his ear, his left hand raised as if hailing a cab. "You can't . . . Please! Wait!"

I peeked around the wing of my armchair in time to see the guy's brown coattails disappear around a corner.

The receptionist sat down with a resigned and audible thud that sent his chair, which must have been on wheels, rolling backward into the wall. "Shit."

"Who was that?" I asked.

He looked up, startled. "Oh, sorry about that. I shouldn't swear in front of the clients."

"That's all right," I said. "It's a technical term. I use it every day."

The young man grinned, relief flooding his face.

"So," I asked again, "who was that impatient son of a gun?"

"Nick Pottorff," he replied. "One of the investors."

My father cleared his throat importantly. "Excuse me, but we're investors, too," he complained.

"I'm sorry, sir, but . . ." He extended his hands, palms out, and shrugged.

I laid a hand on my father's arm. "That's okay, sweetheart. Pottorff's an impatient jerk. It's not the young man's fault."

I beamed at the receptionist. "Your name is Matt?"

"Matthew," he replied.

"Well, Matthew, my husband has a theory about brown-suited men."

Daddy raised an eyebrow as if trying to remember what, if anything, he had ever said to me about brown-suited men.

"Tell him, sweetheart," I prompted. "Tell him your theory about brown-suited men."

"Brown suit," Daddy said, sounding puzzled.

I nodded.

"Brown socks."

"Uh-huh."

"Tacky tie."

I shook my head to disagree. "Cheap. The Three

Stooges on a tie is tacky. Or Christmas elves. Brown and orange triangles are just plain cheap."

"Cheap tie, then," Daddy amended.

"Right."

"And therefore . . ." Daddy scanned my face, desperate for help.

"Untrustworthy!" I concluded.

Matthew laughed out loud. "You're right," he said. "Pottorff's a royal pain in the ass. If I didn't need this job . . ." His voice trailed off. "I'm in school. University of Maryland," he explained. He raised a chemistry textbook from where he'd had it concealed under the counter. "Working here usually gives me plenty of time to study."

Daddy had returned his attention to *Field & Stream*, no doubt thinking I'd lost my mind with the brown-suited man bit. It was a little dopey, I admit. Just my feeble attempt to lighten the situation for a clearly embarrassed Matt.

"I'd like to go back to school," I embroidered dreamily. "Maybe to study fashion design."

Daddy looked up from the magazine and rolled his eyes. "The wife," he said carelessly, "is an expert on fashion. She has charge accounts at Saks, Neiman Marcus . . ."

I made a fist and punched him, hard, on the arm. "Stop it, George!"

". . . Nordstrom, Lord and Taylor." Daddy might have continued the litany of department stores forever, had the telephone not rung.

Matthew answered, then looked up, relief plain in this eyes. "Mr. Steele will see you now."

The young receptionist escorted us down the hallway to a conference room where C. Alexander Steele, CEO, was seated at a round mahogany table. On a nearby credenza, a tray of coffee paraphernalia sat next to a silver bucket brimming with ice. Next to the ice, neatly arranged on a matching tray, was an assortment of bottled fruit juices and colas. There was no sign of the obnoxious Mr. Pottorff.

Steele stood up as we entered and extended a hand. "Captain and Mrs. Alexander. Welcome. Please sit down."

Steele gestured toward a sofa, chair, coffee- and end-table grouping that reminded me of a living room, or what a living room might look like if one were married to Donald Trump. Daddy and I perched next to each other on the gold brocade sofa, and Steele settled his elegant, silk-clad buns into an adjoining armchair.

"May I offer you some refreshment?" Steele asked.

Daddy turned to me. "Sweetheart?"

Although my mouth was dry, I shook my head. I was so nervous I knew that if I tried to drink anything I'd probably end up sloshing it all over Steele's beautiful upholstery.

"Nothing for me, either." Daddy reached into his breast pocket, pulled out a piece of paper and laid it on the coffee table. I could see it was a printout from the Internet: *Viaticals: The Perfect High Return/Low Risk Investment*. For the moment, though, Daddy ignored it.

"I don't want to waste any of your time or mine, Steele, so let's get down to it," Daddy began. "One of my tech stocks went up like a rocket. I've decided to cash in and take my profits. So, I've got close to ninety thousand floating around that I'd like to put to work in something that has potential for a quick turnaround."

Steele nodded. "I hear you."

"I've got a unit trust that's maturing in a year," Daddy continued with easy confidence, although as far as I was concerned, he might as well have been speaking in tongues. "If I can turn that ninety thou around fast, then I'll have a substantial piece of change to work with.

"Viatical investments were new to me," Daddy admitted, "so I did some research." As he tapped the printout, his Naval Academy class ring captured the light from the lamp and flashed it across the ceiling.

I stole a quick glance at Steele and suspected that he noticed the ring, too. If he'd done his homework, he'd have known that Dad was an Academy grad. Couldn't help but add to Dad's Wall Street cred.

"Sounded too good to be true, if you want to know the truth," Daddy added. "This guy I play racquetball with told me he bought a policy that matured in six months. Made a bundle. So, I asked around the club, and your name came up."

Steele was nodding. "Those results are not at all unusual. In fact, you can't *lose* money in this market. The worst you can do is not make *a lot* of money."

Steele leaned forward, resting his elbows on his knees. "Supposing you buy a one-year, $100,000 life insurance policy for $88,000. If the person dies in the sixth month, you've earned a twenty-four percent annual rate of return! If he lives one year, your rate is about twelve percent. At two years, your rate drops to about six percent, but even if he lives fifty years, you still make money!" He spread his hands. "In comparison to a certificate of deposit earning, say, five percent, or, God help us," he chuckled, "dealing with the inconsistencies of the stock market, viatical settlements are virtually risk-free!

"And there's always the humanitarian aspect to consider." Steele aimed his expensive, laser-bleached smile at me. "Naturally, purchasing a viatical settlement helps you, the client, but this is one purchase you can really feel good about! Your investment helps a terminally ill individual make it through a time of great emotional and financial stress."

I reached out and laid a hand on top of my father's. "That's *really* important, isn't it, George?"

"Yeah yeah. Always happy to do my part." Daddy slipped his hand out from under mine. "Look, Steele, getting back to what you were saying. I'm not interested in waiting around for fifty years."

"Of course, I understand, I was just giving you a for instance." Steele uncrossed his legs and stood up, inviting us to join him at a conference table near the window.

As Daddy held my chair, he flashed me a wink. Thank goodness! Clearly he had embraced his role as Wall Street cowboy, but I had begun to wonder whether aliens had landed and taken over his body!

Once we were seated, Steele fanned a handful of slick brochures out on the table in front of us. "We've got quite a few plans here, Captain Alexander. The five-year program has a higher fixed rate of return, of course, but those policies are almost exclusively senior settlements, expected to pay out within sixty months. I'm thinking you'll find our one-year program the one that best meets your needs. These are policies expected to pay out within the next twelve months at a very attractive rate of return."

Steele paused, allowing my father time to review some of the information he'd put before him.

It all sounded pretty dicey to me. Even if your rich uncle Joe is ninety years old and has been smoking cigars since he began sneaking puffs behind the barn at the age of twelve, how could you predict when he'd die? Statistics don't apply to individual cases. You might as well go to Madame Stella and have your palm read.

When I tuned back in again, Daddy was saying, "Okay, Steele, one-year it is. What exactly do I receive for my investment?"

"You become the owner and the irrevocable beneficiary of an existing, investment grade life insurance policy which is presently in force and covering a terminally ill person with a life expectancy of one year or less."

"Okay. Say I decide to invest my ninety thousand. What happens next?"

Steele shuffled through the brochures. "Ah, here it is. It's a common question, so we've prepared a checklist." He slid it across the table. "First," he explained, "your investment is placed in our viatical escrow account at BB and T."

"That sounds reassuring," I said. BB&T was as solid a bank as they come.

Daddy grunted.

"Next," Steele continued, "our viatical provider secures a policy of an appropriate face amount, which meets both medical and insurance underwriting criteria."

I tried to catch my father's eye. There was no doubt in my mind that the "viatical provider" Steele was referring to was none other than our good friend Gilbert Jablonsky. Good God, what did Steele do? Place orders with Jablonsky for life insurance policies as if they were used cars?

"Then what?" Daddy wanted to know.

"Once the insured person has agreed to sell his policy, he receives a purchase agreement in which the insured person and his beneficiaries relinquish all rights to the policy by signing a change of beneficiary form. These documents are forwarded to the insurance company, where the changes are officially recorded. Then, a copy is sent to the viatical escrow agent who reviews it, and if the documentation is in order, the funds are released and the deal is closed."

"How do I know this is a legitimate policy you're selling me?"

Steele's face crumpled. We were questioning his honesty. "All our policies are with insurance companies that are A rated or better by A.M. Best, Standard & Poor's, or an equivalent rating company."

"I see," my father said. "And now, no point beating around the bush. How do I tell when my viator has died?"

"Each viator receives a viator number." Steele pointed to the bottom of the brochure, where an Internet address was printed in large black type. "You log on to that website whenever you like, type in the viator number we give you, and you'll receive an updated status report on that person."

"What do you do, Steele, have somebody call up the viator and ask 'So, how you doing today, Harry? Feeling poorly?' "

"Oh, Daddy! That's disgusting," I cried. Instantly, I could have bitten my tongue off. I flashed a smile at Steele, hoping he hadn't noticed my slip. "Isn't he just *awful?*"

Daddy, smooth as silk, saved my sorry skin. He pinched my cheek, "That's my little girl!"

You've got to give Steele a little credit. He didn't roll his eyes, although I'm sure he wanted to.

Daddy pushed back his chair and stood. "Once the viator dies, how soon will I receive my money?"

"The benefit is paid by the insurance company, of course, so that varies company by company, but we've been averaging six to eight weeks."

That seemed to satisfy my father. "Well, Steele, I think we'll probably be able to do a little business here. Let me get my ducks in a row and get back to you." He pumped Steele's arm up and down vigorously.

"If you have any questions or concerns, please give me a call," Steele added. He reached into the inside breast pocket of his jacket, took out a silver card case and extracted a business card. "Call me, any time, Captain. That has my cell, as well as my office."

"Thanks, I'll do that," Daddy said. He handed Steele's business card to me and I slipped it into my bag.

"C'mon, sweetheart. Time to go," Daddy added. "We'll be late for the theater."

"*The Producers,*" I said airily. "We've had tickets for simply *ages!*"

Steele checked his watch. "You'll have plenty of time to get to the Kennedy Center," he said as he ushered us down the hall, then through the glass doors and into the elevator lobby.

"Oh, it's not in D.C.," I chirped. "It's in New York."

If Steele had any response to that remark, it was lost as the elevator doors closed silently in his face.

Once the elevator began its descent, I fell back, exhausted, against the wood paneling. "Captain Alexander, you were terrific," I said. "You really did your homework."

"I was up late bopping around the Internet," Daddy replied. "I didn't want to blow it."

"So, what do you think?" I asked as the elevator disgorged us on the lobby level.

"I think that if we can prove that the Ginger Cove residents on Mrs. Bromley's list did not die of natural causes, our friend Steele has to be in it up to his impeccably groomed eyebrows."

"We need to talk to Dennis," I said, referring to my brother-in-law, the Chesapeake County cop.

With one arm, Daddy held the lobby door open for me and we passed out into the bright June sunshine.

Unexpectedly, Daddy tapped my shoulder. "Look, Hannah. There's your brown-suited man."

"Where?"

Daddy pointed to the far end of the parking lot, where a man who looked a lot like Nick Pottorff was climbing into a BMW. Pottorff started his car, revved the engine a couple of times to show how macho he was, backed out of the parking space, and sped past us, tires squealing.

I'd seen that car before. As it flew by, I got a good look at the license plate, too: N4SIR.

I grabbed my father's arm. "That's the same car I saw in Gilbert Jablonsky's lot!" I leaned back against the fender of a blue Volvo. "Oh my God, Daddy! That means there's *got* to be a connection between Steele and Jablonsky!"

"Ba-da-bing, Ba-da-boom," Daddy said.

"What?"

"Haven't you been watching *The Sopranos* on HBO?"

Of course I had, but I wasn't in the mood for lighthearted banter. "Listen to me! I am positive that car and its license plate were parked next to mine in Jablonsky's parking lot in Glen Burnie just one week ago! How can you not remember a vanity plate like N4SIR?"

"I don't know." Daddy stood straight and tall, hands

thrust deep into his pockets, shaking his head. "Isn't that a little obvious, Hannah? Do you think he'd drive around with a plate like that if he really were a mafia enforcer?"

"I don't think the word 'subtle' appears in Nick Pottorff's dictionary," I said.

"In that case, sweetheart, we need to share what we know with Dennis ASAP and see what he advises."

"Are you busy tomorrow night, Daddy?"

"I don't think so. Why?"

"If Connie and Dennis are free, I thought we'd cook out in the backyard."

"Haven't had a good hamburger in a long time," Daddy said. "Count me in."

Daddy held the passenger door of the Chrysler open and I slipped in, ladylike, remembering, just in case anybody was watching, to keep my knees together, slide and swivel.

When Daddy got behind the wheel, he turned the key in the ignition, then leaned back in his seat. "*The Producers*?" he chuckled. "In New York City?"

"Sorry, Daddy. Steele was so full of shit, I just couldn't help myself."

CHAPTER 18

I didn't ask for much. Just a casual backyard cookout, a small, intimate get-together in a friendly, stress-free environment where my brother-in-law could grab a few beers, sprawl in a lawn chair, put his feet up and forget, for a time, the rigors of keeping Chesapeake County a safe place for its citizens to live, work, and play.

I planned to ask Dennis what to do about ViatiPro later. After the burgers with everything on them. After the corn on the cob, drizzled with butter. After the still warm from the oven, deep-dish apple pie. (From the bakery. Fresh.)

A policeman in the family is an asset, I know. One mustn't abuse the privilege. Rule one: Don't ask him to bend the law for you. Rule two: Don't waste his time with trivialities. Rule three: Don't put yourself into situations where he has to ride to the rescue with a platoon of United States Marines.

I've never asked him to bend the law. Never knowingly wasted his time. Two out of three? Not bad.

So, like I said, it was to be a simple backyard cookout, two Rutherfords and two Iveses, plus Daddy, of course. And after Dennis was relaxed, I'd ease into the ViatiPro business, feeling my way.

But no.

I was dicing celery, green pepper, and scallions when Daddy called, asking to bring Cornelia Gibbs. Neelie was

Daddy's girlfriend. How could I refuse? I lobbed another potato into the pot and kept on chopping.

Then my sister Ruth popped in bearing a singing bowl. "Something new I'm carrying in the store."

"Thanks, Ruth. I didn't know bowls could sing." I held it in my wet hands. It was about the size of a rice bowl, and heavy.

"It's made from brass and six other metals. You hit it with this wooden striker." She produced a cylindrical mallet from the pocket of her skirt and gave the bowl a whack. "Nice, huh? It clears negativity from the room, especially before you meditate." She narrowed her eyes. "You have been meditating, haven't you?"

The correct answer would have been no. "Whenever I get the chance, Ruth. Whenever I get the chance."

Ruth smiled semiapprovingly, then turned her attention to other things. "What'cha cooking?"

I had to confess. "Potato salad."

"Oh my God, I *love* your potato salad!"

It wasn't my recipe, it was our late mother's, but what could I do? The next thing I knew, Ruth was joining us, too, bringing along her lawyer friend, Maurice Gaylord Hutchinson, Esquire. What a perfect opportunity for "Hutch" (as she affectionately called him) to meet the parental unit. Hutch, an introspective, comfortable, reliable man (the polar opposite of Eric, Ruth's ex), had worked his buns off when some turd stole Ruth's identity and she'd nearly lost both Mother Earth, her new age store on Main Street, and her sanity.

When Ruth breezed out the door to fetch Hutch, her long, salt and pepper hair streaming like a banner behind her, I tossed two more potatoes into the pot. I kneaded an egg and a cup of raw oatmeal into the hamburger, hoping it would stretch to serve eight.

And I kept chopping.

Paul came home from work around five, bearing a dozen ears of corn and a Box o' Wine he insisted we try. I sent him out on the patio to shuck the corn while I scraped the chopped vegetables into a bowl and took care of more important things: I opened the wine.

With my thumb, I punched a hole in the cardboard box and wrestled the plastic spout out of the hole, skinning my knuckles in the process. *This is supposed to be easier than a corkscrew? No way.*

I found a glass, thrust it under the spout, and pushed the button. Considering the way I'd tortured the spout while trying to extract the darn thing from the box, it was a miracle that it worked. I watched as the dark ruby liquid filled my glass halfway, then I swirled it around, testing its legs. I raised the glass to my lips and took a sip, for medicinal purposes. My skinned knuckles were feeling better already.

The wine was a merlot. Velvety, according to the label. Lush plum flavors, gently spiced, with a soft touch of oak. Who makes these terms up? Paul and I once went to a tasting where the wines were described as "assertive," "barnyardy," or even "flabby." I took another sip of the merlot. Definitely not flabby.

When the potatoes were done, I drained the pot, doused them with cold water, and left them in the sink to cool. I grabbed another glass, tucked the wine box under my arm, and headed out to the patio to join Paul.

"Corn's shucked," he said. The naked ears were stacked up like a pyramid on the picnic table next to his elbow, and a paper grocery bag of corn silk and husks sat next to his feet.

I handed him the glass. "Have some wine."

Paul served himself from the box. "Thanks, hon."

We sipped in silence for a while.

"Nice of the weather to cooperate."

I nodded. A gentle breeze was discouraging the average, run-of-the-mill mosquito, and I'd lit citronella candles in small, galvanized buckets and placed them around the garden to intimidate any insects with kamikaze tendencies.

"Do you think I'm crazy, Paul?"

A smile spread slowly across my husband's face. "No, not crazy. But I think you have to be prepared, Hannah. All this could turn out to be some sort of weird coincidence."

"I don't think so. Neither does Daddy. And you should have seen Mrs. Bromley, Paul. She's usually so level-headed. And she was frightened. Really frightened!" I paused to take another sip of wine. "In fact, she's so rattled, she's gone away for the weekend. She's hiding out at a B and B in Chestertown."

He squeezed my knee. "The trouble with you, Hannah, is you care too much. I know Valerie's death hit you hard and that you *want* to believe her chemotherapy wasn't responsible. . . ."

His words hit me like a bucket of cold water. If my own husband wouldn't believe me . . . *et tu* Paul? I covered his hand with my own. "Let me ask you this, Paul. If I died tomorrow, would you say, 'Oh well, must have been the chemo'?"

Paul blinked, clearly rattled.

"You saw how fit Valerie was," I said. "Trust me, it wasn't the chemo."

"Maybe not. But isn't it possible, just possible, that your concern over Valerie's death has caused your vision to be slightly skewed? You've convinced me that Jablonsky and this Steele fellow are crooks . . . but murderers? Are you sure you aren't blowing things just a bit out of proportion?"

I pressed my palms over my ears. "I'm not listening to you!"

"Okay, let's see what Dennis has to say and go from there. But Hannah?" He pulled one hand off my ear. "At least sit the man down with a beer before you pounce. Promise?"

I leaned over and kissed his cheek. "Promise."

*　*　*

It should have been a wonderful party.

Daddy arrived first, Neelie on his arm. "Good to see you again, Hannah." She kissed both my cheeks, then thrust a bag of designer cheese straws into my free hand.

"Thanks, Neelie," I said. "You look sharp." And she did, in a bright red blouse tucked into crisp white slacks, neatly belted. Her snow-white hair was parted slightly to one side, pulled into a low ponytail at the nape of her neck and finished with a silver barrette.

Daddy beamed. The man was besotted. The last time he'd looked at a woman that way, it'd been Mother.

I took a gulp of wine and swallowed, hoping to dull the ache in my heart. "Paul's manning the bar," I said, gesturing with the bag of cheese straws. "Club soda and lime, straight ahead."

"Is Dennis here yet?" Daddy asked me as Neelie pushed her way through the screen door and went out onto the patio ahead of him.

I shook my head. "Paul made me promise to give Dennis a few minutes before we spoil his evening. So if I open my mouth too soon, you may have to sit on me." I put Neelie's cheese straws down on the kitchen table.

"Hannah, Hannah," Daddy said. "I think you were three years old the last time I was able to keep you from doing something once you set your mind to it." He started to follow Neelie, then turned back. "I know it was serious business yesterday, sweetheart. Thanks for trusting me to go along."

"Are you kidding? I would have been lost without you. You were terrific! Academy Award material. Now, shoo! Check in with Paul. I'm sure the charcoal needs starting."

Daddy patted my head and left me to my salad dressing.

Using scissors, I cut fresh herbs into a bowl, added a clove of garlic, and smashed them together with a pestle. I scraped the green goo into a bottle, added oil and vinegar, and shook vigorously. I tasted it. Bleah! Forgot to put in the salt. I corrected the seasonings, shook the mixture again, and dumped the dressing on the potato and vegetable mixture, tossing it lightly.

Through the kitchen window, I could see that Ruth and Hutch had arrived via the side gate. Ruth wore lavender harem pants and a loose, Indian-style shirt. In his business suit, Hutch was overdressed. As I watched, Ruth helped him off with his jacket. Smiling, he loosened his tie and drew it slowly out from under his collar. *Take it off, take it off, take it all off,* I chanted silently. *Performing nightly at Chez Ruth's! Heeeeeerre's Hutch!* At least I hoped so. Ruth had been through a long dry spell.

I went out to greet the new arrivals.

"Hutch." I extended my hand. "Nice to see you again."

"Ditto," he said, shaking mine.

"Drink?"

"G and T, if you have it."

I smiled. "I think that could be arranged." I pointed to Paul. "Check with the bartender over there."

"Mind if I smoke?" Hutch patted his pocket. Through the cotton I could see the outline of a pack of Marlboros.

Yes, I minded. I minded a lot. If I had my way, every pack of cigarettes would carry this Surgeon General's warning: *Danger: Smoking killed my mother. Do you want to die, too?*

"Just not in the house," I warned, already moving away.

I went looking for Paul, slipped my arm around him, held up my glass. "Barkeep, more wine!" He was happy to oblige.

When Connie and Dennis finally arrived, the corn water had just come to a boil. I clapped a lid on the pot and turned the heat to low. "Hello, hello!" Connie caroled as she made her way down the hallway to the kitchen.

She burst through the door, all smiles. I hugged her tightly. "Connie, I've missed you."

"It's only been three weeks," she said.

"I know. But I missed you all the same."

With one arm still wrapped around Connie's shoulders, I extended my hand to Dennis. "Thanks for coming, Dennis. I'm looking forward to talking with you."

Dennis stared at me. "You okay, Hannah?"

I swiped at my eyes, astonished to find that my eyelashes were wet. "Onions," I lied.

Connie shot me an oh-yeah-sure look. "Hannah, what's wrong?"

My face grew hot. Connie and Dennis began to shimmer, as if they were about to be beamed up to the starship Enterprise. "I'm sorry. It's just that the last time I saw you, at the race, Valerie Stone was still alive."

Connie located the tissues in a box on top of the refrigerator and handed one to me, standing by while I used it to dab at my eyes. "Is there anything we can do to help?"

I flapped a hand in front of my face, waving away my tears. "I'll be fine in a minute."

"Here," Connie said, taking charge. With a sweeping glance, she surveyed the kitchen. "Is the potato salad ready?" When I nodded, she said, "Dennis, you take that out and put it on the table. I'll join you in a minute. Is there wine?" she asked me. I nodded again. "Fix me a glass of wine, too, Dennis, will you?"

I'd left my wineglass on the table. Connie picked it up and handed it to me. "Here. Drink this. You'll feel better."

"Thanks." I took a couple of swallows then looked up at my sister-in-law. "It's not just Valerie," I said. I walked my wineglass over to the window. "Come here. I want you to see something."

When Connie joined me, I pointed out to the garden swing where Daddy and Neelie were sitting side by side. As we watched, Daddy said something and Neelie threw back her head and laughed. He grinned slyly, reached out and took her hand.

"I know nothing can bring my mother back . . . nothing. And I'm happy for my father, I really am. I *adore*

Neelie. But when I see him like that, laughing. Ooooooh," I moaned. "It makes me miss my mother so much!"

Using both hands, I pressed the tissue into my eyes while Connie rubbed my back sympathetically. "I understand, Hannah, believe me. And I'm sure Paul does, too. It's been years since our mother died, but not a day goes by that I don't miss her. Sometimes I think of something I want to tell her and I'll actually pick up the telephone. . . ." She shuddered.

"That's happened to me, too."

Connie stood with me silently by the window for a few more minutes, then took a breath and let it out slowly. "So, madam, what can I do to help?"

I crumpled the tissue and lobbed it into the trash. "Here," I sniffed. I handed her the platter of hamburger patties. "Can you take these out to the chef?"

"Who's cooking?"

"Paul volunteered."

"Just don't give them to Dennis," she warned. "The last time I put him in charge of the grill, he earned the nickname the Great Incinerator."

I laughed, feeling better already. "And can you bring in the corn? The water's ready."

The burgers were juicy, the corn sweet, the pie was like manna from heaven. I'd enlisted Ruth's help—she and Neelie were on cleanup crew in the kitchen—while Hutch blew smoke rings all by himself in the back garden.

All evidence of our recent feast had been cleared from the patio table except for the Box o' Wine, a carafe of decaf coffee, and a plastic tray of cream and sugar. As a courtesy to the kitchen crew, we'd graduated to plastic cups and spoons.

"More coffee, Dennis?" I asked.

He held out his cup. "Thanks."

Daddy looked at me.

I tugged on my right ear. It was our prearranged signal. Time to begin.

With his chair legs screeching against the concrete, Daddy scooted closer to the table. "Hannah and I would like to talk to you about something."

Dennis glanced from my father to me, the cup halfway to his lips. "I think I hear my mother calling."

Connie punched her husband in the arm. "Be serious, Dennis."

"I am serious! When have you not known me to be serious?"

Connie smiled helplessly. "You can dress him up, but you can't take him out."

"Dennis," I said, "we need your advice."

"Is this going to get me into trouble?"

I glanced sideways at Daddy. "I don't think so."

"That's a relief." Dennis looked straight at me.

"But it might take a little time to explain," Daddy amended.

Dennis sipped his coffee. "That's okay. As long as my beeper doesn't go off, I have all the time in the world."

"Have you ever heard of viaticals?" I asked.

"No. What's a viatical?"

And so I began. I told Dennis how I'd learned about viaticals from Valerie, what I found out about the business when I visited Jablonsky, how I took that information to Brad and ended up working for Victory Mutual, and how, eventually, Daddy and I ended up playing dress-up in Steele's fancy office in Laurel, Maryland.

In the flickering light from the citronella candles, Dennis looked puzzled. "So, let me understand this. People are making money selling secondhand life insurance policies."

I nodded.

"How can that be legal?"

I don't know how long Hutch had been standing behind

me, listening. He pulled up a chair. "Oh, it's perfectly legal," Ruth's boyfriend confirmed. "First people like this guy Steele were trying to make money from people on their deathbeds. Now they're trying to make money from the people who want to make money from people on their deathbeds."

"And sometimes," Daddy added, "they get greedy."

"Remember my friend, Valerie? She was terminally ill. She was supposed to die within a year. So she sold her life insurance policy to Steele through Jablonsky. Some total stranger became her beneficiary. And then . . ." I paused and looked around the table. ". . . she went into remission."

Dennis started to say something, but I held up a finger. "Hold that thought," I said. "Let me fast forward."

I filled Dennis in on what I'd learned from Mrs. Bromley about senior settlements and the missionary work Jablonsky seemed to be doing at Ginger Cove.

"Jeesh," Dennis said.

"Sick," said Connie.

"It gets worse," Daddy added.

On cue, I pulled Mrs. Bromley's list from my pocket and spread it out on the table. "Here's a list of nine people, all of them residents of Ginger Cove." Reading down the list, I ticked them off on my fingers. "Clark Gammel, dead. Tim Burns, dead. Wyetha Hodge, dead. James McGowan, dead . . ." I paused. "Of the nine people on this list, six of them are dead. And the one thing they all had in common is that they sold their life insurance policies to ViatiPro through Gilbert Jablonsky."

Connie laid a hand on her husband's arm. "And Hannah's friend, Valerie? Don't forget she died unexpectedly, too."

I drank some more of my wine. "Tell Dennis about Pottorff, Daddy. Enforcer?"

"Enforcer?" Hutch's eyebrows went up.

Daddy frowned. "N-4-S-I-R. That's his vanity plate. Cute, huh? The guy must be a mental giant." Once again he turned to Dennis. "Anyway, Hannah saw this guy in a brown suit, Nick Pottorff, coming and going from both Steele's and Jablonsky's offices, and we don't think he's simply carrying company papers."

I nodded vigorously.

"So, where's this going?" Dennis asked.

"I think Steele persuaded a lot of people to invest in viaticated life insurance policies. I think he used Jablonsky to meet that demand. Then, I think Steele got greedy. People who were supposed to be terminally ill, like AIDS patients on protease inhibitors and people like my friend Valerie, weren't dying fast enough, so Steele hired Pottorff to speed things along."

"We think Pottorff's job was to make sure the policies 'matured' in a timely fashion," Daddy explained.

In the candlelight, Dennis's eyes flashed. "You think Pottorff's a contract killer?"

I nodded. "I think he murdered Valerie, and I think he murdered the people on this list."

"But there'd be evidence—" Dennis began.

I shook my head. "Only if you're looking for it. Who's going to think twice when an eighty-five-year-old man is found dead in his bed? Who's going to ask questions when a terminally ill cancer patient simply doesn't wake up?"

Perhaps it was the wine lubricating my brain cells, but suddenly I knew how it was done. "They were smothered," I said with confidence. "Someone put a pillow over their faces. There'd be signs then, wouldn't there? I saw it on *CSI*." I leaned forward and laid my hand gently on top of Mrs. Bromley's list. "I want you to dig them up, Dennis. I want you to dig them all up. I want you to look for signs of petechiael hemorrhaging."

Paul, who had been silent until then, finally weighed in. "Hannah—"

But I wasn't going to be silenced. "And I want you to exhume Valerie Stone's body, too."

They probably didn't think I noticed, but I did. A look passed between Dennis and Paul. I'm sure Connie caught it, too. Dennis unfolded his long legs and stood up, walked around the table, and stopped behind my chair. "Come with me for a minute, Hannah. I want to talk to you in private."

With one hand resting on the table for support, I rose unsteadily to my feet. Dennis took my elbow and led me into the back garden where—was it my imagination?—the stale smell of Hutch's last cigarette still clung to the leaves of the rhododendron.

"Hannah," Dennis began when he got me alone. "Even if I wanted to, I couldn't exhume even one of those bodies. You seem to forget, I'm a Chesapeake County police officer. Anne Arundel County is not in my jurisdiction." He took a deep breath. "And even if it *were* my jurisdiction, I couldn't even justify a search warrant with the information you've just given me. I'm quite sure my colleagues in Anne Arundel County couldn't, either."

"But . . ." I felt ill.

"Octogenarians and desperately ill women die every day," Dennis continued reasonably. "This business about life insurance policies, it's all circumstantial."

"But Pottorff . . ." I began, tears welling up in my eyes. "The license plate."

Dennis rested his hands on my shoulders. "Sure, there could be a connection, but it's probably perfectly legitimate. The men were in business together, Hannah. Think about it!" His voice softened. "I know how close you were to Valerie Stone, but the police simply can't go forward with this. There's no probable cause."

"But—"

"You're bucking the Supreme Court, Hannah. Rumor, mere suspicion, and even strong reason to suspect are not equivalent to probable cause. We'd need a lot more to go on than a license plate and a hunch."

It was crystal clear to me. Daddy was on board. How could someone as bright as Dennis Rutherford fail to see it, too?

"But how about ViatiPro? And Victory Mutual?"

"That's about the only thing you're doing right," he said gently. "Informing the insurance company the way you did. Let them sort it out with the Maryland Insurance Administration. That's their job."

Although I'm sure he didn't mean to, Dennis's words stung: *The only thing you're doing right.* I began to sob.

"Hannah!" he said, and drew me to his chest. He was warm, slightly sweaty, and his shirt smelled of barbeque smoke and Tide.

My head spun, my stomach roiled. I wanted the ground to open under my feet and swallow me. After all I'd done, how could this be happening? Why wasn't Dennis listening to me? How could he let Valerie down? How could he let Mrs. Bromley continue to live in fear?

The breeze freshened, cooling the tears on my cheeks. I pushed my brother-in-law away. "Just go away, Dennis! Go away and leave me alone!"

Reeling, I swept past him, past my guests still seated around the patio table, past Neelie and Ruth as they polished up my kitchen. Somehow I managed to get up the stairs and into my bedroom, where I threw myself face-down on the bed and began to bawl.

Like I said. It should have been a wonderful party. Leave it to me to foul things up.

CHAPTER 19

Saturday morning I slept late. I awoke awash in a sea of regret with a hangover the size of a satellite map of Hurricane Floyd. Paul had already gone to his office at the Academy, thank goodness, so he wasn't there to waggle a finger and say "I told you so."

I took three aspirin to deaden the pain caused by whatever was knocking my prefrontal lobes against my temporal lobes and lay down on the sofa until the jackhammering stopped.

Somewhere in all the confusion, two lost thoughts came together with a drum roll and a crash of cymbals. If Nick Pottorff worked for Jablonsky, then maybe Gail Parrish could tell me something about him. Besides, Gail owed me. The last time we'd talked, she promised to call me back, and I still hadn't heard from her.

I waited until ten, then telephoned Jablonsky's office.

The phone rang six times before somebody picked up. "Mutually Beneficial, how may I help you?" The voice was an octave deeper, decades older, and three times more sophisticated than Gail's.

"This is Hannah Ives," I said. "I'm returning Gail Parrish's call."

"I'm sorry, madam, but Gail Parrish is no longer with the firm." The woman spoke with an Oxbridge accent so obviously fake that I wanted to crawl down the telephone line and slap it out of her.

I sat back in the hard kitchen chair, stunned. "But I just talked with Gail last week!"

"Would you like to speak with Mr. Jablonsky, madam? Perhaps he can help." I hated the woman. Instantly. She sounded like Margaret Thatcher, with a cold.

"I don't want to talk to Mr. Jablonsky," I insisted. "I want to talk to Gail."

"I'm sorry I can't be of more help, madam, but they didn't tell me anything at the temporary agency, just that the receptionist had moved to Las Vegas."

"I beg your pardon?" I clenched my fist, trying to keep my voice under control.

"Miss Parrish has moved to Las Vegas," she repeated, slowly and distinctly, as if I had the IQ of a garden gnome.

Las Vegas? Hah! That was a pile of manure. More than likely Gail figured out she was working for a crook. Maybe she quit before the cops could show up with squad cars *whoop-whoop-whooping* to measure her boss for a bright orange one-piece. But there wasn't any point in arguing. Unless the new receptionist was Jablonsky's wife or sainted mother, there was no reason for her to know any more about the missing receptionist than I did.

I advised myself to stay calm. "Did Gail leave a forwarding address?" I inquired.

"None that I'm aware of," she said. "Shall I put you through to Mr. Jablonsky, then?"

That was the last thing I needed, for Jablonsky to think that Gail and I had become friends. It wouldn't help Gail any, either, wherever she was. "No, no. Don't bother. I'll just call Gail at home."

"Very well," the woman said, barely concealing her exasperation with an "if you knew her home phone number all along why are you getting testy with me" kind of long-suffering sigh. "Is there anything else?"

"No, thank you."

"Thank you for calling Mutually Beneficial," the woman droned, and hung up.

"Suck eggs," I said into the dead air.

I didn't waste any time pulling the Annapolis phone book down from the shelf. I turned to the P's. There were plenty of Parrishes, George, and several Parrishes, Gerald, but no listing for Parrish, Gail, or Parrish, G.

Of course not, dummy. Gail is house-sitting. Unless I could remember the name of the homeowners, I was fresh out of luck.

But Gail had never mentioned the name of the people she was house-sitting for, only that they lived in Eastport and were blue water sailors.

Gail had an ex-boyfriend, I recalled. Even if he knew her present whereabouts, though, it would do me not one damn bit of good, because Gail had never told me his name, either.

One thing I was one hundred percent sure of: Gail had *not* moved to Las Vegas. She loved Annapolis. She was saving money for a sailboat. I'd never been to Las Vegas, but I'd seen the ads on TV. I didn't think you could do much sailing in the Nevada desert unless you wanted to launch your boat in the Grand Canal at the Venetian Casino and Resort or tack your way around the dancing fountains at the Bellagio.

My hopes were raised when I remembered that Gail had telephoned me the week before and that her number might still be in the memory chip of my telephone. But, alas, when I went to the phone and scrolled through the menu, the number that popped up was Jablonsky's, and I was reminded that she'd called me from Jablonsky's office, not from home.

Other than asking Jablonsky, then, I was running out of options.

I worried about Gail as I ran my Saturday errands. Had she discovered something about her boss that caused her to quit, using a move to Las Vegas as an excuse? Or, more chilling, had she discovered something about her boss that put her in danger? Had the lie about Las Vegas originated with Jablonsky?

The dry cleaners was a short, two-block walk down Prince George Street, but once I'd lugged the cleaning home and hung it up in the closet, I needed a car to take care of the other chores on my To Do list.

West Marine had telephoned to say that Paul's hand-held GPS had been repaired and was ready for pickup, so my next destination was the shopping plaza near Hillsmere to retrieve the device. I continued to worry about Gail as I drove, wondering as I wound my way through Eastport if I was unknowingly passing by her house. Was she reading the Saturday paper in that yellow bungalow at the corner of State Street and Bay Ridge Avenue? Doing her laundry, as I needed to do, in the basement of that three-story brick town house at Chesapeake and Americana? I hoped so.

I waited patiently while the clerk at West Marine wrapped the GPS in bubble wrap, then I tucked it carefully into the bottom of my handbag. I drove west on Forest Drive, cutting over on Spa Road to West Street so I could return my overdue library books.

My civic duty done, my good name restored, I cut through the library parking lot and drove out the back along the old railroad right-of-way to Taylor and across Rowe Boulevard to Graul's, the market where I do the bulk of my shopping.

Graul's carries a marvelous assortment of gourmet items I can't seem to live without, and as usual I walked through my front door with shopping bags bulging after spending at least fifty dollars more than I planned. Saturday's "must have" was a round loaf of crusty olive bread, $3.75. I rest my case.

I put the groceries away, listened to my phone messages—only some Congressman's lackey wanting Paul's

opinion on a prescription drug benefit for seniors (For!)—
then gathered up the laundry, including the dirty linens
from last night's picnic, and trudged downstairs to the
laundry room.

As I sorted the whites from the darks, I noticed that one
of the place mats had a plum-colored ring on it, probably
from the base of a wineglass. I pretreated the place mat
with laundry spray, recalling, with embarrassment, how
rude I'd been to Dennis the previous evening. Yet, even in
the cold, sober light of day, his words still stung: *the only
thing you're doing right.*

I knew that everyone has a Constitutional right to pro-
tection from unreasonable searches and seizures, and I
also knew that Dennis, as a cop, had to adhere to higher
standards than I would. Yet the evidence I had collected
against Steele and Jablonsky seemed, at least to me, much
more than circumstantial. It seemed compelling. Still,
there was no excuse for my taking Dennis's head off, even
if it had been the wine talking. Dennis was my brother-in-
law, and my guest. I'd have to call him to apologize.

I added detergent to the washer, punched a few buttons
and started the machine, then took a quick detour to my
office across the hall.

Ruth had sent me an e-card from the "Get Well Police."
Har-de-har-har. Maybe I'd been drunker last night than I
thought. I sent her a thank-you, and since I was already at
BlueMountain.com, I picked out an e-card for Dennis: a
Chesapeake Bay blue crab saying "Sorry I've been so
crabby." I personalized the e-card and sent it off, feeling
slightly better about myself.

Emily had e-mailed that Jake was cutting a new tooth;
Chico's wanted to offer me twenty-five percent off; Paul
had forwarded several jokes from his usna.edu account,
one of which, about a cat that survived a close encounter
with a garbage disposal, made me laugh so hard I nearly
fell off my chair.

I quickly deleted the obvious spam—Viagra (Deep discount!), eager teenage Russian brides, offers of creative ways to enlarge certain portions of my anatomy, none of which I possessed—until I got to an e-mail address I didn't recognize: sailingphool@aol.com. The subject line was "Hello, Hannah!"

I suspected it came from a gal I met at Womanship, a popular sailing school for women. (Their motto? Nobody yells!) Tina races a Cal25 and keeps urging me to sign up for the Annapolis Frostbite Series. Sailing in the summertime is a delight, but in November? If you have to wear long underwear, fleece pants, three sweaters, two pairs of mittens, foul weather gear, and plastic Baggies over your toes in order to stay warm, I draw the line.

But when I opened the e-mail, fingers poised to type "Brrrrrrrrrr, no way!" I was astonished to find the message was from Gail Parrish.

"Hey, Hannahmail! Snitched your address from Gil's Roladex. Need to talk to you. Seriously. Call me at home. Gail."

Gail's signature line included a telephone number, thank goodness. I dialed it at once, but the line was busy. I was surprised that no voice mail kicked in, especially in this day and age, but then, it wasn't exactly Gail's telephone. It belonged to a couple of diehard sailors, and sailors, in my experience, don't always live on the cutting edge of technology.

Maybe it was busy because Gail was working on-line and had *70'd the call to keep voice mail from knocking her off-line. We both used AOL, so I added Sailingphool to Hannahmail's buddy list, then checked to see if Gail was logged on. She wasn't.

Just to be sure, I sent her an instant message. I waited a few moments. Sent another one. Waited. There was no reply.

I went back to Gail's message and clicked on Reply.

"Dear Gail," I e-mailed back. "Tried to call. Line busy. Where the hell are you? Hannah."

At one o'clock I tried telephoning again, with equal lack of success. Gail could still be on-line, of course. I imagined her cruising the Internet, searching Yacht-world.com for the previously owned sailboat of her dreams, or for one in her price range, at least.

Although I was desperate to talk to Gail and wanted to hit my "redial" button every four or five minutes until she picked up, I had a problem. I had told Harrison Garvin on Friday that I was close to finishing my report. "Just a bit of tweaking here and there," I'd boasted. "It'll be on your desk first thing Monday morning."

Garvin had beamed. He was meeting with his management team on Wednesday, he said, and would move my report to the top of the agenda.

Now I had to make good on my promise.

I toasted a bagel for lunch, washed it down with the last of the coffee, located my security card and drove out to Victory Mutual.

Once I got settled in the cubicle I'd borrowed from Mindy, I tried Gail again. Busy. Damn the woman! She wanted to talk to me. I wanted to talk to her. The least she could do was stay off the phone.

Then again, maybe it wasn't Gail's fault. I decided if I hadn't been able to get through by three o'clock, I'd call the operator and ask her to check to see if the phone was out of order or off the hook. There was probably a perfectly reasonable explanation. No use stewing about it.

I logged onto Mindy's computer, and after several trial runs my SQL scripts finally ran flawlessly. I'd been massaging the data for so long that the results didn't surprise me, but I felt quite certain they would knock the socks off Harrison Garvin.

One data table proved that forty-five percent of the policies that had changed from personal to corporate ownership over the past five years had been reassigned to ViatiPro, and that sixty-two percent of that number had been paid, meaning the viator had died.

Another table showed that fully seventy-six percent of the total number of policies that had changed hands had been for amounts under $100,000. Clearly, ViatiPro wasn't the only investment company scrambling aboard the gravy train, but thanks to me, that train was about to come to a screeching halt.

I revised the script and reran it, this time limiting my results to policies for $100,000 or less that had been written during the past two years. Like most insurance companies, Victory Mutual had a two-year contestability period. If the company's investigators could prove any of the policies had been falsely obtained before the two years was up, the policies could be cancelled and crooks like Steele and his unwary investors would be left holding worthless pieces of paper. As far as I was concerned, Steele could take his lumps. It was the unwary investors—like my friend Mrs. Bromley—whom I felt sorry for.

In my opinion, the reports said it all, and in terms so clear that even my three-year-old granddaughter could understand. Nevertheless, I had to spend another hour converting the data I had collected into graphs and pie charts that Garvin could plug into the PowerPoint presentation he planned to show his team. I fiddled with the slide layouts and backgrounds for a while, then ran the slide show, sitting back and impressing myself with the results. *Damn, Hannah, you haven't lost your touch.*

When I was satisfied, I printed a paper copy of the presentation and slipped it under Donna's door. I also e-mailed the file to her as an attachment just in case she logged in over the weekend. Donna struck me as the type who liked to get a head start on her Mondays, and I was happy to oblige. In any case, there was no way I would take the report to Garvin without discussing it with Donna first. Although information on specific underwriters had not been captured in Victory Mutual's database, I had the feeling that when the actual policies were pulled, some of Donna's underwriters were going to have a lot of explaining to do. Donna deserved to be the first to know.

On my way back to my cubicle from Donna's office, I grabbed a Coke out of the vending machine in the staff lounge. I popped the top and took a long, refreshing swig. Then I logged onto the Internet and went to aol.com to check for any messages from Gail. Zero. Zilch. Nada.

I stared at the screen for a good two minutes, sipping my Coke and planning my next step. *You're supposed to be good with computers, Hannah Ives. Don't just sit there, do something!*

I put the Coke down and lifted my fingers to the keyboard. When in doubt, Google.

I Googled "Gail Parrish." There was an African-American playwright by that name, and a jazz musician, and a Gail Parrish who, according to a genealogy website, had married her first cousin in Spartanburg, South Carolina, in 1837. That would make her 166 years old. Not the Gail I was looking for.

I browsed through Google's features: calculators, street maps, spell checkers, phone books. When I clicked on phone books, I was delighted to see a new feature. Type in a phone number, with area code, and Google would look up the address for you. *Hot damn!*

I typed the telephone number Gail had given me into the Google search box. Reverting to an old childhood ritual, I crossed my fingers for luck, closed my eyes, and hit the Enter key.

When I opened my eyes again it was like magic: next to a telephone icon, the address of the house Gail had called me from was staring back at me from the screen. "Thank you," I breathed aloud to whatever angel had sprinkled me with fairy dust that afternoon.

Before it could disappear in some cataclysmic computer meltdown, I jotted the address down on a Post-it and lifted the note off the pad. Then I hightailed it out of Victory Mutual so fast that the barrier arm at the security turnstile scraped alarmingly across the canvas top of my convertible. It was some measure of my eagerness to see Gail that I didn't even care.

When I got to the address in Eastport, I found that Gail Parrish was living in a lovingly restored, three-story colonial in the third block of Second Street, a short walk from the Severn River. A yellow VW Beetle was parked out front. I'd seen a similar car in Jablonsky's parking lot, so I figured the VW belonged to Gail.

I parked my LeBaron behind the VW and stepped out onto the sidewalk.

Gail's house had a porch the size of a postage stamp and a bright red door with a brass knocker shaped—no surprise, considering its owners—like an anchor. I trotted up the steps, lifted the anchor, and rapped loudly three times.

Nobody came to the door.

I looked around for a doorbell and finally found it, tucked into a space barely two inches wide between the door frame and the side of an oversize bronze mailbox. I stuck a finger into the crevice and pushed the bell.

No cheerful chimes, no clever tunes. From somewhere inside came a rude buzzing sound. No wonder they had installed the knocker. But still, nobody answered the door. Gail's car was out front, so where the hell was she?

There were all sorts of perfectly reasonable explanations.

Perhaps she was taking a bath. Or a nap.

Maybe she'd gone for a walk, or taken in a movie. The Eastport Cinema was less than a mile away.

Or somebody could have picked her up. Maybe her ex-was no longer an ex-? Had he come back into her life and swept her away to the Poconos for a weekend of romance and reconciliation?

I pulled the cell phone from my purse and punched

Gail's number for what seemed the zillionth time. While I waited for the call to go through, I used my other hand to shade my eyes and peer through the front window. Although it was covered by sheer curtains, I could see enough through the glass to determine that there was nothing going on in the living room.

Gail's line was busy, surprise, surprise. Frustrated, I tossed the phone back into my purse.

I was heading around to check out the back of the house when something rubbed against my legs, scaring me witless. When I could breathe again, I looked down and saw that the culprit was a black and gray tabby. Gail mentioned she was taking care of the owners' cat. What was its name? Gail had told me, I was sure. Nemo? Nimitz?

I kneeled down and stroked the animal's soft, slate-colored fur. "What's your name, young fellow?" I fumbled for the tags that hung from the cat's collar. "Nitro," I read.

"Hey, Nitro old boy." Or was it a girl? With fur so thick, it was hard to tell. I rubbed Nitro behind the ears, then used the fingers of both hands to massage the bumps along his spine—a bit of pseudoshiatsu, modified for cats, that I'd picked up from Ruth.

Nitro purred like a well-tuned car. He stretched extravagantly, then rolled onto his back, reclining like an odalisque on the concrete sidewalk. "Ah, you *are* a girl," I observed, massaging down the full length of the shameless hussy's tail. "So, Nitro, anybody home but you?"

Nitro closed her eyes. Her nose drew ecstatic little figure eights in the air. I imagined her little kitty brain saying, "Don't talk, woman. Keep on rubbing."

I was working on one of Nitro's front paws, caked with dirt, when a woman stepped out of the house next door. Her eyes flitted in my direction. As I watched, she meandered down the sidewalk, then bent to fetch her Saturday morning paper, pressing one hand against the small of her back as if she were in pain.

"Excuse me," I called out, "but have you seen Gail?"

Gail's neighbor straightened. "She was out in the yard this morning, trimming the hedge." The woman waved her newspaper vaguely at the boxwood hedge that separated Gail's driveway from her own. Lying on the ground next to the hedge about halfway down the drive was a pair of electric hedge trimmers. A bright orange power cord snaked across the concrete and was plugged into an outlet in the foundation of the house.

"Golly," I said. "Why would Gail go off and leave an expensive piece of equipment like that lying on the ground?"

The neighbor shrugged. "Maybe she got interrupted and just forgot they were out here." She grinned. "Happens to me all the time. Know what I call it?"

I shook my head. "No, what do you call it?"

"Losing the rabbit."

I smiled at the odd but strangely apt allusion to hunting. "I find myself losing the rabbit a lot these days."

The woman limped back up her walk. "Hysterectomy," she said in response to my unasked question.

"Ouch, sorry," I said.

She shrugged. "Oh, well. What'cha gonna do?"

"Did you notice if Gail had any visitors?"

"No, sorry, I didn't."

I advanced several steps onto her lawn. "Look, I'm kinda worried. Gail e-mailed that she wanted me to call her about something important, but when I telephoned, the line was busy. It's been busy for five hours." I had a sudden thought. "Your circuits aren't down, are they?"

"Not that I know of." She reached into the pocket of her sweater and pulled out a portable phone. She punched a button and put the phone to her ear. "Nope. Got a fine dial tone."

"That's what I was afraid of. Frankly, I'm more than a little worried. Gail's car's on the street, so she should be at home."

"You knocked?

I nodded.

"Maybe she's in the bathtub."

"For five hours?"

She raised a finger. "The Frasers gave me a key ages ago. They were away a lot on weekends, you know, sailing, and they asked me to feed the cat." She bobbed her head in Nitro's direction. "I see you've already met Nitro."

"Oh, yes." For all intents and purposes, the cat had passed out, cold, in a patch of sun on the warm cement. "You said something about a key?" I prodded.

"Oh! There I go again, losing the rabbit. If you'll wait a minute, I'll go see if I can find it."

"That'd be great. Thanks!"

She handed me the newspaper. "Here, take a look at this while you wait."

I'd barely had time to scan the headlines before she returned, waving a key. "Got it!" she crowed. "My name's Cindy, by the way."

"I'm Hannah."

"Nice to meet you, Hannah."

"Likewise." We had started up the walk, side by side, but I stopped and turned to face her. "Cindy, I really appreciate this. I'm sure it'll turn out to be nothing, but—"

"Oh, I understand completely," Cindy said. "I worked with this woman once, never late, never took a sick day, never once in three years! Then one day, she didn't show up for work. Didn't call in. Didn't answer the phone." She touched my arm. "I called the *po*-lice," she drawled.

"What happened?"

"Well, it took some major league convincing, but they finally agreed to send an officer to meet me at her apartment. We pounded and pounded on the door. Eventually got the super to open up." Cindy and I had reached the porch.

"And?"

"She was home, all right. Sitting on the floor in her bathrobe, like a zombie, surrounded by dirty laundry, spoiled food, unwashed dishes, and bags and bags of garbage."

"Gross." I waited for Cindy to climb the steps. "What was the matter with her?"

Cindy turned the key in the lock and pushed the door open. "Severe depression. She had to be hospitalized. Never did come back to work."

"Sad," I said. "Although I'm pretty certain we won't find Gail like that!"

Cindy laughed. "Oh, no way! She's just about the most outgoing person I know."

We were standing in the living room. "Gail?" I called out. "It's Hannah. Gail?"

Directly on our right, a flight of stairs led to the second floor. "I'll check upstairs," I volunteered, remembering Cindy's recent surgery. "Can you look around down here?"

Cindy nodded.

While Cindy limped off in what I assumed would be the direction of the dining room, I climbed the stairs to the second floor. Nothing seemed out of place in the master bedroom and bath.

Across a narrow hallway were two smaller bedrooms. If the unmade bed was any indication, Gail appeared to be using the larger of the two rooms. I opened her closet. Since I wasn't familiar with Gail's wardrobe, it was hard to tell if anything was missing, but every hanger had something hanging on it.

In the bathroom, a towel had been draped to dry over the shower curtain rod, as if Gail planned to reuse it. A makeup bag yawned open on top of the toilet tank, and a toothbrush stood at attention in a cup on the bathroom sink. The bristles were still wet.

If Gail were on her way to Las Vegas, I hoped she took

a lot of cash, but not for gambling. She'd need to buy some new clothes and a toothbrush once she got there.

I checked the remaining bedroom, but like the master bedroom, it appeared untouched, so I trotted back downstairs and joined Cindy in the kitchen. I found her standing at the sink, her back to me. The odor of burnt coffee hung in the air.

"Phew! That smells awful!"

"Pot boiled dry. Probably forgot to turn it off before she left." Cindy had filled the coffeepot with soapy water and was swirling it around. "Did you find anything upstairs?"

"Nope. Guess I was worried over nothing."

While Cindy took a Brillo pad to the pot, I glanced around the kitchen. With the exception of a mug and spoon sitting out on the polished granite countertop next to the fridge, Gail's kitchen was practically spotless.

"Is this it?" I asked.

Cindy ripped two sheets of paper towel off the roll, spread them out on the counter and inverted the coffeepot over them to drain. "Yup. Except for a little laundry room in the back. Judy Fraser used to put together flower arrangements on a table back there, but Gail fixed it up real nice for her computer."

"Was Gail on the computer a lot?"

"God, yes. She buys and sells antique jewelry on eBay." Cindy's brows scrunched together. "Didn't you know?"

Nitro saved me the embarrassment of having to admit I didn't know about Gail's jewelry business when the cat suddenly appeared, meowing pitifully. She trotted over to Cindy and rubbed against her ankles.

"You hungry, Nitro, baby? Poor kitty." Cindy opened a cupboard next to the sink and pulled out a plastic canister of dried cat food. She dumped a half scoop of kibble into Nitro's bowl, then grinned up at me. "She's a regular P-I-G!"

Something about the cat was bothering me. "Did you let Nitro in?" I asked.

"She's got a cat flap," Cindy explained.

"Duh," I said.

Cindy replaced the cat food canister. "Yeah, Gail's always complaining about how slow the dial access is. She's getting cable real soon." Cindy swept the mug and spoon into the sink. "We can check out the laundry room if you want." Clearly, Cindy thought it would be a complete waste of time.

"Let's," I said. "Just to make sure."

I followed Cindy down a narrow hallway, past a powder room no larger than a phone booth. At the end of the hallway was a swinging door, like on a Wild West saloon. Cindy pushed through the door, faltered, and took a step backward. Her hands flew to her face and a horrible keening sound—half scream, half moan—leaked out from between her fingers.

It had to be bad news.

I elbowed Cindy aside and stepped into the room.

It was worse, far worse, than anything I could have imagined.

Gail Parrish lay on her left side on the white tile floor, curled into a fetal position. Next to her was an overturned chair.

I couldn't pretend Gail had merely fainted. Under her body, a pool of blood had spread, running downhill on one side until it disappeared under the washing machine. On the other, where a filing cabinet and a table leg met the floor, the blood had formed a puddle. Small white boxes and cotton squares seemed to be floating like tiny boats on the incarnadine sea, and the floor all about was littered with computer printouts, bubble wrap, padded mailers, and packing tape, as if someone had made a clean sweep of the tabletop. The whole obscene pool was beginning to darken and dry at the edges.

Gail had to be dead. Nobody could lose that much blood and survive.

"Call 911!" I screamed. "Now!"

I knelt down and pressed my fingers to the vein in Gail's neck, praying for a pulse. Nothing moved under my fingers, and Gail's neck was rigid and cold. Her face was turned to one side so that her hair fell softly over her cheek. Instinctively, I reached out and smoothed it back behind her ear, like I might have done for a sleeping child, but regretted the gesture at once. Beneath that curtain of lustrous, mahogany hair, Gail's eyes stared, vacant and unseeing.

My head swam alarmingly, and I fell back against a table leg, my blood pounding in my ears so loudly that it nearly drowned out Cindy's moaning. *Breathe in, breathe out!* Gradually, as I got my breathing under control, I realized that the moaning was coming from deep within my own throat, not Cindy's. *Poor, poor Gail!* What had she done to deserve this?

By then I was practically huddled under the table, but from that vantage point I could see the cause of all the blood: a small, round hole near Gail's left breast. I'd never seen a gunshot wound before, but I was certain that was what it was. If what I'd seen on TV was any indication, a small hole meant a small caliber bullet, probably at close range.

I glanced around quickly, but didn't see a gun. That didn't mean there wasn't a gun; it could very well be hidden under the mess of printouts and bubble wrap, but I knew better than to muck about with a crime scene any more than was necessary in order to give aid to the victim. Not that there was anything I or the paramedics could do to help save Gail now.

Except for the whine of an attic fan, the house was oddly silent. I'd almost forgotten about Cindy. "Have you called 911?" I yelled again.

Cindy's answer was a wail and the sound of painful retching coming from the powder room. I'd have to make the call myself. I found my purse where it had fallen to the floor, pulled out my cell phone and punched 911.

The 911 operator was a pro: calming me down, soliciting details, and issuing instructions all at the same time. Once she had determined that Gail's assailant was no longer in the house, she said, "Don't move, don't touch anything. The police are on their way."

Don't move. I wouldn't, *couldn't*, leave my friend.

Too stunned to cry, I sat on the floor next to her, knees drawn up and pressing into my chin.

Don't touch anything. Who's to know? I thought. I reached out and took Gail's ice cold hand in mine, almost believing that if I held it tightly enough, rubbed it briskly enough, I might coax some warmth back into those frozen fingers.

Was all this *my* fault? Had Gail been killed because of something she was going to tell me? Did somebody intend to silence her . . . forever?

A tear ran hotly down my cheek. Then another. And another.

"Ma'am? Ma'am?"

Who the hell was that? It took me a moment to realize that the operator was still on the line, trying to get my attention through the cell phone pressed to my ear.

"Yes? I'm here."

"The police are turning into your street right now," she said.

"Uhhhhhh," I managed. I closed my eyes and rested my head against the table leg, willing the nightmare away.

"They're on the porch now," she advised. "The next knock you hear will be Officer Tracey."

I turned my head toward the swinging doors, imagining Officer Tracey moseying through, strong, silent, and dependable, like Gary Cooper in *High Noon*.

But Tracey didn't knock, he buzzed, and at the front, not the laundry room door. The raucous sound seemed a vulgar intrusion in the otherwise respectful silence of the house. It must have taken Cindy by surprise, too, because she screamed an interminable, bloodcurdling, *Friday the 13th* kind of scream. Even today, it haunts my dreams.

"It's okay, Cindy!" I screamed back. "It's the police. Please, go let them in!"

After a moment I heard Cindy's rapid footsteps receding down the hall, and I began to relax. *Officer Tracey will be here soon. Officer Tracey will help me. Officer Tracey will find out who killed Gail.*

And then I saw them: paw prints. Kitty prints, to be precise. Kitty prints that meandered through the gore, circled the overturned chair, trotted over a computer printout and faded, step by bloody step, before disappearing into the hall.

That wasn't mud I had been working out of Nitro's toes, it was Gail's blood.

CHAPTER 20

Blood. Gail's blood. It seemed to be everywhere.

Paul led me up to the bedroom and waited while I stripped. He wrapped me gently in a multicolored beach towel, hugged me for a long minute, kissed the top of my head, then stuffed the ruined slacks and sweater I had been wearing into a plastic garbage bag. "Bath," he ordered.

I eyed the bag. "My clothes?"

"Do you really want to keep them?" Paul asked.

I shook my head.

Paul chewed his lower lip, a sure sign he was worried about something. "The police . . ." he began.

Somewhere in my paralyzed brain comprehension dawned, and I finished the sentence for him. The police might want to examine my clothes for evidence. I stared at my husband and tried desperately to swallow around the lump that seemed to have taken up permanent residence in my throat.

"Bath," Paul repeated, taking hold of my shoulders and turning me in the direction of the bathroom.

This time I obeyed.

Shut away in the womblike comfort of our master bath, I turned on the tap, dumped in some lavender bath salts, and crawled wearily into the tub. I lay down, closed my eyes and waited, enjoying the sensation as the hot water rose up my neck, crept over my cheeks, and covered my ears. When only my nose was exposed, I used my toes to push the tap off. In the relative silence beneath the water I could hear nothing but the air moving in and out of my lungs and, faintly, the sound of the television downstairs.

With my hair floating and swirling lazily around my head, I tried to wipe my mind clean, to fill it with nothing but white space. It was a losing battle. It would be a long time, I thought, before I would be able to close my eyes and visualize anything but an image of Gail Parrish curled up on a white tile floor in a pool of her own dark red blood.

Could I try TM? After my cancer diagnosis, Ruth had insisted I learn Transcendental Meditation; she'd even paid for my lessons. TM had helped lower my stress, but I'd never achieved that altered state of consciousness that Ruth had rambled on about so passionately.

I relaxed, hands floating by my sides, breathing in and out, repeating the mantra I had been taught: *Hirim. Hirim. Hirim. Hirim.*

A disorganized army of lights and shapes floated aimlessly about the interior landscape of my eyes, my breathing slowed, and I drifted away on an undulating wave, alternately both radiant and dark.

I was awakened by Paul knocking gently on the door. "Hannah?"

"Mumph."

"You okay in there?"

I lay in the tub silently, collecting my wits.

"You have to eat something," Paul said.

I rallied enough to answer. "I can't. I'll be sick to my stomach."

"Mind if I come in?"

I grunted.

The door swung open, followed by Paul, who perched on the edge of the tub. He wrung out a washcloth and used it to wipe the perspiration from my face. "You have to eat something, Hannah."

I grabbed my husband's hand, washcloth and all. "What if it's my fault Gail is dead?"

"It's not your fault, Hannah. It's the fault of whomever pulled the trigger."

"Please! Save the NRA platitudes for somebody who gives a damn!" I dropped his hand. "Of course I could be responsible! The other day when I was talking to Gail on the telephone, it was clear she had stumbled onto something. 'That's odd,' she told me. She was supposed to call me back. She never did."

"There could be all sorts of reasonable explanations."

"That's what I kept telling myself when I couldn't reach her today, that there was a reasonable explanation why her phone was constantly busy." I took a deep, shuddering breath. "She was working on eBay, Paul. Somebody shot her before she could log off."

"And do you have a theory as to who that somebody might be?"

"I think that Gail uncovered something when she was compiling that list of Ginger Cove residents for me. Maybe after she hung up, she went digging around in Jablonsky's files. Maybe he caught her at it and fired her. Or, maybe she simply panicked and quit."

"That would explain the substitute receptionist," Paul said. "But not the murder."

"My theory is that Gail quit. I also think that Jablonsky figured out *why* she quit and decided he couldn't trust her to keep her mouth shut. I think he had her killed to keep her from blowing the whistle on him."

"Enter Nicholas Pottorff," Paul said.

"Exactly. Jablonsky is far too fastidious to get his own hands dirty."

"Have you shared your theory with the Annapolis police?"

I nodded.

"Do you want to talk to Dennis, too?"

"God, no! I'm still embarrassed by what I said to him last night. I've been lying here thinking about it, and you know, Dennis is right. Maybe that's why he made me so angry. I know he can't interfere with cases in other jurisdictions, and it's not fair for me to ask him to."

I glanced up at my husband through lowered lashes. "Besides, Dennis thinks I'm a pain in the ass. He's only being nice to me because he's married to your sister."

"That's not true! Dennis likes you."

"Hah."

"Well, I'm not going to argue with you about it. I think you're being pigheaded and foolish. *Of course* we should call Dennis. Things are different today than they were last night. Gail's death has changed everything."

"Particularly for Gail," I said.

Paul frowned. He was only trying to be helpful, and I'd hurt his feelings.

I sat up in the tub and opened the drain. "I'd rather not bother Dennis, if you don't mind, Paul. He already thinks I'm a kook. Besides, I have confidence in Officer Tracey. He seemed a take-charge kind of guy. I don't think he's going to drop the ball."

Paul pulled a towel off the rack and handed it to me. "Tell me about Tracey."

I dried myself briskly. "He was a prince." I lowered my head, wrapped the towel around it and twisted the ends under. "I swear to God, I've never seen anybody work so fast," I said, looking up. "In the two minutes between the time he got there and the arrival of the paramedics, he corralled Cindy and had her sitting in the living room with a female officer, coaxed me out from under Gail's computer table and sat me down on the sofa next to Cindy, and cornered Nitro—that's the cat—and shut her up in the powder room."

"I told him everything," I added. "And he gave me his card. I have a feeling I'm going to need it."

I turned, reached under the sink for my dryer, and began working on my hair. I didn't mention it to Paul, but I was grateful, too, that Mike Tracey had escorted me to my car, running interference with the reporters who had materialized on the scene and were crawling all over it like ants at a picnic.

"You okay to drive, ma'am?" he'd inquired as he closed the car door after me.

I had nodded.

Then he'd gone back to sit with a distraught Cindy until her mother arrived to take her off his hands.

In the mirror, I saw Paul was still standing behind me, watching with an amused smile as I worked mousse into my hair and began fluffing it with my fingers. "Go away, now," I told my husband. "Find a good DVD. I need some cheering up."

After Paul left the bathroom, I finished drying my hair, dressed in my flannel pajamas, and wandered downstairs to the living room, where he had cued up *Ruthless People*, our favorite "feel good" movie. He aimed the remote at the TV and clicked the movie on.

"Sit," he said, pointing to the sofa. When I sat, he handed me an afghan. I tucked it around my legs.

Paul disappeared into the kitchen and returned a minute or two later with a steaming bowl of oatmeal he'd apparently cooked up while I was passed out in the tub. He'd dotted it with butter and sprinkled it with brown sugar, just the way I like it.

"Thanks," I said, accepting the spoon he was dangling in front of me.

Paul watched me while I ate, then took the dirty bowl to the kitchen.

When he rejoined me on the couch, I stretched out my legs and lay down with my head in his lap, and we watched the movie, laughing ourselves silly, which was the whole point. When it was all over, I felt let down, as if I'd been holding a big, red balloon and it had suddenly deflated.

"What do you want to watch now, honey?"

"It's almost eleven," I said. "Turn on the news."

"Are you sure?"

I nodded, the denim on his leg moving roughly over my cheek. "Uh-huh."

We watched the final credits of a popular TV drama crawl by, minimized and distorted to unreadability in order to make room on the screen for the bronzed face and bleached buzz cut of the news anchor, cheerfully giving us a "heads-up" on what to expect at the "top of the hour."

Gail Parrish's murder was the lead story.

Anne Arundel County Police are investigating the murder of an Annapolis woman who was found shot to death in her Eastport home earlier this afternoon. The body of the woman, a thirty-two-year-old receptionist, was discovered by neighbors who grew worried when they saw her car in the driveway and she didn't answer the telephone. Police have no suspects. Release of the victim's name is pending notification of next of kin, but TV6 has learned that the house is owned by Ian and Judith Fraser and that the Frasers are presently out of the country. Neighbors tell us that the victim was house sitting for the Frasers. . . .

Before the anchor had finished reading the story, I was astonished to see myself appear on camera, emerging from the Frasers' front door—still red, still with that ridiculous knocker—accompanied by Officer Tracey, with Cindy tagging along behind.

As Tracey hustled us down the sidewalk, dodging cameras, a reporter was thrusting a microphone in my face, and I was waving it away as if I were Demi Moore or Madonna or something. But unlike Demi Moore, I looked like hell. My face was the color of grits, the subtle lines at each side of my nose had deepened to ravines, and since when had those railroad tracks been carved into my forehead?

After failing with me, the reporter tried to interview Cindy, but she merely gazed stupidly at the camera, sobbing uncontrollably.

Perversely, the reporter seemed pleased with that. "The neighbors are clearly shocked by this senseless act of violence in what has always been a friendly, quiet neighborhood," he was saying as the camera panned from his well-coiffed head to a view of a house across the street, where a youngster was shooting hoops in the driveway.

I thought I was going to barf. "Turn it off," I said.

Paul took aim with the remote and obliged. "I warned you."

"Why do they have to turn everything into a goddamn circus?"

"It's their job," Paul said reasonably.

We were discussing what movie to watch—I voted for *Overboard*, while Paul argued for *Goldmember*—when the telephone rang.

Paul raised an eyebrow. "Let the machine pick up?"

"No," I said, thinking about Officer Tracey. "Nobody calls after eleven at night unless it's important."

Paul let the phone ring once more before he answered it. He listened for a moment, then held the receiver out to me. "It's Dennis."

"I don't want to talk to him," I whispered. "Tell him I've gone to bed."

"I think you'll want to hear what he has to say."

Two against one. I was outnumbered.

I took the receiver from my husband's outstretched hand. "Hi, Dennis," I said, and before he could say anything, I forged ahead. "Look, I'm sorry about what I said to you last night. I was a little tipsy."

"I figured that. Don't worry about it. I didn't take it personally."

"Are you sure?"

"Yup. But that's not why I called. I just caught the news.

I couldn't believe my eyes when I saw you on TV. Was that the woman you were telling me about? Works for Jablonsky?"

"Worked. She either quit or was fired last week. Why, I don't know. That's one of the things I was going to ask her."

"How did you end up discovering the body?"

Body. I cringed. Already the living, breathing Gail was being reduced to a thing. I cleared my throat and tried to explain about Google and the phone number, about Cindy and the house key. "The Annapolis police were great, Dennis, but they aren't telling me anything."

"Who's handling the case?"

I told him. Then I shared my theory. "I really think Gail was killed to prevent her from talking to me."

Dennis grunted. "But how would the killer have connected Gail with you?"

I hadn't really thought about that.

"Is it possible Nick Pottorff recognized you when you and your father went to Steele's office?" Dennis continued.

"No. I never saw Pottorff at Jablonsky's. Just his car."

"Do you think Gail said anything?"

I thought for a moment. "No. I can't think of any reason why she might have done that."

Dennis started to speak, but I interrupted him. "I think the key is Ginger Cove. That's what Gail was looking at when she talked to me. And that's where six people connected with Jablonsky have died."

"You may be right, Hannah. Look. Let me make a few calls and get back to you."

Paul handed me a tissue. I used it to wipe my nose. "Thank you, Dennis."

"You get some rest, okay?"

"I'll try."

"Put Paul on, will you?"

"No. You'll just tell him to make me some hot tea and send me to bed."

"That's good advice, actually. Put him on."

I handed the phone to Paul. "Yeah." Paul listened for a few seconds, then said good-bye, looking worried.

"So, what did he say?"

"I'm supposed to give you some tea and send you to bed."

I pinched Paul's cheek, hard. "Seriously!"

"Seriously?" Paul gathered me into his arms, resting his chin on top of my head. "He wants me to double lock all the doors and asks me to make sure you don't take any long walks by yourself."

My heart began to pound. "You're serious."

"Dead serious. Dennis thinks you may have stirred up a hornets' nest. And he doesn't want you to take any unnecessary chances."

I burrowed my head more deeply into the fleecy softness of Paul's Navy sweatshirt. At least I had someone warm to curl up against, I thought grimly, while Gail Parrish was lying on a refrigerated slab at the Office of the Chief Medical Examiner in Baltimore.

I shivered.

"Decided on a movie?"

"I'm not in the mood for another movie, Paul."

"Me neither."

"Paul?"

"Hmmmm?"

"I've just thought of something." I sat bolt upright. "If Jablonsky didn't know about the connection between Gail and me before, he's sure to know about it now."

"Shit! TV, the newspapers."

"Exactly."

His arm snaked around my shoulders. "Don't worry, Hannah, I won't let you out of my sight."

We sat in uncomfortable silence for a few more minutes, then arm in arm made our way upstairs to the bedroom.

While Paul pulled down the covers on the bed, I stood

in front of the bathroom mirror, slathering Neutrogena cream all over my face, working it into the creases that, I swear, had not been there only the day before.

In the mirror something caught my eye and I stopped rubbing. I stared at my reflection, then checked my hands.

There were rust-colored traces underneath my fingernails.

I grabbed a metal nail file and started digging.

It was going to be a long and sleepless night.

CHAPTER 21

When I pried my eyelids open, Paul was standing over me with a mug of coffee in one hand and the Sunday paper in the other. "Wake up sleepyhead!" He'd accomplished that task by jiggling the bed with his slipper-clad foot. Mathematicians are not noted for their subtlety.

I groaned and glanced at the clock on my bedside table. It was nearly noon.

The digital clock and I were old friends. The previous night, as I lay in bed, I'd watched the lighted number indicating the hour click from two to three to four before I fell into a light and troubled sleep.

"Good morning," I mumbled around a tongue that was as dry as the Mojave Desert. "Or perhaps I should say good afternoon."

Paul held the mug out where I could reach it.

I rearranged the pillow more comfortably between my back and the headboard and accepted the coffee from him gratefully.

Paul waited until I'd taken a sip before tossing the newspaper onto the bedcovers. "You made the front page," he said.

I cringed. With my free hand, I picked up the paper.

The story about Gail had made the *Baltimore Sun* front

and center, directly above the fold. The police must have contacted Gail's parents, because she was named in the story and they had published a picture of her, one that I recognized from her desk at MBFSG: Gail and the Labrador retriever she'd had as a teen, with the dog neatly Photo-Shopped out.

My picture was featured on A12, where the article continued from the front page. Fortunately, it'd been taken at a distance, and in profile. I still looked like hell, but that might be a good thing. If Jablonsky were reading the paper that morning, he'd have a difficult time connecting the haggard old woman pictured in the newspaper with that well-dressed, impeccably made-up, ditzy dame who had showed up in his office last week, all chirpy and ready to charm his socks off.

According to *The Capital*, the police had interviewed Gail's employer. Predictably, Jablonsky had told them that Gail quit work the previous Friday, giving him no notice.

Jablonsky was shocked, *shocked* by this, of course. Gail had always been so reliable. Blah-de-blah-de-blah. It was Jablonsky's understanding, the paper went on, that the murdered woman had been planning a move to Las Vegas to join her boyfriend, Ross Bankson.

Ross Bankson. Ah-ha. Ross must be the ex-.

The paper had gotten one thing right. According to one witness (that was Cindy), Ms. Parrish had been estranged from Mr. Bankson. Naturally, police were hoping to talk to him. Through the dead woman's telephone records, they had traced Bankson to an apartment in Baltimore, but when they called at the apartment, Bankson had not been at home.

"It says here that the police are looking for Gail's ex-boyfriend," I read out loud. Paul was standing in front of the bathroom sink in his undershirt, shaving. The door to the bathroom stood ajar.

"Uh-huh."

"I think they're barking up the wrong tree," I commented. "Gail hinted that her boyfriend was a jerk, but sure as God made little green apples, I don't think Bankson had anything to do with her murder."

"Uh-huh."

I closed the paper angrily. "Paul? Are you even listening to me? This is important. My God, it looks like the cops are falling for all this crap Jablonsky is feeding them. Oily bastard!"

Paul emerged from the bathroom, patting his face dry with a towel he had draped around his neck. "Of course I'm listening. Boyfriend didn't do it. Jablonsky's an S.O.B." He bent down to kiss me.

I kissed him back, letting my lips linger on his for a while before gently pulling away. I grinned at my husband, then used a corner of the bedsheet to wipe a dollop of shaving cream off his ear.

Paul lobbed the towel into the bathroom, missing the dirty clothes basket by miles, then opened the door to his closet and pulled out a pair of gray pants and a light blue dress shirt.

I stared in disbelief. "It's Sunday, Paul. We missed church. Why on earth are you getting all dressed up?"

Paul stepped into his pants. "Sorry, sweetheart. While you were sleeping, Bailey called. I've got to go into the Academy. There's an emergency meeting of the department at one-thirty. Not sure what's up, but it's something big because the superintendent's legal officer is going to be there."

"Shit."

"My sentiments exactly."

I crossed my arms, rested my head back against the pillow and scowled at the ceiling. Bailey was chairman of the math department. The last time he'd called a meeting like this it was because a final exam had been stolen.

"This can't be good news."

"Nope." Paul leaned closer to the mirror, adjusting his tie. "If it's a compromised exam, then we're screwed. The mids are gone for the summer. We'd have to decide whether to call them back for a retake."

Midshipmen spent their summers sailing the seven seas. Calling them back would require a military mobilization not unlike that of Operation Desert Storm. "Maybe it won't come to that," I said.

Paul slipped into his loafers, then crossed the room to sit on the edge of the bed. He picked up my hand. "I hate to leave you alone, Hannah, particularly after yesterday." He brought my hand to his lips and held it there. "Promise me . . . *promise me* you'll keep the doors locked. Promise you won't go anywhere until I get back."

I stared at him without speaking. Paul really thought my life might be in danger! Since I'd seen the newspaper, I felt a little less freaked. The article hadn't mentioned my name, and the picture could have been of any bag lady.

"Hannah?"

"Okay," I agreed. Paul had enough to worry about with his stupid meeting. He didn't need to be worrying about me, too. "But only if you escort me out to dinner when you get back. I have a hankering for some good, old-fashioned Irish stew."

Paul kissed my forehead. "Galway Bay it is. That's one promise I'll be happy to keep."

By the time I crawled out of bed and got myself dressed, it was already one-thirty; Paul's meeting at the Academy would just be getting underway. As I wandered around the house making sure all the dead bolts were in place, I worried about the meeting. Not because Paul's job was in danger—this wasn't one of those one-on-one, call you on the carpet, hand your head to you on a platter kind of meetings. I worried because however it came out, especially if the legal officer was involved, it would mean extra work for Paul and his colleagues.

And if the press got wind of it? I could forget about seeing my husband until the dawn of the next Ice Age. Paul spent most of his waking hours at the Academy already. I would begrudge them even one hour more.

I decided to spend the first half hour of my voluntary home arrest composing a condolence message to Gail's parents. From the newspaper, I learned that Gail had been brought up in a rural town in western Kentucky. A quick search of the Internet provided her parents' mailing address.

I sat at my desk and selected a suitable note card from a packet of all-occasion cards I'd bought at a Naval Academy crafts fair. I chewed for a while on the retractor button of my pen, trying to decide on an equally suitable sentiment. When my mother died, I'd received dozens of beautifully illustrated, well-meaning sympathy cards but only one that had spoken directly to my heart. I combed my memory for the exact wording.

I began with a brief paragraph about how I'd met Gail and how much I had liked her. I mentioned our joint love of sailing. I closed with, "Sorrow is not forever. Love is." And signed my name.

I was rummaging through the cubbyholes on my desk, trying to find the first class stamps, when the telephone rang.

"Hello?"

"Hannah! Oh, thank God I got you!" It was Mrs. Bromley, speaking in a hoarse whisper.

"Mrs. B! What a pleasant surprise. But why are you whispering?"

"Don't talk, just listen." Her voice trembled. "I'm on my cell phone and I don't know how much time I have until he comes back."

"Comes back? Who comes back?" I found myself whispering as well.

"Oh, Hannah, I was tailing that so-called gardener, trying to take a clearer photograph, when he caught me at it. He smashed my camera, threw me into the back of his van, and took off! I've been kidnapped!"

CHAPTER 22

Kidnapped?

I felt like I'd been struck squarely between the eyes with a two-by-four. Here I'd been sitting at home, keeping my own comfort-loving derriere well out of harm's way, believing that Mrs. Bromley was safely ensconced in a B&B on Maryland's bucolic Eastern Shore. How could she have been kidnapped?

It didn't seem like a good time to ask.

"We've stopped now, for some reason," Mrs. Bromley whispered, before I could say anything else. "Frankly, I think he's lost. He didn't seem to be the sharpest knife in the drawer, if you know what I mean. Lights are on, but nobody's home."

"Can't you open the door?"

"I tried. I think he's got it tied together on the outside."

"Can you tell where you are, Mrs. B?"

"No! The cargo doors have windows, but they're all painted over. And there's a sliding Plexiglas panel that opens into the cab, but it's so scratched up I can barely see out of it. Just a minute." I heard banging and scraping sounds, then Mrs. Bromley came back on the line. "Damn thing has a lock on it, too."

"Thank goodness he didn't notice your cell phone. Tell me you called 911!"

"Of course, dear. The minute he drove away. I gave the

operator a description of the van and my general impression that he was traveling north on Riva Road, but then I lost the blasted signal."

"As long as you have the cell phone, the police can locate you by tracking your signal through the cell towers. Right after I hang up, call 911 again."

"I don't know how long I have before the batteries run out." Mrs. Bromley drew a quick breath. "Wait a minute! I hear something!" She paused, and I strained to hear what she was hearing, too, but the only thing that came over the line was silence. "There's traffic going by, so I must be near a well-traveled road, but I can also hear music. Just a minute."

The line went quiet again while I nearly expired from tension. "Somebody's playing music," she said at last. "No, wait a minute, it's chimes. Westminster chimes!"

One block away from where I stood, the Naval Academy chapel bells had just finished ringing the half hour. "Oh glory!" I cheered. "I can hear the chapel bells! You can hear the chapel bells! You've got to be nearby!"

But where? I could eliminate the Naval Academy grounds. Because of heightened security following the commencement of the war in Iraq, no vehicle was allowed inside the Academy walls without a Department of Defense sticker. Marines behind barricades armed with M-16 assault rifles saw to that.

I needed more clues.

"Can you see *anything* out of that cab window?" I asked. "Anything at all?"

"A chain-link fence and something yellow. Wait!"

I waited, panic making a crescendo in my gut. I felt ready to blow, like a geyser.

"It's construction equipment," Mrs. Bromley said brightly. "One of those back hoe things."

Construction. Construction within earshot of the chapel bells. Not far from a main road. Nobody was building anything on King George Street, at least not that I knew of. The other main road into town was Rowe Boulevard. Holding the telephone, I paced back and forth across the carpet, searching my memory banks.

Wait a minute! The state of Maryland was building a public housing project at the far end of St. John's Street, just one block off Rowe. That might be it!

"Listen carefully, Mrs. B. When you call 911, tell them it's possible that you're on St. John's Street somewhere near the Bloomsbury construction site."

"All right."

"Now, hang up, Mrs. B. No, wait a minute! Can you set your phone on vibrate? When I call you back, I don't want your kidnapper to hear it ringing."

"His name's Chet."

"Chet? Your kidnapper's name is Chet? How do you know his name is Chet?"

"It's embroidered right on his shirt."

"Okay. Noted. What does the van look like?"

"It's a dark blue Ford with 'All Seasons Lawn and Landscaping' painted on the side in orange letters."

That was certainly inconspicuous. Chet, whoever he was, didn't sound like a pro, otherwise he'd have chosen a plain white van to transport his victim in. I didn't know whether his status as an amateur kidnapper would spell good news or bad news for Mrs. Bromley. "Stay put!" I ordered. "I'm coming to look for you."

"You think I'm going anywhere?"

"Duh. Sorry. And call 911!"

I hung up quickly and, just as quickly, dialed 911 to report the kidnapping myself. I also called Paul on his cell phone. He'd have it turned off during his meeting, of course, but I could leave him a message. I had promised on a stack of Bibles that I wouldn't leave the house. Well, lightning could strike me dead, I didn't care. This was an emergency. I knew God would understand. I wasn't so sure about Paul.

I raced up the stairs to the kitchen, grabbed my purse

and the house keys, rammed an Orioles baseball cap over my curls, and added a pair of Jacqueline Kennedy Onassis sunglasses that had been sitting in a basket on my kitchen counter ever since a house guest had left them behind more than two years ago. As a disguise, it was piss poor, but it'd have to do.

I eased out the back door, locking it carefully behind me.

I ran west on Prince George Street, dashed across Maryland Avenue and made it all the way to where Prince George intersected with College Avenue without collapsing. Astonishing! I would never have been able to do that before the race training.

Directly in front of me the St. John's College campus spread out in both directions, dominated by McDowell Hall, a grand, pre-Revolutionary brick mansion on top of a hill, and anchored by Greenville Library on one end and Woodward Hall on the other.

I could have turned left on College Avenue then right on St. John's Street, but if the van holding Mrs. Bromley was where I thought it would be, I could reach her more quickly if I cut across campus and through the parking lot adjoining Key Auditorium. I took off at a run, praying that either I or the cops would get there before Chet returned to the van and drove it away.

I jogged left, passing a replica of the Liberty Bell, and cut diagonally across the lawn, just your ordinary, Sunday jogger, panting like a hound dog in August, holding her sunglasses to her face to keep them from sliding off her nose.

The parking lot was jammed with cars and I burst out onto St. John's Street near the Maryland state parking garage, both sides of the road were clogged with vehicles, too. Damn! Something must be going on at the college.

I checked my watch. Only three minutes had passed since I left my house.

I cut to the right, and as I drew even with the back of Key Auditorium, I could hear piano music. Ah, yes. The Heifetz piano competition. I'd read about it in the paper.

Under ordinary circumstances I might have paused to listen, might even have stuck my head inside the auditorium, but I found myself pausing only to catch my breath, my hands resting on my knees, eyes scanning the street ahead for any sign of a blue van.

There were three of them.

I jogged down the street, scrutinizing each van as I passed. None carried anything even remotely resembling an orange logo.

I jogged on.

Ahead of me, at the end of the street, behind a chain-link fence and not far from the banks of Weems Creek, sat a knot of construction trailers. I raced in that direction, passing row after row of two-story town houses, sheathed in Tyvek, which were rising to my left out of the red Maryland clay. Just beyond the town houses, I came to a rutted road. I turned into the road and continued running, my ankles taking a punishment on the well-pocked surface as I thundered past a battered Ford pickup and a bulldozer.

Past the bulldozer and hidden between two construction trailers I found the blue van. Just as Mrs. Bromley had said, it had ALL SEASONS LAWN AND LANDSCAPING painted on the sides in bright orange letters.

As much as I wanted to rush over, wrench the door open, and haul Mrs. Bromley out, I stood there quietly for a moment, looking in all directions, just to make sure Chet wasn't anywhere in the vicinity.

I checked my watch again. Five minutes. Where the hell were the cops? Several couples strolled along the banks of the creek, taking advantage of the afternoon sunshine. Just ahead, traffic rushed by on Rowe Boulevard, slowing now and again at the light on Bladen Street. But no cops.

I used my cell phone to call 911 and report our exact location, then approached the van cautiously from the side, so I could peer into the cab. Chet had not returned. I pulled the door handle. The cab was locked.

I crept around to the back of the van and knocked quietly on the rear cargo door. "Mrs. B. It's Hannah. I'm going to get you out of this thing."

"Thank goodness! Let me know how I can help."

"I don't think there's much you can do from the inside, except push when I tell you to."

Indeed, the back door of the van was securely locked and, just to make sure his prisoner couldn't escape, Chet had woven a bicycle chain through the door handles and secured it with an oversized combination lock. "Damn!" I called through the door. "He's put a chain on it. No wonder you couldn't get it open."

I dropped my purse to the ground and glanced around the deserted construction site, desperate for a tool I could use to pry the lock off the door. Failing that, I thought, something big and heavy. I'd bash the door in.

About twenty yards away was a Dumpster, loaded with debris, sitting next to another pile of debris. I patted the side of the van. "I'll be right back!" I told her.

I scrabbled over the pile, tossing aside bits of plywood, odd-shaped pieces of Sheetrock, squares of pink insulation, and leftover shingles and vinyl siding. My sunglasses finally gave up the ghost, sliding off my nose and disappearing under a pile of wood chips. I didn't care. I pawed on.

Beneath the remains of a roll of tar paper, I found a tangle of iron rods of the kind normally used to reinforce concrete. I picked carefully through the rods, tossing several aside before selecting one about two and a half feet long. Brandishing it like a sword, I scrambled back to the van, banging my shins several times on the corners of protruding plywood boards.

"Hold tight! It's going to take me a minute or two to bust this thing open."

A minute or two. That was optimistic.

I studied the chain and the padlock, trying to decide which was the more vulnerable. Finally, I inserted one end of the rod between the jaws of the padlock, braced the rod against the door of the van, and yanked down.

I succeeded only in bending the rod.

I eased the rod out, turned it around and threaded it through one of the links of the chain. "A chain is only as strong as its weakest link," I muttered as I applied pressure to the link. Nothing happened, except a searing pain shot up my arm.

I removed the rod and reinserted it halfway, beginning at the point where the chain met the padlock. I began turning the rod clockwise, hand over hand, winding the chain up. When I'd wound it as far to the right as it would go, I grabbed the right end of the rod with both hands, hung on and pulled down with all my weight, lifting my feet up off the ground.

Once. Twice. I rocked the van.

Three times. Four. The chain groaned.

Suddenly, the chain snapped, throwing me, my hat, the rod, the chain, and the padlock to the ground all in one great, glorious heap.

Fueled by adrenaline, I shot to my feet and was reaching for the handle to the cargo door when a heavy hand fell on my shoulder and squeezed hard.

"Oh, no you don't!"

Instantly, every ounce of energy seemed to drain from my body. I felt limp and defeated. I turned to face my assailant.

Chet loomed over me, lean and muscular, tall as a tree. He was dressed in khaki pants and a navy blue shirt with *Chet* embroidered on it in orange script. Without doubt he was the gardener I'd first seen in Mrs. Bromley's clandestine photos. His shirt matched his van, I remembered thinking. You pay extra for that.

Out of the corner of my eye I noticed that Mrs. Bromley had managed to open the door from the inside. The crack widened as the door swung slowly outward.

Hoping to distract Chet, I dropped to the ground and

scrambled to retrieve my iron rod. I grabbed the rod, rolled over, and swung it at Chet's shins, connecting with one of them with a resounding crack.

"Ooooow! You bitch!" Hopping on one leg, Chet managed to grab my arm and twist it behind my back, iron rod and all, pulling my arm painfully skyward. With his free hand, he grasped my weapon, twisted, and by sheer strength, pulled it out of my clenched hand. The last time I saw the rod, it was sailing over the chain-link fence. After what I'd done to his shin, I was counting myself lucky he didn't beat me to death with the thing.

In the meantime, Mrs. Bromley's tennis shoes had hit the ground. She picked up my purse and swung it at Chet, like a Biblical slingshot, but it bounced ineffectually off his head.

Chet tugged me back against him, reached around and clamped my neck in the crook of his arm. He jerked us both around to face Mrs. Bromley. "Get back in the van," he ordered, "or I'll break her fucking neck."

Mrs. Bromley froze, my purse dangling by its strap from her hand. Her eyes darted from my face to Chet's, apparently weighing her options.

Her eyes flashed. If she'd had a gun, I don't believe she would have hesitated to shoot the bastard, but with only my purse as a weapon, what choice did she have? She set my purse carefully inside the van, turned and climbed obediently back in.

Unless the police showed up within the next five seconds, our geese were cooked.

Chet released his grip on my neck but was still twisting my arm so painfully that tears came to my eyes. Holding me securely, he duck-walked me over to the cargo door, boosted me up with a well-placed, retaliatory knee kick to my butt, and dumped me unceremoniously in a heap on the floor.

"I'm sorry," Mrs. Bromley whispered.

I gathered my legs under me and sat up, shading my

eyes against the glare of the sun that poured through the door. "That's okay," I said. "You gave it your best shot."

Suddenly, the sun was blocked by Chet's bulk as he stood framed in the doorway. "How'd ja find . . . ?" he drawled.

A light in his attic blinked on. "Yeah." Chet picked up my handbag, rummaged through the pockets until he found my cell phone. "Naughty, naughty!" he said. He drew his arm back and sent my cell phone flying in a wide, high arc until it landed somewhere on the Bloomsbury Square construction site where an enterprising youngster would find it the following morning and use up all my minutes having phone sex with some call girl in Miami.

Chet tossed my purse back into the van, where it landed at my feet with a thud. "Now you'll stay out of trouble."

His hard, dark eyes settled on Mrs. Bromley. "You must have one on you, too, then." He held out his hand. "Give."

Mrs. Bromley unclipped her cell phone from her belt and reluctantly handed it over. Soon it was sailing over the chain-link fence in the general direction of mine.

Chet started to close the door, but seemed to think better of it. "You ladies are too damn much trouble," he muttered. He rubbed the spot on his head where Mrs. Bromley had clipped him with my purse, then limped back a few steps, staring into the van, thinking. It was probably a relatively new experience for him.

While he stared, I looked around the inside of the van, too, hoping to find something I could use as a weapon.

Whatever else Chet might be, he was definitely a gardener. The van was chock full of the wherewithal required to provide fairly competent lawn care service. A lawn mower was lashed to one wall with bungee cords; hedge clippers, a chain saw, pruning shears, shovels, rakes surrounded us. Any one of them would have been useful as a weapon if they hadn't been stowed away so securely. Zero chance of getting any into my hot little hands while Chet's beady eyes were upon us.

Chet seemed to be cataloging the contents of the van, too. Hanging on a metal hook near the door was a bright orange extension cord, neatly coiled. He reached out and lifted it off the hook.

"You two sit together now."

I scowled. "We are sitting together."

"No. Back-to-back."

I turned obediently until I was sitting directly behind Mrs. Bromley.

"Closer," he said. "Now link your arms together."

When he was satisfied with our position, Chet stepped into the van. He paused a few cautious feet away. "No funny business now."

"We'll behave," I assured him. We were confined in such close quarters, I feared that if I tried anything, I'd end up injuring Mrs. Bromley.

I never knew an extension cord could be so long. Chet managed to wrap it around our waists, twine it about our necks, draw it tightly across my chest, loop it down around my ankles, and pass it back around our waists again. By the grunts, I could tell when he got to the knot tying part, somewhere out of reach in the vicinity of Mrs. Bromley's ankles.

Apparently satisfied, he climbed down and slammed the cargo door behind him. A few seconds later the shock absorbers squeaked and the van heeled to the left as he climbed into the driver's seat. The engine roared to life and, tires spinning on the loose dirt, our kidnapper peeled out onto St. John's Street.

"Keep track of the turns," I said in quiet desperation.

We turned right, then stopped. "This must be the light on Rowe Boulevard," I guessed, struggling to loosen our bonds.

We turned right again, then made another right, then a left, and an almost immediate right. By this time I figured we were in West Annapolis. But then the van made a series of zigzags, perhaps intentionally, or perhaps because Chet was lost again, and it wasn't long before I lost all track of where we might be. We could have been in Admiral Heights or Ferry Farms or all the way out in Cape St. Claire, for all I knew.

Suddenly, Chet took a sharp left, and both Mrs. Bromley and I toppled over. "Ouch!" she cried.

"What is it?"

"Something's digging into my side!"

"Hold tight!" I struggled to work us back into a sitting position, but the van took another hard turn and we rolled again, sliding along the floorboards. This time I knocked my head on a corner of the lawn mower and saw stars.

For what seemed like hours, but was probably only twenty minutes, we careened around like tennis shoes in a dryer, before the van finally screeched to a stop, throwing us back against a plastic, five gallon gasoline tank. There was an electronic beep from within the cab.

"What's that?" Mrs. Bromley whimpered.

"I think it's a garage door opener."

The van inched forward, then lurched to a stop. There was another beep, and the sound of a garage door grinding down.

Mrs. Bromley and I waited, hardly daring to breathe. "I wonder where we are?" she whispered after a moment of silence.

In the dark, I shrugged. "I don't have the vaguest idea," I whispered back.

Chet turned off the ignition and climbed out of the cab. We heard the sound of a door opening, and muffled conversation. After a few minutes more, the cargo door opened and Chet climbed into the van. Without saying a word, he went about the business of releasing us from the extension cord, then hopped out.

Mrs. Bromley and I were rubbing our arms and checking each other for damage when a hand appeared at the

222 • Marcia Talley

door, followed by a brown sleeve and a face only a mother
could love.

"Well, ladies, what a pleasure to see you today."

It was Nick Pottorff.

CHAPTER 23

I looked Nick Pottorff straight in the eye. "Who the hell are you?"

Mrs. Bromley crossed her arms over her bosom and glared at him, too. "And what do you want with us?"

Pottorff ignored her, keeping his eyes on me. There was no flash of recognition, thank goodness, just a hint of ill-concealed amusement. "Your friend, here, she's been a busy little bee with her camera."

"She's not my friend. She's my mother," I lied smoothly.

"I'm president of the Ginger Cove garden club," Mrs. Bromley pouted. "I was photographing the *tulip* beds, for heaven's sake, and the next thing I knew, this *thug* . . ." She glared at Chet so fiercely that he actually backed away.

"Nice try, Mom." Pottorff held out his hand and helped Mrs. Bromley alight from the van.

He offered me the same assistance, but I kept my hands to myself. If I actually had to touch the loathsome toad, I knew my fingers would drop off. "No thanks. I can manage."

When my feet hit the ground, I nearly collapsed. My left leg had gone to sleep. I pounded on it with my fist, trying to get the circulation going again. "Are you all right, Mom?"

Mrs. Bromley's smile was unconvincing. "As well as could be expected, dear."

We were standing on the spotless concrete floor of a modern, three-car garage. Except for the van, it was empty. No tools lined the back wall, no paint cans, no old snow tires, no broken-down bicycles or rusty shovels. A Stepford garage. It wasn't natural.

Pottorff extended an arm and bowed slightly, like a head-waiter about to escort us to our table. "Please, follow me."

With Chet bringing up the rear, we followed Pottorff up a short flight of stairs, through a mud room where winter coats and rain slickers hung on hooks in an orderly row, into an eye-poppingly gorgeous gourmet kitchen. Valerie would have loved this, I thought. As we trooped past a high-tech appliance island, I stole a glance out the window, hoping to recognize the neighborhood, but it was impossible. Nick Pottorff's house, if this was his house, had been built on a heavily wooded lot. Through a thick canopy of leaves I thought I caught a glimpse of water, but I couldn't be sure.

Chet prodded me in the back. "Move along, lady."

Pottorff opened a door next to an antique Dutch cupboard and led us down a flight of stairs.

I feared we would find a dungeon at the end of it, or a dark, dank basement, but the stairs were broad and carpeted, and when we reached the bottom, we found ourselves in a luxurious family room right out of the pages of *House Beautiful*. A sixty-inch HDTV plasma screen was mounted on one wall, flanked by floor-to-ceiling bookshelves. To our right was an extensive bar of carved oak, modeled on an English pub. At least two kinds of beer seemed to be on tap, as well as a wide range of hard liquor, if the number of bottles on display was any indication. A beveled mirror reflected the light from a Tiffany-style light fixture, and mounted above the mirror was the pièce de resistance: a copy of Goya's *Naked Maya*. From her vantage point over the bar, the Maya enjoyed a view of a massive stone fireplace.

"You have a lovely home." My voice dripped acid.

Pottorff turned and studied me without smiling. "Please, give me a moment." He lifted a key from a hook mounted next to a decorative chalkboard that had "Happy Hour" painted on it, then ambled down a short hallway, at the end of which was a door made of dark wood, inset with etched glass. I squinted. Curlicues and dolphins, I thought, or maybe they were mermaids. Hard to tell.

Pottorff unlocked the door, turned and waggled his fingers in a come-hither way.

With Chet at our backs to hustle us along, we toddled down the hallway past a glass front refrigerator filled with beverages. Like at 7-Eleven, only fancier.

"Please. Wait in here," Pottorff said, stepping aside.

"Wait for what?" I asked.

"Please." He opened the door wider.

"But it's a wine cellar," I said, stepping with some reluctance into the room.

Nick Pottorff turned to Mrs. Bromley. "Your daughter has remarkable powers of observation."

"And it's cold in here," Mrs. Bromley complained. "We don't have sweaters."

"Wine cellars are maintained at fifty-five degrees," I informed Pottorff. "Like a cave."

"Are you a tour guide now?" Pottorff grinned, revealing a row of crooked teeth. "You aren't going to be in here all that long," he said.

"We hope," added the despicable Chet.

Pottorff scowled. "Shut up, Chet, and get the ladies a blanket."

Chet turned and sauntered down the hall. With his back to us, I noticed the gun for the first time, tucked inside the waistband of his khakis. I felt my lunch beginning to crawl back up my esophagus. Chet returned in less than a minute carrying a red plaid blanket he'd snatched from the back of a leather sofa; I'd noticed it in the family room when we walked by. He tossed the blanket into the room, where it landed on the floor in an untidy heap.

Pottorff left, making an elaborate production of closing and locking the door behind him. The only light in the room came through the glass pane in the door. I managed to retrieve the blanket and draped it over Mrs. Bromley's shoulders.

"Whose house is this, do you know?" she whispered.

"I wish I did. Not Nick Pottorff's, surely. Every time I've seen him, he's been wearing the same brown suit. I doubt he could afford a place like this."

"His teeth need work, too," said Mrs. Bromley. Next to me, she shivered. "Jablonsky, then?"

"That'd be my guess. It's fancy enough for Fishing Creek Farm, although I didn't have the impression that Chet was driving in that direction. Whoever he is," I mused, "the guy's got money."

In the light coming through the glass pane, I could see Mrs. Bromley's worried face. "Help me find a light switch," I said. We ran our hands along the walls on both sides of the door, without success. "Must be on the outside," I grumbled, angry at myself for feeling defeated by a simple thing like a light switch.

Mrs. Bromley spread the blanket on the floor and sat down on it, leaning back against the stout leg of a tasting table that dominated the center of the room. She patted the floor next to her. "Sit, Hannah. Let's consider our options."

To tell the truth, I didn't think we had many options, but I plopped down next to her anyway. We sat in companionable silence for a few minutes while my eyes gradually became accustomed to the semidarkness.

At home, my "wine cellar" consists of six pine shelves that Paul brought home from IKEA and banged together in the pantry. Mrs. Bromley and I were being held captive in the kind of wine cellar you read about in *Wine Spectator*. I knew that nobody actually *owned* a wine cellar like this, except movie stars and dot-com kings.

"I'm going to case the joint," I told Mrs. Bromley. I stood and worked my way clockwise around our prison, running my hands along the wine racks like a blind man. They were smoothly polished and made of wood. To the left of the door, diamond-shaped bins lined the wall. When I turned the corner, my hands met more bins, then an alcove that included a small sink set flush with the countertop—marble, from the coolness of it. I reached up. Stemware was suspended from racks mounted overhead; when I touched them, they tinkled like wind chimes. This had to be a decanting table.

I moved on past the decanting table, where there were more bins, mostly with single slots, extending straight up to the ceiling, ten feet or more above my head. Set into a niche near the ceiling was an air conditioner that kept the wine at a constant 55 degrees, as I suspected. Even in the dim light, I could distinguish the two saucer-sized air vents that blew cool air into the room.

Suddenly inspired, I grabbed a bottle by the neck and eased it out of its slot. I stuck my hand into the slot up to my elbow, hoping I'd discover the walls were made of Sheetrock or something equally flimsy, but my fingers met only rough, cold stone.

I plopped back down next to Mrs. Bromley. "Well, that was the grand tour. Now what do I do?"

"I'm sorry, Hannah. This is all my fault."

"Not entirely your fault," I assured her. "I'm the one who lit the fire under Jablonsky, remember?"

I studied her profile, and even though her chin was quivering, I asked her the question I'd been meaning to ask for several hours. "I thought you were staying in Chestertown at a B and B! How did these creeps find you?"

Mrs. Bromley lowered her head and stared at her thumbs. "I changed my mind. I didn't go to Chestertown."

"Mrs. B!"

"I just said I was going to Chestertown so you wouldn't worry about me."

"So you *planned* to go after Chet with your camera?"

Mrs. Bromley nodded miserably.

I had toyed with the idea of not telling her about Gail, but this didn't seem like the time to begin keeping secrets from one another. "Mrs. Bromley, we're in real danger here." I informed her of Gail's murder, skipping over the details about my finding the body.

"Gail makes eight," she muttered when I'd finished my story.

"Yes, and if we don't want to be numbers nine and ten, we need to get ourselves out of here! If Pottorff killed your friends at Ginger Cove, and Gail, and Valerie, I don't think he'll have any qualms about offing a middle-aged woman and her meddlesome mother."

On the other side of the door the television had come on, so loud it could blister paint. Chet had figured out how to work the DVD player and was watching a movie, *Twister*, from the sound of it. A storm came howling out of every speaker in the room.

I padded across the tile floor and tried the door, just in case, but it was securely locked.

"Hand me my purse, will you, Mrs. B?"

I extracted my Visa card and slid it along the crack between the door frame and the lock, but a metal flange prevented the edge of my card from reaching and tripping the latch. "Shit!" I sat down on the floor, cross-legged, resting my back against the tasting table. "He must have some valuable wines in here. It's locked up like Fort Knox."

"No need to whisper, dear," she said. "Chet's not going to hear anything over that raging storm!"

"The door's glass," I observed. "Wanna break a few bottles?"

"I'd break *all* the bottles if I thought it would help, but we'd have to get by Chet, and he has a gun."

So Mrs. Bromley had noticed the gun, too.

"If only we had a window." I surveyed the room again, but wine racks covered every floor-to-ceiling inch. If there were ever any windows in this part of the basement, they had been covered up during construction.

Mrs. Bromley pointed up. "Hannah, that air conditioner has to exhaust out to somewhere. Could it be installed in a window?"

I jumped to my feet. The woman was brilliant! "Help me," I said.

Standing directly under the air conditioner, I pulled a bottle out of its slot and handed it to Mrs. Bromley, who set it on the floor. Working as a team, I pulled another, and another, handing the bottles off to her. Bottle after bottle, I reached higher and higher, until I had cleared a ladder of makeshift toeholds. Then I started to climb.

"Be careful!" Mrs. Bromley called after me.

Once at the top, I held on with one hand and studied the air conditioner, a Whisperkool. I wanted to shut off the cold air that was blasting into my face, but the controls were locked behind a Plexiglas panel.

The Whisperkool itself was secured to the wall with long metal bolts. Above it, though, a wooden panel had been fitted into the space between the top of the air conditioner and the ceiling. It was what lay behind that panel that looked promising.

Holding onto the air conditioner with one hand, I moved my foot gingerly to another toehold and leaned as far forward as I could to examine the panel. I poked at it with my finger. It didn't budge. I grabbed the top of the Whisperkool and pulled down. The panel moved a fraction of an inch. Encouraged, I jiggled the air conditioner up and down and was elated when the panel responded, admitting a welcome sliver of daylight.

A muffled "Yay!" drifted up from below.

"If I can just work this panel loose, I think I can reach the window!"

"Will we be able to climb out?" she asked.

"I don't know, Mrs. B. The air conditioner might be in the way."

I continued jiggling the air conditioner up and down, up and down, like a kid on a pogo stick. The sliver of light became a slit, and the area I was working in grew marginally brighter, but it was slow going, and I was afraid I might pull the air conditioner clean off the wall. If the falling air conditioner didn't kill us outright, then Chet would probably finish the job when he came in to see what we had been up to.

"Mrs. B, look around down there and see if you can find me a corkscrew, something I can pry with."

"Right." I heard a drawer slide open, then another and another before Mrs. Bromley said, "The only corkscrew he seems to have is one of those pull-screw models, and it's mounted on the tasting table."

"Damn!"

"How about this?" From my perch, I turned carefully and looked down into Mrs. Bromley's upturned face. She was holding up a wine funnel.

"Let me give it a try." Holding tight and fighting vertigo, I stretched my hand down. On her end, Mrs. Bromley stood on tiptoe. I captured the funnel between my index and middle fingers and tucked it under my arm. When I was securely in position in front of the air conditioner again, I examined the funnel. The spout was curved, but it was made of sturdy stainless steel.

Holding the funnel end, I used the spout to dig around a corner of the panel. I made a hole, then rammed the funnel between the panel and the wall and pulled. I moved to the opposite corner and did the same.

Hoping to speed things up, I ran my fingers over the wood, feeling for nails I could work on. I never thought my fingers were particularly sensitive, but even in the dark I could tell that the panel was attached with screws, not nails.

"Mrs. B! I need a screwdriver."

If only this guy hadn't been so modern, I complained bitterly to myself. I didn't ask for much. Just an average, run-of-the-mill corkscrew with the name of a liquor store stamped on the side and a stainless steel, foil-cutting blade that folds up inside.

I heard drawers opening and closing again. "I'm not finding anything."

"A cheese knife?"

"No, nothing." A cabinet door opened, then closed. "Wait a minute! How about this?" She held up a thin piece of metal about a foot long. "I think you dry decanters on it. It's got a plastic tip." She grunted. "There, I got it off."

The drying stem was the thickness of a chopstick, much thinner than the funnel. It fit perfectly in the narrow space I had created between the panel and the wall. I crammed the rod in and yanked it toward me.

"It's coming!" With a screech, the screws began to surrender and the wooden panel started to pull away from the wall. I worked my fingers around behind it, stuck the rod in and pulled again. Suddenly, the panel came off in my hands. I waved it in the air like a trophy, and turned to smile at Mrs. Bromley. She stood below me, silently clapping her hands.

Behind the panel was a nest of wires and white plastic duct work. With growing excitement, I tore away the duct work to reveal the window.

It was six inches tall, large enough to accommodate the air conditioning exhaust, but not nearly tall enough for a human body to pass through.

"Damn, damn, damn!" I didn't realize I'd been sweating until the sweat started to cool on my forehead. "Oh, the big F-word!" All the other words I thought of contained four letters, too.

"It's too small, isn't it?"

"Yes," I whimpered. "We could sneak in a pizza, maybe."

"Come down, Hannah. You did your best."

So Pottorff wouldn't be aware of what I had been doing, I shoved the panel back into place, pushing the damaged corners in as best I could. Then I backed down the wall, carefully avoiding the wine bottles that Mrs. Bromley had arranged in neat battalions on the floor.

Outside the room, Chet was still watching *Twister*. From the sound of it, Cary Elwes was about to get his, or maybe the cow had just flown by. We were about to replace the wine bottles in their slots when the room outside suddenly grew quiet. I held tight to Mrs. Bromley's hand, hardly daring to breathe.

Chet's shadow darkened the door. He seemed to be listening, but we kept quiet. Chet grunted, and his shadow moved away. We could have frozen to death in there, for all he cared. I heard the refrigerator door slide open and the clink of bottles. Chet, it appeared, was helping himself to a beer.

A minute later Chet crawled back into the fury of the storm and we began to relax. "Just in case we don't get out of this, Mrs. B, I want you to know how much your friendship has meant to me."

"I feel the same way, Hannah."

"I just wish I could get a message to Paul. The last time I talked to him, he made me promise not to leave the house. When he gets home and finds me gone, he's going to kill me." I chuckled ruefully. "So to speak."

I reached for my purse and started rummaging.

"What are you looking for, dear?"

"Something to write with. I want to leave Paul a note, if they . . ." I swallowed, unable to continue.

For want of something better, I located my checkbook and tore a deposit slip out of the back. It would have to do.

With tears streaming down my cheeks, I wrote Paul a note that came straight from my heart.

When I finished, and had pulled myself back together, I turned to Mrs. Bromley. "Where should I hide it?"

Mrs. Bromley didn't even pause to think. "You could empty out a wine bottle, put the note in, and recork it."

"I like that idea."

"I used it in a novel once. *The Broken Promise*."

"Really? When we get out of here, I'll have to read it." Tucking the note into my pocket, I crossed the room. Starting at the lower left-hand corner nearest the door, I counted nine slots up and seventeen over. I pulled a wine bottle out of the slot and carried it over to the door so I could see the label more clearly.

"Michael LeBois Pinot Noir Santa Maria Highlands 2001," I read aloud.

"Sounds complicated, but lovely," Mrs. Bromley said.

"I'm sure he's waiting for this little beauty to mature." I took the bottle over to the decanting table and positioned it under the corkscrew. "Well, too effing bad!" I pulled down and rammed the corkscrew home. I lifted the handle to release the cork, then held the bottle over the sink.

"Want a taste?"

"Are you kidding?"

I tipped the bottle to my mouth. "God, this is good." I took another swig and swished the wine around in my mouth before turning the bottle upside down and watching every last ounce of Michael LeBois's finest gurgle down the drain.

I rolled my note into a tube, stuck it in the bottle, and replaced the cork, pushing it all the way in with my foot. Then I returned the pinot noir to its proper slot.

"In case something happens to me, Mrs. Bromley, remember: nine up and seventeen over. It's my birthday."

From her position on the floor, Mrs. Bromley looked up at me and smiled. "Under the circumstances, Hannah, don't you think it's time you started calling me Naddie?"

CHAPTER 24

"Naddie," I said, trying it on for size. "Naddie."

Next to me, Mrs. Bromley began to weep quietly. "If anything happens to you, Hannah, I'll never forgive myself."

"Please, Mrs. B, uh, Naddie." I wrapped my arms around her, wanting so much to comfort her, to reassure her that everything would be okay, but at that point, neither one of us was likely to believe it.

Tears glistened on her cheeks.

"Here," I said, "let me find you a tissue." I plunged my hand deep into my purse. I had a packet of tissues in there somewhere.

I pushed aside my wallet, my lipstick, an appointment book, my car keys—fat lot of good they were going to do me now. I found an old AAA battery, a stick of gum, and somebody's business card. Then my hand touched something soft and squishy.

Squishy? I tried to think. I felt it on all sides. Something squarish, in bubble wrap.

Bubble wrap. Paul's global positioning system was wrapped in bubble wrap.

Carefully, lovingly, realizing the potential of this miraculous discovery, I pulled the GPS out of my purse and laid it gently on the blanket.

Carefully, lovingly, I began to remove the bubble wrap, praying, as I did so, that the GPS had been returned from the West Marine repair shop operationally complete, including fresh batteries.

"What's that?" Mrs. Bromley asked as the device began to emerge from the plastic.

"This, Mrs. B, may be our salvation." I looked straight into her eyes. "And if not our salvation, at least a means of bringing these criminals to justice after we're gone."

"What? With a PDA?"

"No, not a PDA, Naddie. It's Paul's GPS." I turned it around so she could see the screen. " 'I lift up mine eyes . . . ' " I quoted. "I *knew* there was some reason we needed that window!"

Naddie looked puzzled. "Does it send out some sort of signal?"

"No," I explained. "Just the opposite. It picks up satellite signals and tells you exactly where you are. Paul uses it when he's sailing, to navigate."

"Well that's all well and good," Naddie said, wiping her eyes with her sleeve, "but knowing exactly where we are isn't going to help us get *out* of where we are."

"No, but when we *do* get out, it will tell us how to get back."

"Get back? Why on earth would we want to come back?" And then she got it. "Ah, the police! I must be senile."

I got to my feet. "Here, hold onto this—carefully!— while I climb back up to the window."

"Why do you need the window?"

I eased a toe into an empty wine slot and began to pull myself up the wall. "It needs to see the sky in order to pick up satellites."

When I reached the ceiling, I used the decanter drying rod to remove the panel, laying it aside on top of the Whisperkool.

Light poured into our prison cell.

Naddie handed me the GPS, and I held it as far out the

little window as I could before turning it on. I waited, watching anxiously for the screen to light up. When it did, I said a silent prayer, thanking God and the Energizer Bunny. Then I cheered as, one by one, the device glommed onto the satellites orbiting overhead.

When the GPS was done acquiring satellites, it beeped. "Now, to save our position."

Below me, Mrs. Bromley was bouncing up and down on her toes. "How do you do that?"

"Remember when I said Paul used this for sailing? Well, what we do is push the man overboard button." With my thumb, I mashed the M.O.B. down. "If we get out of here alive, Naddie, this little baby will tell us exactly where we've been. It'll even lead us here, like a mechanical bloodhound."

I kissed the GPS, tucked it into my waistband, and scrambled back down.

"You know what?" I said as I rewrapped the GPS in its protective plastic. "I'm tired of waiting. I think we need to make it happen."

I tucked the device tenderly into my purse, slipped the strap of my purse over my head and positioned the bag comfortably against the small of my back. "You know what else I think? I think Chet's waiting for instructions. He doesn't have *permission* to use that gun, otherwise he would have shot us already."

"Perhaps we should get his attention." Naddie squared her jaw and grinned. She picked up a bottle of chardonnay, and when I nodded, she smashed it on the floor.

We stopped to listen. Chet had switched channels. He seemed to be watching a stock car race.

I picked up another bottle of chardonnay and hurled it against the wall. It crashed into a bin of merlot with a satisfying *thwack*.

The television went silent.

Just to make sure Chet was listening, I threw another bottle of wine against the door, hoping to shatter the pane.

Surprisingly, the bottle broke, but not the glass. God only knew what kind of space age material it was made from.

A shadow appeared on the other side of the glass. "Hey, you ladies, cut it out. I know what you're trying to do."

I stood to the left of the door, well out of pistol range. "Aw, Chet. We're just having a little fun! There's wine in here, Chet. Lots and lots of wine! What do you think we've been doing in here, Chet? We've been drinking wine! Lovely, lovely wine!" I dashed another bottle against the tiles.

"You can break every goddamn bottle in there, I don't give a fuck. It's not *my* wine."

"C'mon, Chet," I wheedled. "Let us go. Before your friend gets back. We'll never tell."

"No fucking way."

Chet's shadow disappeared for a minute, and then it returned, dragging a chair. He positioned the chair directly in front of the door and sat down in it. I imagined him with his arms folded across his chest, a deputy sheriff in a spaghetti western.

I used the corkscrew to open a bottle of merlot, then poured it carefully under the door. Chet seemed to be ignoring the wine that had to be wicking into the carpet at his feet. Every few seconds he'd tip his head back, and I could see the vague outline of a bottle. Chet was drinking beer.

"Chet," I called through the door. "You really should let us go. You know why?" I giggled drunkenly. "Because my brother-in-law is a policeman, that's why! You don't believe me? His name is Rutherford, Chet. *Lieutenant* Dennis Rutherford. You can look it up. And if anything happens to me, he's going to come looking for you. And he's going to find you, and when he finds you he's going to cut off your balls and feed them to his cat!"

On the other side of the door Chet drained his bottle. I saw him set it on the floor next to his chair. Then he paid another visit to the refrigerator. I heard the door slide open and the *psssst* of a bottle being uncapped.

"You know something, lady? You are full of shit!" Chet faced the door defiantly. He tipped the bottle up and took a long swig. "I gotta do what I'm told. Ain't no independent thinking in this outfit. Last time I tried, he ripped me a new one."

I turned to Mrs. Bromley and rolled my eyes. "If Chet ever had an independent thought, the *New York Times* would report it."

"Boss not very understanding, then, is he?" Naddie was getting into the act.

Chet plopped down in his chair. "No way. Don't *ever* want to screw up with this dude or you could end up a floater."

"It can't be that bad," she drawled.

"Wanna bet? Kee-rist!" He snorted and upended the bottle. "Was supposed to get papers back from this broad. Ended up capping her instead. Didn't mean to. Was he *pissed*!"

The image of Gail's body swam before my eyes. I clapped my hand to my mouth, trying to suppress a scream.

Naddie touched my arm. To Chet, she said, "Why don't you get out of this business, then. Do you have a mother, Chet? Go home to her. Get a job at Wal-Mart."

"I don't usually work with guns," he mused, ignoring her. "Too fucking loud."

"Messy, too, I'll bet," Naddie said.

The refrigerator door slid open. *Psssst.* However this comes out, I thought, it'd probably be the last time Pottorff stationed Chet next to an unlocked refrigerator door.

"So, Chet, if you don't like guns, how come you got one stuck in your belt?" I asked.

"That?" He snorted. "Adds to my street cred, you know? Gets respect."

"So, what do you usually work with, Chet?" I hiccuped. "I really want to know. Knives? Poison?"

Chet laughed. "Nah. I make it look like natural causes, you know, like those geezers at the nursing home."

Naddie's fingers dug into my arm.

Chet was on a roll, so I pressed him. "And just how did you do that, Chet?"

"I burked 'em," he said simply. He tipped up his bottle and took another drink.

Somewhere a horn blared. Chet arose from his chair. When the horn blared again, Chet disappeared.

I turned to Naddie. "What the heck is burking?"

"My God," she said, grabbing onto the edge of the tasting table for support. "It dates back to nineteenth-century Edinburgh," she whispered. "Burke and Hare were these two fellows who dug up bodies to sell for anatomical dissection. When digging got to be a lot like work, they decided to streamline operations. They'd get a victim drunk, and while Burke sat on his chest to keep the lungs deflated, Hare would cover his nose and mouth, neatly asphyxiating him. It's extremely difficult to detect," Naddie continued, "unless you're looking for it."

"Jesus," I said. I thought about Valerie and Clark and those other poor folks at Ginger Cove and felt an overwhelming urge to force a pillow over Chet's face and hold it there until he quit squirming. Then I'd let him breathe. Then I'd mash the pillow over his face again. And again.

"Quick! Before he gets back!" In the light coming in from the window, I was able to identify the bin holding the champagne. I rushed over and pulled out a magnum. I held it in both hands and was about to use it like a club to smash down the door when I realized Chet was no longer alone.

"Hey, Nick. What's happening, man?"

"What the fuck?" It was Pottorff. His shadow, shorter and bulkier than Chet's, blocked the light coming in through the door. He was lifting his feet, examining his shoes. He'd stepped in the wine.

"Asshole! I thought you were supposed to be watching them?"

"I am watching them. They didn't go nowhere."

"Son of a bitch!" Stepping high, Pottorff's shadow receded.

"I didn't break them bottles, Nick. Them bitches did." Chet sounded desperate.

"Fuck, fuck, fuck! Look at this mess!"

"Look, man—" Chet began.

"Just get rid of them!"

I wrapped an arm around Naddie and dragged her with me as I retreated to the far corner of the wine cellar. I handed her my magnum and picked out another one for myself. Whatever happened, we'd go down fighting.

I braced myself, expecting Chet to burst in at any moment, gun blazing.

Then, from somewhere upstairs, a new voice shouted, "Not here, you morons!"

"Who is that?" Naddie whispered.

"I don't know!"

We heard muffled conversation, and within minutes the door opened and Pottorff slunk in, followed by Chet.

I raised the magnum to my shoulder like a baseball bat and got ready to swing.

"Drop the bottle, lady." It was Chet, backing up the order with his gun pointed directly at Mrs. Bromley. "You, too," he snarled.

Prudently, we did as we were told.

Pottorff grabbed my arm and dragged me roughly out of the wine cellar. Chet escorted Naddie, a bit more courteously. Maybe he hadn't emerged fully formed out of the primordial slime. Maybe he had a mother after all.

Retracing our steps, they hustled us back through the family room, up the stairs, through the kitchen and into the garage, where they shoved us into the back of the van and slammed the door.

Once again we heard the garage door grind open, and with Chet at the wheel and Pottorff riding shotgun, the van peeled off into the late afternoon sunshine.

* * *

The plan, apparently, was to pummel us to death.

Traveling at a high rate of speed, the van lurched through our captor's neighborhood with Naddie and me ricocheting off the walls as it careened around corners and joggled over potholes.

Naddie held onto the lawn mower. "Can you get the door open?"

On my hands and knees, I crawled to the cargo door and tried the handle. "It's locked!" I yelled over the roar of the engine. "But even if I could get it open, they're driving too fast. We'd be killed if we tried to jump."

Chet slammed on the brakes and I slid forward into a bag of grass seed. I looked up to check on Mrs. Bromley. She was still hanging onto the lawn mower, but under its tie-downs the mower had shifted alarmingly. I crawled forward, dragging the grass seed with me. Before the van began to move again, I helped Naddie into a corner on the passenger side of the van and cushioned her on both sides with seed bags. "You okay?"

She nodded, looking pale.

I piled two more seed bags around her for good measure, then the van took off and I slid back toward the cargo doors.

Where the hell were they taking us?

I cast a desperate eye around the van. A canvas bag containing gardening tools dangled from a single handle, its contents jingling and clanging like pie tins. I crawled across the floorboards and dumped the bag out: a cultivating fork, some pruning shears, a bulb planter. I set the Garden Weasel miniclaw aside, thinking it might come in handy later, grabbed the trowel and crawled back to the cargo door. Kneeling, I used the trowel to scrape at the paint covering the window.

"It's coming off, Naddie!" A peephole began to take shape. I scraped some more, enlarging the opening until it became a nickel, a quarter, a silver dollar. I put my eye to the window.

Traffic was light, but then, it was Sunday. I counted three cars behind us, and then four. Chet was traveling fast, passing everyone in his path. We sped past a highway sign, but I could see only its back side.

We were on an expressway, though. I shifted my gaze to the right, across the median to the other side of the divided highway. A green sign announcing the Route 50 split for Annapolis and Washington, D.C., was receding into the distance. "We're heading north on I-97," I told Naddie.

I started in again with the trowel. I'd made a hole about six inches in diameter when Naddie said, "Listen!"

It was the first of the sirens.

The van slowed. Chet must have heard it, too.

I cupped my face and put it to the window, searching the road behind us for any sign of a police car. The siren grew louder. The van slowed again, but I couldn't see any flashing lights.

"Come on! Come on!" I chanted. "Where the hell are you?"

Suddenly, out of the corner of my eye, I saw it. A two-tone blue cruiser pulling a U-ey, pitching and yawing over the median strip, siren *whoop-whoop-whooping* and blue lights flashing.

"Naddie! They're coming! Oh, thank God, thank God!"

But Chet wasn't planning to wait around for the Anne Arundel County police. The van lurched and I was thrown against the cargo door. As the van sped up, I crawled forward, pounding with my trowel on the Plexiglas partition that separated us from the driver's compartment. "Slow down, you idiots! You're going to get us all killed!"

As if they cared. They had seat belts, after all.

I turned to check on Mrs. Bromley. "You okay, Naddie?"

Looking small and frightened between the seed sacks, Mrs. Bromley nodded.

I crawled back to my peephole. The cop car was still behind, easing into the fast lane. He was going to force us over.

Then the cop drifted back. In a moment I saw why. A funeral procession, headlights blazing, had been crawling up the slow lane. Model citizens all, they tried to get out of the way, but some had pulled to the shoulder, some to the median, others, in confusion, still clogged the slow lane. Chet barely slowed. Like a stunt car driver gone berserk, he threaded his way between the mourners, horn blaring.

We passed the exit for BWI Airport. In a few minutes, I knew, we'd reach the Baltimore beltway. The cop was still behind, but his lights were receding. Had he determined that the chase was an unreasonable risk to innocent bystanders? Had he given up? Damn! If he didn't catch us before the beltway, Chet could go east on I-695. He could go west. He could drive north through the Harbor Tunnel. Unless the cops called in a helicopter, we might never be found.

I needed to stop Chet. But how?

Still holding the trowel, I crawled around the van, searching desperately for a weapon. I banged into buckets and flower pots, muddy work gloves and boots, a compost pail and a rusty wheelbarrow. It was like crawling through a minefield. Then I saw it, like a beacon in the night: a yellow canister strapped to the wall with a bungee cord. I tucked the trowel into my waistband and, pitching and weaving drunkenly, made my way toward the canister, thinking it would make an excellent bludgeon. Bracing myself against the wall, I unhooked the bungee cords and pulled the canister down. I checked the label. Insecticide. *Oh, ho, ho, better yet,* I thought as I tucked the canister under my arm. Some painters' masks hung on a peg nearby. I snatched them as I passed and staggered forward.

"Here, Naddie, put this on."

I fastened a mask to my own face, then, dragging the canister, made my way clumsily toward the front of the van.

I studied the sliding window. It had a lock, like on a jewelry display case. It didn't look too sturdy.

I pulled the trowel out of my pants, rammed it into the space between the sliding panels and pulled back, hard.

"What the hell?" Pottorff was pounding on the window with his fist. "Get back there!"

I pulled even harder. The lock turned out to be sturdier than the Plexiglas it was attached to. The Plexiglas crackled, then cracked, then split in two.

Pottorff's hand shot through the opening, but I whacked it with my trowel. "God damn!" he yelled, hastily retracting his paw.

I picked up the insecticide, aimed the nozzle into the cab, pulled the trigger and sprayed. I sprayed right and left, up and down, I sprayed until the canister was empty.

Pottorff coughed, he gagged, he tore at his eyes.

Chet stared straight ahead, but his eyes were streaming; he swiped at them with his shirtsleeve. The van swerved, hit the rumble strip, then pulled back onto the road.

"Stop!" I screamed. "Stop now!"

Chet was aiming for the exit to I-695 when the cop car appeared outside his window. Chet swerved, accelerated and tore up the ramp, but was going too fast to make the turn. The van hit the Jersey wall, scraped along it, gradually slowing. Just when I thought we'd be okay, my head crashed into the ceiling as the van jumped over an object on the shoulder and shot across the ramp to bounce off the Jersey wall on the opposite side.

In the cab, Chet was wrestling with the steering wheel, struggling for control. With the cop crowding him on the right, Chet kept to the shoulder, still driving like a madman. Up ahead, a disabled vehicle blocked his way. "Look out!" I screamed, and ducked, covering my head with my arms. By the time Chet saw it, though, it was too late. He slammed on the brakes, sending the van into a slow skid. It screamed along, teetering on its right-hand tires, tipped and toppled on its side with a sound of breaking glass and shredding metal.

Suddenly everything was quiet.

I opened my eyes. I was lying on what had been the right side of the van, and I had the headache from hell.

I struggled to my knees. "Naddie! Where are you?"

"I'm over here."

Wiping at my eyes, I crawled to her. Secure in her corner, cushioned by seed sacks, she had survived the crash fairly well, but she was pinned in by the lawn mower, which had become unattached from its moorings.

"Are you okay?"

Naddie clutched her arm to her chest. "I think I've broken my arm."

"Anything else?"

She sucked in her lips against the pain and shook her head. A tear rolled down her cheek. "I don't think so, but the arm hurts like the devil."

"I'll have you out in a minute."

I'll have you out? That was a laugh. I poked my head through the window. There was no one in the cab. What I saw in the sideview mirror was the backside of Chet and a brown blob that was Pottorff, crawling over the guardrail and hightailing it off into the underbrush, heading, I presumed, for nearby Arundel Hills Park.

"Help!" I screamed to anyone who might be listening. "Help! Get us out of here!"

There was the wail of more sirens. "Reinforcements!" I cheered. I crawled back to the cargo door and began flailing at it with my feet.

Suddenly the door was wrenched open. With "Thank God!" on my lips, I launched myself forward, falling into the arms of a very surprised Anne Arundel County cop.

"My friend," I muttered into his uniform. "Her arm's broken."

The officer held me at arm's length. He looked puzzled, as if I'd been speaking Greek. Where had all that blood on his uniform come from?

"Ma'am?" he said. "Are you all right, ma'am?"

The next thing I remember was sitting in the backseat of the police cruiser holding a compress to a gash on my forehead, watching as Chet and Pottorff, handcuffed, shuffling and staring at their shoes, were assisted into the backseat of a second cruiser.

"Please, check out my friend in there. I think she needs an ambulance."

"You both need an ambulance," the officer said. "It's on its way."

I shivered. "My friend. Is she okay?"

The officer smiled. "She's fine. Just a little beaten up. We've made her comfortable. Don't worry."

A blanket appeared from somewhere and I pulled it over my head and around my shoulders. "What took you so long?" I complained. "I called 911 and told them where we were."

The tips of the officer's ears reddened. "Do you know how many blue vans All Seasons has?"

Under the blanket I shook my head.

"Six. And one of them was parked on Rowe Boulevard in front of the Hall of Records. The crew was weeding the median." He grinned. "We had a very surprised driver and his assistant spread-eagled among the pansies when your call came in. By the time we'd realized our mistake and got around the corner to the construction site, you were gone."

Although it wasn't particularly funny, I smiled. "So near and yet so far."

"Something like that."

"They took my cell phone," I said.

The officer immediately got my drift. "Is there somebody we can call?"

I thought about Paul. If he had already gotten home, he

must be frantic. "My husband." I gave the officer our number. Then I ticked the others off on my fingers. "And my brother-in-law, Lieutenant Rutherford with the Chesapeake County Police. And Officer Mike Tracey. He's one of you. He's working on the case this is related to."

"Ma'am," the officer said with a broad grin, "are there any cops you *don't* want me to call?"

I smiled. "It runs in the family."

"Do you mind if I ask?" the officer said after a moment.

"Ask what?"

He tapped the painter's mask that still dangled from my neck. "Why this? Your friend has one, too."

"I'll show you," I said.

He followed me over to the van, where I pointed out the yellow canister. "I sprayed 'em with that."

"What's in it?" he asked, picking it up and hefting it in his hands.

"Nothing now," I grinned. "But it used to be insecticide."

"'Kills chewing, sucking, and other hard-to-kill insects,'" the officer read off the label.

I thought about Pottorff in his beetle-brown suit. "Sounds about right to me."

CHAPTER 25

The next time I saw Officer Mike Tracey, I was perched on a gurney in the emergency room of Anne Arundel Medical Center, and the plastic surgeon was humming "I've Been Working on the Railroad" while sewing six stitches into my noggin.

Tracey had been leaning against the wall, silently watching the doctor work. "That's quite a gash," he said as the doctor moved aside and the nurse began to apply a bandage.

"I'll live. How's Mrs. Bromley?"

"She's just a few cubicles away. Why don't you ask her yourself?"

Holding my head stationary, I waggled a hand at the doctor. "Almost finished?"

The doctor nodded, smiling. "Call my office and make an appointment. I'll want to see you in five days." He pulled a prescription pad from the pocket of his lab coat, scribbled something on it, tore off the page and handed it to me. "This is for Percocet, if you need it for pain. My phone number's there, too."

"Thanks, Doctor." From the throbbing going on in my forehead, I predicted I'd need to corner the market in Percocet.

The nurse put the finishing touches on my bandage then took us to see Naddie. She was in a nearby cubicle, lying on a gurney. "We've given her a light sedative," the nurse told us. "And we're keeping her overnight for observation. Don't tire her out," she said before slipping out.

I approached the gurney from the side and gazed down at my friend. Mrs. Bromley's eyes were closed and her breathing was slow and regular. "How peaceful she looks," I whispered to Officer Tracey. "I can't believe that I put her life in danger like that."

Mrs. Bromley's eyes fluttered open; she turned her head in my direction and smiled. "Hi," she said groggily.

"Hi yourself," I said. "How are you, Naddie?" Mrs. Bromley usually wore a headband, but sometime during all the excitement, it had disappeared. I smoothed the snow-white hair back from where it tumbled over her forehead.

"I could use a drink," she said.

I filled a blue plastic cup with water from the sink and supported her head with my hand while she drank it. When she was done, Naddie relaxed against the pillow, looked up and seemed to notice my bandage for the first time. "What happened to you?"

I touched my bandage gingerly. "A bump on the head. A few stitches." I smiled reassuringly. "Don't worry, I'll be just fine. How about you?"

"They just read the X rays," she said. "My arm's broken in two places. They're going to set it. Ouch! I'm really looking forward to that! And I'll have to wear a cast."

"Casts come in a full range of designer colors, I hear."

Mrs. Bromley's face clouded over. "But my art show? It's next week!"

"Don't worry, Naddie. I'll help you with your show. You just relax, now. Everything's going to be fine."

"Do you ladies feel up to answering a few questions?" Mike Tracey extracted a notebook from his pocket and flipped it open to a blank page. When we agreed, he disappeared into the hallway, returning a few moments later, dragging a couple of chairs.

After we were comfortably seated, Mrs. Bromley launched with surprising enthusiasm into her version of our recent adventure, while I offered my two cents' worth about Jablonsky, Pottorff, and Steele. We had begun to describe the house where we'd been held prisoner when Paul burst into the cubicle, with Dennis only a few steps behind.

"My God, Hannah!" Paul fell to his knees in front of my chair as if he were about to propose marriage. He touched my bandage with his fingers, took my face gently in his hands and kissed me softly on the mouth. "What on earth am I going to do with you?"

"Why didn't you call me?" Dennis's scowl said it all.

"I'm always bothering you, Dennis. I thought you'd be proud of me. I called 911, like a good girl." I grinned, to let him know I was teasing. "I would have called you next," I added, "but they took away my cell phone."

"Who's 'they'?" Paul asked.

Mike Tracey leaned forward, elbows resting on his knees, notebook still in hand. "We picked up the gardener and a guy named Pottorff when they tried to escape after the crash. Pottorff, it turns out, works for a fellow named Jablonsky. We've picked him up, too. They're so busy pointing fingers at each other it'll be a while before we get it all sorted out."

Dennis turned to me again. "Do you have any idea where you were being held?"

"Yes and no," I said. "I think it may have been Jablonsky's house in Fishing Creek Farm, but there's a way we can find out for sure." I looked around the cubicle for my purse but couldn't see it. Where the hell was it? I'd had it with me in the van, I knew that for sure. Had it gotten lost in the accident? Was it still in the ambulance? Had it been stolen? The warm pride I had been feeling about my coup with the GPS was quickly turning to ice cold panic. "My purse! It's gone!"

Mike Tracey laid a comforting hand on my shoulder. "Don't worry. It's probably back in your cubicle," he said. "I'll take a look."

It seemed like hours, but it was only minutes before Tracey returned with my purse. "Whew!" I took it from his outstretched hand and crushed it to my chest. "If I'd lost it . . ."

I handed the purse to Paul. "Look in the bottom," I instructed.

His brow furrowed, Paul set the purse on the foot of Mrs. Bromley's gurney, opened it and plunged in with both hands. He came out holding the GPS, still carefully cushioned in bubble wrap. I prayed that it hadn't been damaged in the accident.

"What does this have to do with anything?" Paul asked as he unwrapped the device.

"They may have taken away my cell phone, but they missed your GPS. I hit the M.O.B. button, Paul."

Like my husband, Connie and Dennis were sailors. I watched, amused, as a slow smile spread across Dennis's face when Paul explained to Officer Tracey what the M.O.B. meant.

Lieutenant Dennis Rutherford grinned at his colleague. "Hey, Mike. Ever applied for a search warrant on the basis of a latitude and longitude coordinate?"

They knew where the house was, of course. They'd looked it up.

Mrs. Bromley, the GPS, and I had given them plenty of probable cause, but I was needed to identify the place, positively, once they got inside.

With Paul's GPS mounted on the dashboard, Paul and I rode in the backseat of Tracey's cruiser from our house on Prince George to College Avenue. We turned left on College and right on Rowe, heading due west out of town, rather than east toward Fishing Creek Farm. Well, I thought sourly, that eliminates that creep Jablonsky.

When we made a right turn on Melvin, my heart began to race. At the end of Melvin was the community of Wardour, one of Annapolis's oldest high-rent neighborhoods. But before we reached the Wardour roundabout, Tracey surprised me by steering his cruiser left on Claude. At the end of Claude he stopped; we'd reached a dead end.

Directly in front of us, on a heavily wooded and beautifully landscaped waterfront lot, stood a modern, four-story home built entirely of brick. Tracey pulled into the drive and the GPS began to beep. "We have arrived," Tracey said. I didn't need the GPS or Mike Tracey to tell me that. I was staring at a brand new three-car garage.

"Who does the house belong to?" I croaked.

"Somebody you know," Dennis said, turning in his seat to face me. "Mr. C. Alexander Steele, president and CEO of ViatiPro."

Why was I not surprised?

Surveying the house in front of him, Tracey whistled. "The business of death must be good." He opened the door of his cruiser, leaned out and motioned to an unmarked vehicle that had pulled into the driveway just behind us.

"Who—" I began.

"Evidence technicians," he replied.

Mike Tracey himself led the charge up the sidewalk. We stood behind him, like a tag team of Jehovah's Witnesses, while he rang the bell.

A middle-aged Filipina dressed as a maid answered the door. "Mistah Steele, he no home," she replied to Tracey's question. She stared, wide-eyed, first at us and then his badge, before backing away, bobbing at the waist. "I go get Missy Steele, okay? You wait."

A few seconds later a willowy woman dressed in a white tank top, black capris, and leather flip-flops came to the door. "I'm Claudia Steele. How may I help you, officer?" Diamond studs twinkled in her ears.

Tracey introduced the lot of us, then handed her the

search warrant. "We're here to search the premises," he told her. "For evidence of a kidnapping."

If Claudia Steele was surprised, she didn't show it. While we waited, jockeying for position on the narrow landing, Mrs. Steele flipped quickly through the pages of the warrant. "I'm sure everything's in order here, officer, but I'm confident that you're making a huge mistake."

"We'd like to begin in the basement," Tracey said.

"Be my guest." She turned. "Please, follow me."

How could she be so cool, so collected? Naddie and I had trashed the place. Did she think we wouldn't notice? She moved ahead of us with such poise and confidence that I was almost ready to believe I'd dreamed up the whole thing, until we stepped into the family room. There was the fireplace, the bar, the humongous TV, and, bless her little painted toes, the *Naked Maya*.

"This is it," I said firmly. "This is definitely the place."

Claudia Steele lounged against the bar while I led the officers to the wine cellar. The door, of course, was locked.

"They keep the key under the chalkboard," I told Tracey.

Once inside the wine cellar, I stared in disbelief. It had been only twelve hours since Naddie and I laid waste to the room, yet not a single bottle was out of place. There was no trace of the wine we'd spilled on the floor, no hint of a stain in the grouting. I looked up. The damage I'd done to the air conditioner had been repaired. I went to the door and looked down: even the carpet was miraculously clean. I felt like a fool.

As I wandered around the wine cellar, muttering, Claudia Steele stood next to the decanting table, holding the key in her hand and glaring at me with ill-disguised contempt. "I don't have the slightest idea what you're talking about, Mrs. Ives. You'd think if somebody had been tossing wine bottles around my cellar, I'd have noticed."

I didn't believe for a minute that C. Alexander Steele had cleaned up the mess by himself, and Nick Pottorff and his buddy Chet had been busy. Tracey would interview the maid, I was sure. Perhaps she'd tell a different story.

Mrs. Steele's arms were folded over her chest. "Will that be all now?"

"One more thing," I said, turning to Officer Tracey. "Our fingerprints will be all over the place, of course, but I think I can save you a little time. If you'll look over there? Next to the door?" I pointed. "Count nine bottles up and seventeen bottles over. You should find a bottle of pinot noir."

Mike Tracey started to cross the room, but Claudia Steele stepped in his path, blocking the way. She was used to being in control; my giving orders didn't seem to suit her. Tracey simply stared, waiting her out. "Will you excuse me, ma'am?"

Her face a mask of loathing, Claudia Steele stepped aside.

Tracey turned to a technician. "Gloves?" He snapped them on, then counted the bottles. ". . . fifteen, sixteen, seventeen." He stopped, his gloved finger touching the neck of the bottle, my special bottle. I held my breath as he withdrew it from the slot and set it on the tasting table.

With slow deliberation, Tracey patted his pockets, searching for his reading glasses. Once the glasses were on his nose, he laid the bottle in his palm and bent over it. " 'Michael LeBois Pinot Noir,' " he read.

"That's right, 2001, if I'm not mistaken."

"The bottle's been opened."

Claudia Steele's eyebrows shot up.

Mike Tracey wrapped his fingers around the cork and twisted, but it wouldn't budge. He scanned the room, spotted the corkscrew. "Do you mind?"

Claudia Steele shrugged. "Do I have a choice?"

Tracey removed the cork, shook the bottle, then peered

inside. After a thoughtful moment, he tapped out the note I'd written to Paul. He unrolled the note, scanned its contents, his face passive, then handed the note to the technician, who sealed it inside a Baggie. "We'll need it for evidence, of course, but after that. . ." He looked at Paul. "I'll think you'll want to have it, Ives."

"Well," Claudia Steele huffed. "I don't have the slightest idea how *that* got there. I haven't been home. I spent the weekend with my mother in Pennsylvania. You can check."

Strangely enough, I believed her. There hadn't been any cars in the garage when Chet pulled in with the van.

"I have nothing to do with my husband's business, or with his associates," she insisted.

Tracey reached into the inside pocket of his jacket and pulled out a photo lineup, six mugs to a page. He laid it on the tasting table. "Do you recognize any of these men?"

Claudia Steele tapped Pottorff's face with the tip of a French manicured nail. "That's Nick Pottorff. He's a messenger for MBFSG. My husband does a lot of business with them." She waved a hand. "I don't recognize any of these others."

"Where can we find your husband, ma'am?"

"Where you can always find him on Monday," she commented dryly. "At his office."

Leaving the evidence technicians to do their work, Paul and I left with Officer Tracey. As I climbed into the car, I turned to Paul. "Remind me to find out who her cleaning lady is."

Late Tuesday evening my brother-in-law showed up after dinner, bringing us a progress report. While we waited for the decaf to brew, I telephoned Daddy. Within ten minutes he joined us at the kitchen table, where I was already serving dessert.

"I don't even know his last name," I said as I set the container of half and half on the table.

"Whose name?"

"That gardener, Chet."

"He goes by Laidlaw," Dennis told me. "But he's got a record in Louisiana under Charles Lewis, the name his own sweet mama gave him."

"So, what's happening with those creeps?" I asked, sitting down.

"There's a whole lot of speechifying and finger-pointing going on, and that's just the lawyers!" He grinned. "It'll take Tracey and his crew a couple of days to sort it all out, but Chet Laidlaw's been a busy boy, implicating Pottorff and Jablonsky in the murders. They've got Laidlaw dead to rights on the shooting of Gail Parrish. The slug we took out of her body matches the gun he was carrying. As for the others." He held out his cup for a refill. "Tracey's getting an exhumation order for Clark Gammel and Tim Burns. After that, we'll see."

"Chet Laidlaw *admitted* to smothering those people," I reminded him. "So, what are they looking for?"

"If they were burked, there'll be petechiael hemorrhages in the eyes, perhaps some blue-hued congestion about the face and neck caused when blood with a low oxygen content got trapped above their lungs."

"Oh," I said simply, thinking again about Valerie and being almost sorry I asked.

"How about Steele?" my father wanted to know. "He's the one *I* want to see behind bars."

Dennis sipped his coffee. "Well, Jablonsky is pointing the finger back at Steele and being quite forthcoming in describing their joint role in a multistate viatical investment scam."

Daddy shook his head. "But I still don't understand why *Jablonsky* wanted Valerie Stone, Gammel, that Burns fellow, and all those others dead. Jablonsky already sold their policies. It was Steele and *his* investors who stood to gain by their deaths."

"I think I can answer that question," I said. I'd spent the afternoon with Donna Hudgins and Harrison Garvin at

Victory Mutual, briefing them on my report. It had turned out to be a very interesting meeting.

"At first," I said, "Steele either didn't know or didn't care that the policies he was buying from Jablonsky were bogus. Steele was under pressure to purchase more policies for the investor money that kept pouring in, some of which he used not to buy policies, but to support his lavish lifestyle."

"Lavish," my husband remarked. "That's putting it mildly."

"Opulent, then." I gave Paul a friendly punch in the arm. "So, when some of Steele's investments turned sour and a significant percentage of ViatiPro's policy portfolio was rescinded by the insurance companies that issued them, it put a serious crimp in his cash flow."

"He would be facing ruin," Daddy interjected.

"Exactly. I figure Steele threatened Jablonsky. Either Jablonsky could arrange for the legitimate policies he sold ViatiPro to 'mature' or Steele would blow the whistle on him."

"Enter Nicholas Pottorff and his good little Do-Bee, Chet Laidlaw," Daddy said.

During the whole course of our conversation, something Dennis *hadn't* mentioned kept nagging at me.

"Dennis, you haven't said anything about Valerie Stone."

Dennis leaned forward, resting his forearms on the table. "Hannah, Laidlaw has copped to the murders of Gail and all those folks out at Ginger Cove, but he insists he had nothing to do with any 'Hillsmere broad.'"

"I can't believe you're telling me this! He must have done it! It can't be just a coincidence!" I shook my head angrily. "Absolutely no way!"

Dennis waited for me to finish sputtering before he continued. "Anne Arundel County is working with the New Jersey D.A. for an exhumation order, but Valerie's family is throwing up road blocks. Eventually I think they'll allow the exhumation rather than put up with all the negative publicity, but so far they're adamant. Nobody's going to dig their daughter up."

"This is ridiculous! I'm going to call Brian. He'll talk some sense into those in-laws of his."

Dennis shook his head. "It's my understanding that Brian Stone doesn't want the exhumation, either."

That was odd. If Paul died unexpectedly, I'd demand an autopsy. If someone were responsible, I'd sure as hell want to know about it.

I'd been waving my fork in the air. Before I put somebody's eye out, Dennis grabbed my hand and pushed it down on the table. "Let the police do their work, Hannah. Trust me, they know what they're doing."

I scowled at my brother-in-law. Maybe the police knew what they were doing and maybe they didn't, but either way, I couldn't see any reason why *I* shouldn't talk to Brian Stone. I'd call him. First thing in the morning.

CHAPTER 26

Brian was avoiding me. He didn't return my phone calls. My e-mails went unread.

I was taking it personally, working myself up to a full-blown sulk until I telephoned Kathy Carpenter. "Oh, Brian's been away," his next door neighbor told me. "He's in New Jersey, visiting with Miranda."

So, Brian had gone over to the Dark Side. I decided to wait until he returned to Annapolis before tackling him about Valerie. After hobnobbing with the country club set, it'd take about a week of beer and crab cakes to deprogram him.

Besides, I'd volunteered to help Mrs. Bromley with her art show, and the day was fast approaching. Naddie had promised to call with details, but I still didn't know much more than what I'd read on the postcard I'd received in the mail. Saturday, eleven to four, Markwood Gallery, Maryland Avenue. And it was Thursday already.

Considering Naddie's broken arm, I was wondering if the show was still on.

"Hey, Naddie," I said when she answered my telephone call. "Sorry to bother you when you must be so busy, but isn't your show this weekend?"

"So it is, and I'm so glad you called! Didn't you say, in some rash moment, that you wouldn't mind helping me out?"

"It wasn't a rash moment, and I don't mind a bit. So, are you feeling okay?"

"Much better, thanks."

Naddie had prevailed upon the local Ginger Cove talent to load the paintings into her station wagon, but needed help unloading the paintings once she got to Markwood Gallery.

"Sure, just tell me what time and I'll be there."

"How about an hour?"

I laughed. "When were you going to call me? When you pulled out of the parking lot?"

"Well, the last time I saw you, you looked a little the worse for wear."

"I still do, thank you very much, but I'm feeling fine. See you in about an hour."

I was bored, and restless, and a little bit glum. As I puttered around the kitchen I turned the radio to WBJC, but it's hard to sing along to Bach, and the Barber "Adagio for Strings" made me feel like jumping off the Bay Bridge, so I switched to WINX Shore Country radio. Stompin' songs from Jimmy Buffett, Alabama, and the Soggy Bottom Boys can perk me up every time.

I was polishing the copper bottoms on my pots when they started playing selections from a Dixie Chicks album. I wasn't very familiar with the Dixie Chicks, but I was really getting into the twangy guitar and the plunky mandolin that introduced the song. Then I froze. Natalie Maines was covering "Landslide," a Stevie Nicks hit from the Fleetwood Mac album that Valerie and I had loved.

"Can I sail thru the changing ocean tides," Natalie crooned. Instinctively, I opened my mouth to sing along, but nothing came out but a strangled whimper. How many times had we sung those words together, Valerie and I, harmonizing on the "uh, uhs" and "well maybes," wondering if, like the singer, we'd survive to grow older, too? I sat down at my kitchen table, wet hands and all, and started to bawl. I felt like the landslide the Chicks were singing about had brought us all down.

My heart ached for Brian and Miranda. I cried for the wedding that Valerie would never see. I wept for the sailboat that Gail would never sail. I wept for my lost breast, all kidnapped children, and the AIDS-afflicted people of Africa.

I was caught in a downward spiral, and if I didn't get out of the house, pronto, I'd cry until my eyelids swelled shut.

I splashed cold water on my face, blew my nose and dried my eyes as best I could, then walked briskly out my front door, down the street to Maryland Avenue. While I waited for Mrs. Bromley, I tried a little retail therapy, but many of the shops had not opened yet, so I was unable to give my Visa card the workout it deserved.

Parking is tough on Maryland Avenue; the street is narrow and cars are allowed on the east side only. When a parking place opened up directly across from the Markwood Gallery, I borrowed a chair from Mimi at Aurora Gallery, centered the chair in the parking spot, and sat down in it, reserving the spot for Mrs. Bromley, much to the dismay of one urban warrior in her monster SUV.

Mrs. Bromley arrived several minutes later, saw me sitting there and grinned. She waved her broken arm, which was encased from elbow to wrist in a cast of bubblegum pink.

"You look spiffy," I said, peering at her through the open passenger side window. "The cast matches the stripe in your blouse."

"Chosen for the occasion," Mrs. Bromley said. "When they change it in a week or two, I'm getting lavender."

I glanced into the back of the station wagon. It was loaded almost to the ceiling with canvasses, wrapped in bubble wrap and cardboard. As Mrs. Bromley took the parking space, I moved the chair onto the sidewalk. I patted its seat. "You sit here and supervise," I ordered when she emerged from the car.

"You are a tough taskmaster," she said, grinning, but she sat down as instructed.

"You look tired, Hannah," Naddie commented as I passed her with an armload of paintings.

So, she'd noticed my eyes. I decided not to mention my little spell. "Bumps and bruises," I said. "A little stiff." I rolled my shoulders. "I don't feel much different from the day after I started taking aerobics. All that exercise was probably good for me."

Inside the gallery, I located the owner and one of Mrs. Bromley's art students who was only too happy to help me unload. Once the station wagon was empty and all the paintings were leaning against the walls in a back room of the gallery, Mrs. Bromley came in.

"Oh, let's not do that now," she said to my suggestion that we start unpacking. "I don't think I could make one more decision today, Hannah. We still have tomorrow. Let's do it then."

As we left the gallery, Mrs. Bromley turned to me and asked, "Would you like to get coffee?"

"Twist my arm," I said.

Arm in arm we walked across the street to City Dock Coffee, one of Annapolis's hidden treasures, always a welcome relief from the cookie-cutter sameness of Starbucks. City Dock Coffee occupied an old storefront, and every square inch had been put to good use.

In the display window on the left, burlap bags of coffee, boxes of tea, cups, teapots, and other decorative crockery had been arranged. In the window on the right, the owner had installed a comfortable sofa, slip-covered in a fabric with a coffee cup design. Two people were sitting on the sofa, coffee cups in hand, but they weren't paying much attention to their coffee.

I recognized the girl, or to be more precise, I recognized her shoes. The last time I'd seen that set of red shoes and slim ankles had been from the vantage point of a four-year-old while kneeling on the floor of the ladies' room at

Kramer's Funeral Home. Now, though, some guy with short blond hair had his nose buried in her neck.

"For heaven's sake," I said. "And on a public street no less."

"That's Corinne Winters," Naddie volunteered, "one of my students." She checked her watch. "Corinne was supposed to be at the gallery today, helping out."

"Looks like she got distracted," I said.

Naddie turned to me. "Corinne is always distracted."

I looked at the girl again. She had closed her eyes, and her companion had begun some major-league nuzzling. "Get a hotel room!" I muttered.

"Too late," Naddie said. "Corinne's pregnant."

I could see that now. Under her stretchy black top the girl's belly gently swelled.

Naddie tugged on my arm. "Don't gawk, Hannah!"

I stood firm. "If they don't want people to see them, why the hell are they sitting in the window?"

Mrs. Bromley punched me playfully with her cast, then reached for the doorknob of the coffee shop with her good arm.

Before I could follow Mrs. Bromley through the door, Corinne opened her eyes and noticed me standing on the sidewalk. She straightened, adjusted her top with one hand and shoved her companion away with the other.

The neck nuzzler turned. He had cut off his ponytail, but there was no doubt about it. The nuzzler was Brian Stone.

Hot rage boiled up inside me as I did the math. Corinne was showing. That meant she was four to five months gone. Four to five months ago, Valerie Stone had still been alive.

I rapped on the window. Brian started. He blushed from the pale curly hairs sticking out of his shirt all the way up to his scalp, where the hair was thinning.

I knocked again. I waggled my fingers.

Brian stood up, tucking in his shirt.

The door had already closed behind Naddie, so I yanked it open and stalked into the coffee shop. I don't know what I planned to do. Punch Brian out, maybe?

"Hannah! Good to see you." He'd decided to play it cool.

Behind him, Corinne was struggling against her low center of gravity, trying to get up from the sofa.

Brian turned and offered Corinne a hand. "You remember my friend, Corinne Winters?"

I glared at Brian as pieces of the puzzle began tumbling into place.

"Coffee, Hannah?" Mrs. Bromley was saying behind me. "Tea?" If she was hoping to distract me, she'd need something more than coffee. A bomb, maybe, with a short fuse, placed directly under my feet.

Corinne was Brian's "friend"? Give me a break! I skewered the creep with my eyes. "Valerie didn't die soon enough for you, Brian?"

He took a step backward. I took one forward, closing the gap.

I poked a finger, hard, in his chest. "Thought you'd have all that glorious money to yourself, did you?" I poked him again. "Thought you'd be able to spend it all on Corinne here and . . . and . . ." I waved in the direction of Corinne's bulging midsection. ". . . and little Whatsitsname.

"When's the baby due, Corinne?" I held up my fingers and counted them off. "Let's see. June, May, April, March, February . . . am I getting close?" Corinne's face was colorless.

"January!" I crowed. "That means you and lover boy were having it off even before he took Valerie on that cruise. How did you feel, Corinne, when he took his wife away on the QE2 instead of you. Jealous?"

"Bitch!" Corinne had found her tongue a last.

I turned to Brian. "So, this is the woman you've chosen to be the mother of your children? The woman who'll be Miranda's stepmother? *Excellent* choice!"

Brian held up his hands defensively. If he hoped to deflect my words, he was dead wrong. "You don't understand—" he began.

"Oh, I understand perfectly. So does Mrs. Bromley here." I turned to Naddie, who was standing silently next to the pastry case.

"Valerie was sick. She was *dying*!" Brian choked. "She was so weak. We couldn't . . . we didn't . . ."

"How fortunate that Corinne was there to comfort you in your hour of need."

"You don't understand," he whimpered.

But I understood perfectly, more than he knew. During my own chemotherapy, Paul had been desperate to comfort me, but I'd kept him at arm's length. By some perverse logic, I'd convinced myself that I was damaged goods, that he was being nice to me only out of pity. I'd actually suspected Paul of being unfaithful, but when the opportunity—in the form of an attractive student—had come his way, Paul had resisted.

"Didn't work out the way you intended, did it, Brian?" I pressed. "Valerie got well, Corinne got pregnant. What were you going to do?"

Out of the corner of my eye I could see Mrs. Bromley tapping her cast against her fingertips, making a desperate "time-out" sign. But I was taking no prisoners.

"The only thing I don't understand is how you did it. How did you murder your wife?"

Corinne doubled over and made a mad dash for the rest room at the back of the shop, where presumably she would upchuck her latte. Brian stared after her with a worried look on his face, but although I must have provoked him, he said nothing.

"I wonder what the phone records will show, Brian?"

"I was miles away when Valerie died, in Harpers Ferry, working on a story."

"So you said. The police left a message on your cell phone, didn't they?"

Brian nodded.

"And you returned the call."

"That's right."

"They can track those things, you know, Brian. Cell phones." I mused, "One hundred forty million human-tracking devices. When you place a cellular phone call, your phone seeks out the nearest receiving tower, which serves a distinct area. Know what they call those areas, Brian? Cells. The tower routes the call to its destination. Your cell phone provider keeps a record of that."

Brian blanched.

"I wonder where your cell phone company will tell the police you were when you made that call?"

Everything about Brian was clenched: his teeth, his jaw, his fists.

"How did you do it, Brian? With a pillow? Did you put a pillow over your wife's face and hold it there until she stopped struggling?"

"You are out of your fucking mind." He emphasized every syllable.

"When you laid her out, Brian, you forgot something very important. I shared a hospital room with Valerie. I know how she sleeps. She gets hot, a foot hangs out. She tosses, she turns. Blankets here, blankets there. The nurses were always picking blankets up off the floor in the middle of the night.

"Do you know *Miranda* found her mother, you worm? Valerie was snug as a bug in a rug with the blankets pulled up neatly under her chin." I shook my head. "You and I both know that's not very likely, is it?"

The way I looked at it, Brian had two choices: he could punch me out, or he could run.

Brian ran. He bolted from the coffee shop, heading south on Maryland Avenue toward State Circle.

Almost at once Corinne appeared, dabbing at her face with a paper towel. "Where's Brian?"

"Brian's gone."

"But—"

"Don't worry, Corinne, the police will find him." I was busily punching Officer Tracey's number into my cell phone. "But I think you'd better find someone else to attend Lamaze classes with you."

"Fucking bitch!" she screamed.

"Oh, I think you already have that territory all wrapped up."

Corinne had run out of steam. She blinked and sputtered and dashed out of the coffee shop, looking both ways as she reached the sidewalk. She must have spotted Brian, because she hustled off in a southerly direction.

I'd almost forgotten Mrs. Bromley, waiting at the counter, behind which stood a paralyzed and wide-eyed barista. I eased into an upholstered chair at one of the tables. "I think I'll have that cappuccino now, Mrs. B."

I punched the talk button. Mike Tracey picked up. "Officer Tracey? This is Hannah Ives. I have some information I think you will find very interesting."

CHAPTER 27

Proving once and for all that they are certifiably insane, Emily and Dante acquired a puppy, a three-month-old chocolate Labradoodle named Coco. They brought Coco along when they came for the Fourth of July, and we soon discovered that the animal had a three word vocabulary: sleep, eat, and rollick.

Chloe and Jake were nuts about the dog, of course. Children and dog, they seemed to be everywhere. They careened around the yard, rolled about on the lawn, ricocheted off the furniture, and whether the children were chasing Coco or Coco was chasing the children, it was hard to tell.

Who would run down first, the children or the dog? My bets were on the dog.

The picnic was in full swing when Brad Perry stuck his head over the fence. "Is this a private party or can anyone come? I can bring my own garbage!"

Paul looked up from the hamburger he was demolishing and grinned. "Sure, come on over. But don't worry about the garbage. We gave at the office."

I used my napkin to wipe the mustard off his chin.

Brad arrived carrying a six pack and a large white envelope. He handed the envelope to me. "Here, Hannah, this is for you."

The envelope had the Victory Mutual logo embossed

where the return address should have been. "What's this?"

Brad dropped his six pack in the ice chest, then popped a can for himself. "Just a little something. Harrison Garvin wants to show his gratitude."

Chloe scampered up and wrapped both arms around my leg. "Gramma, Coco licked me."

I tucked the envelope under my arm, bent down and wiped her runny nose with the hem of my bright green, Kiss My As-paragus apron. "That means Coco loves you, Chloe."

"Okay." Chloe twirled away like a ballerina on speed.

"Now, where was I?" I said.

"You were about to open that envelope," Paul reminded me. "We're all dying of curiosity."

I held it up to the sun, trying to see through it. "It's probably a certificate Garvin had Donna Hudgins print out on her computer," I joked.

"Go ahead, Mrs. Ives, open it!" My son-in-law still could not bring himself to call me Hannah.

I sat down at the table and used a plastic knife to slit open the envelope. There was a letter inside, and clipped to the letter was a check. A "little something"? I nearly had a heart attack. The check was for $25,000.

"Well," I said. "Well well well."

Brad was grinning like a jack-o'-lantern.

I grinned back. "You knew!"

"Of course I knew. Frankly, it was the least Garvin could do. Two crooked underwriters unmasked, millions of dollars saved."

"Millions?"

"Millions and millions, as it turns out, in fraudulently obtained life insurance policies."

"Can I cook marshmallows, Gramma?" Chloe was back.

I slipped the check back into the envelope. "Later, Chloe, after it gets dark."

* * *

When everyone went home, I sat in our backyard swing, gently rocking. A soft breeze caressed my cheek, lifted my hair, then drifted on to coax a tune out of the wind chimes my sister Ruth had hung in our sycamore tree. Across the yard the embers on the barbecue grill glowed a soft orange. For the first time in many weeks I was content. It had been only a month since Valerie and I ran the Race of the Cure, but it seemed like a hundred years. Next year, I knew, I would run the race in memory of Valerie. She would have liked that.

Paul had gone to the kitchen to fetch "a surprise." He returned almost at once, carrying two glasses and a bottle of wine.

He held up the wine. "Guess what label?"

"I can't imagine."

"Guess!"

"Could it be," I ventured, "a Michael LeBois Pinot Noir Santa Maria Highlands 2001?"

It could.

Holding both glasses in one hand, Paul poured the wine. "I thought you'd like to see what you missed when you dumped this down the drain."

I didn't want to admit that I'd already held an impromptu wine tasting when I took a healthy swig of the stuff down in Steele's ritzy wine cellar, so I simply smiled and plucked the glass from Paul's outstretched hand. I swirled it, I sniffed it, I put it to my lips. "Ummmm," I said, "quite a change from the wine that comes in boxes."

"Enormously complex and concentrated," he agreed, parodying the label. "With a sharply focused core of wild berry and blackberry."

"And don't forget, hints of espresso, hazelnut, and smoky oak." I had read the label, too.

We sipped, we swung, and he reached for my hand.

"What are you going to do with the money Garvin gave you?" Paul asked.

"It's a lot of money, Paul. We could save it, I suppose."

"That wouldn't be any fun."

"How would you feel about a cruise?"

"Around the world on the QE2?"

"Don't be silly. Twenty-five thousand dollars will buy only *one* ticket on the QE2."

"So, who're you going to go with?" His eyes sparkled in the lamplight.

"Steele's all tied up," I quipped. "So's Jablonsky."

"I should say so. Murder, kidnapping, conspiracy, wire fraud, mail fraud, and money laundering." Still holding his wineglass, Paul ticked them off on his fingers. "How many counts was it?"

"I lost count."

"Brian certainly won't be taking any more cruises."

"No."

"What's going to happen to Miranda?" Paul wondered.

"That's one story that has a happy ending," I said. "Valerie has a married sister who lives on a horse ranch in Wyoming. Miranda's going to live with them."

"Ahhhh." Paul's arm snaked around my shoulders. "I do love happy endings."

"Me, too. As surrogate parents, The Honorable and Mrs. Padgett certainly wouldn't win any parenting prizes."

"Speaking of happy endings," Paul said, "the Academy's legal officer called today. Those basketball players I was tutoring? They've been cleared."

I slapped my husband's knee. "Way to go, Paul!" I was still pissed off at the Academy for dragging my husband into the cheating scandal, but the students had been struggling, and when they turned in solid B's on an exam, well, eyebrows were raised.

Paul laughed. "Turns out they studied, Hannah. They actually *learned* the material!"

"Imagine that!"

"You know," he mused, after we'd swung quietly for a while. "For $25,000, two people could go on the QE2, but only half as far."

I rested my head on his chest. "When do you want to leave?"

"Now would be nice."

I smiled into his shirt. It was lovely having a husband willing to support my dreams, even if we both knew I'd probably end up investing the money in something far less exciting than a trip to Singapore or Bora Bora—like my IRA.

"Garvin was most generous," Paul remarked.

"Oh, I don't know. I think he felt a little guilty."

"Guilty? Why would Garvin feel guilty?"

"Well, after he had that meeting with his staff and everybody was so impressed with my report, yadda yadda yadda, he called me into his office and asked if there was anything he could do for me, *anything* at all.

"And so, I told him I wanted to buy a life insurance policy. I already have that policy for $250,000 with Mass Mutual, of course, but I had the idea that I'd like to be insured for twice that amount. If I croak, it might be nice to leave something more substantial for Emily and the grandchildren, although I think I might have to change my mind about that." I held out my wineglass for a refill. "Emily cornered me tonight and told me that Dante is thinking about opening his own spa."

"My God!"

"It gets worse. They're looking for investors."

Paul threw back his head and laughed long and hard into the night sky. "Well, I certainly hope you aren't planning to shuffle off this mortal coil for *that*!"

"Don't worry, it didn't happen. Garvin apologized all over the place, but said he couldn't write me a policy. Seems that under current Victory Mutual guidelines, I'm uninsurable because of my medical history." I turned so I could look into my husband's eyes. "You are married to a bad risk."

Paul tipped up my chin and kissed me on the mouth. "Risk, schmisk."

"I still have that other policy, though." I sat up. "You know," I said, poking him in the chest with every word, "at $250,000 I'm worth more to you dead than alive."

He captured my hand and pulled me close. "Hannah, love, exactly the opposite is the truth."